Fleur McDonald has lived and worked on farms for much of her life. After growing up in the small town of Orroroo in South Australia, she went jillarooing, eventually co-owning an 8000-acre property in regional Western Australia.

Fleur likes to write about strong women overcoming adversity, drawing inspiration from her own experiences in rural Australia. She has two children, an energetic kelpie and a Jack Russell terrier.

Website: www.fleurmcdonald.com
Facebook: FleurMcDonaldAuthor
Instagram: fleurmcdonald

FLEUR McDONALD
Something to Hide

ALLEN&UNWIN
SYDNEY · MELBOURNE · AUCKLAND · LONDON

Allen & Unwin
83 Alexander Street
Crows Nest NSW 2065
Australia
Phone: (61 2) 8425 0100
Email: info@allenandunwin.com
Web: www.allenandunwin.com

A catalogue record for this
book is available from the
National Library of Australia

ISBN 978 1 76087 682 1

Set in 12.4/18.2 pt Sabon LT Pro by Bookhouse, Sydney
Printed and bound in Australia by McPherson's Printing Group

10 9 8 7 6 5 4 3 2

The paper in this book is FSC® certified.
FSC® promotes environmentally responsible,
socially beneficial and economically viable
management of the world's forests.

In memory of Sarah, editor extraordinaire. We are so sad you didn't get to hang out your editor's shingle again. Thank you for our five books together.

I am because of who you are.

To those who are precious.

Chapter 1

'I met a friend of yours today,' Mel said as she heaved the heavy shopping bag onto the kitchen bench.

Dave bustled in behind her with Bec in his arms.

'Really? Who was that?' he asked as he set their daughter down and watched her toddle off into the lounge room and turn on the TV. He waited by the door for Mel's answer, listening for Alice's cry from outside.

'I've been trying to remember his name ever since I got back into the car.' Her brow creased with annoyance. 'I don't think I took it in. Just after I met him, Alice started to grizzle, and I was keen to leave. There's nothing fun about being in a supermarket with a crying baby.'

'Hold on, I can hear her now. I'll be back,' Dave said, jogging from the house to lift the newly woken Alice from the car capsule.

The sun was shining, and even the chilly wind that swept down the quiet street couldn't dampen the glow in his chest. Last night, Mel had come into their bed for the first time in many weeks. They'd shared whispered talks, cuddles and occasionally a laugh as memories from better times surfaced. When Alice woke and demanded her mother's breast, Dave had fetched her for Mel, then taken the baby back to the cot. Tonight, the spare room would be empty again, he was sure.

Last week's counselling session hadn't brought out anything he didn't already know. Mel wanted him to leave policing. She was adamant. But so was Dave. He wasn't going to do that. He had insisted they could make compromises that would benefit them both and their family.

The counsellor had convinced them to work together. To each make a little more effort at home: for Dave not to walk out the door and go to work when he was angry; for Mel to listen rather than shut Dave out while he told her something she didn't want to hear. For them both to be a little more open-minded and thoughtful of each other.

'Hey, look at you, Miss Alice,' Dave cooed as he un-buckled the straps and picked her up.

Alice gave a couple of hiccupping cries and closed her eyes.

With his daughter in his arms, he nudged the car door shut and glanced around the street—an old habit—before going inside, where Mel was unpacking the perishables into the fridge.

'How did you and this fellow get talking about me?' he asked as he went through to Alice's room and placed her gently in the cot. He drew up the covers and pulled the door to before checking on Bec. She was curled up on her child-sized unicorn couch watching *George the Farmer*, her hair falling over her eyes. Dave smiled and ducked back into the kitchen.

'So?' he asked again.

Mel straightened. 'Well, it was strange. I didn't notice him, then suddenly he was right there in front of me. Almost like he waited and stepped across my path. Alice was in the sling on my front, and I was busy looking down at what I was buying.'

'Uh-huh,' Dave said. He reached into the shopping bag for two tins of tomatoes and put them in the pantry, just as a trickle of concern ran through him.

'I apologised,' Mel continued, 'and then he just said, "Aren't you Dave Burrows' wife?" Or something like that.' She shrugged.

Dave stilled and turned to look across at Mel. 'And what did you say?'

'Yes, of course, you duffer! Are you still looking for proof we're trying?' She flashed him a half smile.

'What?' Dave was confused, his mind full of criminals who might want to take revenge on him by approaching Mel, rather than on their marriage status. 'No. But you told him who you were?' He knew he sounded incredulous.

'Well, yeah . . .' She gave a sunny smile. 'He wanted me to pass his regards on to you.'

'Mummy?' Bec stood in the doorway. 'I'm hungry.'

Mel gently pushed past Dave and took out a box of Jatz crackers and cut up some cheese. Dave watched as she put it all on a plate and handed it to Bec, who promptly disappeared back into the lounge room.

'And you can't remember his name?' he persisted, stepping closer to her.

'No. It's baby brain, I tell you. I can't remember what I did yesterday!' She looked at him. 'I'm sorry. I *am* trying, you know.'

Dave put his hands on Mel's arms and looked directly at her. 'Mel, this is important. What did he look like?'

'Ah,' Mel frowned again. 'I don't know . . .' Her voice trailed off.

Dave didn't let her finish before he cut in again. 'Tell me exactly what he said.'

Looking up at Dave, her eyes now shone with fear. 'Oh no.' She swallowed hard as realisation hit her. 'He said he was a friend of yours. From—' She paused and thought hard. 'From out bush, I think.'

Dave wanted to shout out names. *Bulldust*? Or *Ashley*? But he knew he couldn't put words in her mouth. One of the first interview techniques taught during detective training was never to do that. 'What did he sound like?' The words snapped out of him.

'Sound?'

Dave's heart was beating hard and a knot of fear was sitting like a stone in his stomach. It was one thing to be an investigator on a case that involved dangerous criminals; it was another to have strangers approach his family. 'Hard voice? Nasal? Deep?' he offered, forcing his tone back to quiet and comforting. 'Did he speak slowly or quickly?'

Mel leaned back against the kitchen bench, her arms folded. 'Um, quietly.' She frowned, the way she did when trying to dredge up a memory. 'Yeah, quiet. He spoke slowly, like he was drawing the words out.'

Dave knew he couldn't prompt her. Couldn't ask about a beard. About vivid blue eyes. About the tattoos on Bulldust's knuckles. Bulldust's features, that he knew by heart.

'Height?'

'Dave,' Mel glanced over her shoulder to the lounge room, then down the passage to Alice's room, 'you're scaring me.'

He wanted to shake her for being so stupid—for admitting who she was to a stranger who approached her out of the blue when she had their baby with her. This turn of events frightened him, which in turn made him angry. It wasn't as if Mel didn't know who Bulldust was, that he was out there somewhere holding a grudge against Dave. In fact, it had been Bulldust's threat to kill Dave, and Mel's reaction to it, that had started their recent spate of marital problems. Actually, if he was honest with himself, all of their problems had stemmed from being undercover.

'How tall, Mel? Measure him against me.'

She put her hand over his head.

'Hair?'

'I don't think he had any. No, I remember glancing at the overhead light reflecting off his head.'

'Other facial features?'

'I don't think so.'

'No beard?'

'No.' She sounded more certain. 'I remember thinking he needed a shave.'

'Just stubble, then?'

She nodded, running her hands up and down her upper arms. Dave knew the gesture. She was trying to comfort herself. He should go to her. Put his arms around her and tell her everything was going to be okay.

He couldn't. It was more important that he remain the professional detective so he could protect them all.

'Any tatts that you saw? An accent?'

'He was wearing long sleeves. Yeah, long sleeves. A blue cotton shirt. Like a work shirt.'

'For a suit?'

She shook her head. 'No, more like what you wear for the stock squad. Like farmers wear.' She paused. 'Dave?' She looked at him questioningly. 'He wouldn't be . . .'

Dave spoke calmly. 'He could be. Now, listen to what I say very carefully. I need you to pack a bag for you and the girls. I have to get you all somewhere safe.'

Mel took a step towards him, then backed away as if Dave were the problem. 'I'm scared.'

He grabbed her in a bear hug, not letting her pull away from him. 'I understand that, and I don't like this much either. But we have to take precautions in case this man *is* Bulldust.' He took a breath. 'You need to take the girls and go somewhere safe.'

'But I've got you.' Mel's voice was muffled against his chest.

He sighed. 'That won't be enough. It's me he's after. And he won't stop.'

❦

Fighting the anger rising inside him, Dave drove carefully, his eyes skipping between the road ahead and the rear-view mirror. He'd had enough dealings with Bulldust over the past two years to know that if he was the one who had approached Mel, he wouldn't have stopped at the supermarket—he would have followed her home. The man was intent on revenge. Dave had gone undercover to gain Bulldust's trust. He'd befriended him, then betrayed that trust, the trust that was between friends. Everything had been taken from Bulldust—his daughter, his business, his freedom—and Dave had seen firsthand what Bulldust did to people who double-crossed him.

Usually they ended up dead.

From Mel's description of the man it could have been Bulldust. The last time Dave had seen him, he'd had a long beard, but that could have easily been shaved off. It was the voice that interested Dave. Quiet. Slowly spoken.

A drawl. A Queenslander.

A little voice popped up in his mind; Spencer, his mate and old partner from his days stationed at Barrabine, had always told him never to assume. Could be someone from the north of Western Australia. Or the Northern Territory.

Dave glanced over at Mel's pale face, then back to the mirror. He didn't believe in coincidences.

Giving evidence against hardened criminals who had no respect for human life was part of the job, one of the perils of working undercover. What wasn't routine was the error made in court when the judge divulged Dave's home city. He wouldn't put it past Bulldust to do everything in his power to track Dave down as soon as he'd heard that he lived in Perth.

'Daddy, where are we going?' Bec piped up from the back seat.

'To visit your grandparents,' Dave said. 'Maybe have a sleepover. Won't that be fun?' He glanced in the rear-view mirror, but so far there was no sign of a tail.

'But it's daytime.'

'I know, but you might stay for a few hours, princess.'

Mel shot him a look of fury. Since they'd piled into the car she'd been silent, and the familiar distance and white-hot anger she'd been carrying around for months had resurfaced.

The very same emotions they had started to overcome last night.

Fuck it, Dave thought angrily. *I'm going to get you, Bulldust, and make you pay for the grief you've caused my family.* If Mel and the kids weren't in the car he would have hit the steering wheel, but instead he looked around, always watching his surroundings, and willed himself to stay calm.

'This isn't the way to Granny's house,' Bec said looking out the window. 'We usually go past the playground.'

'I'm taking the long way,' Dave improvised. 'Just for something different.' He wasn't about to admit he was looking for a tail, although he thought Mel probably had already realised this.

Mel shook her head and stared out the window.

A few more turns and back streets and Dave was sure they weren't being followed. Breathing easier, he started towards his father-in-law's house, already thinking about the frosty reception he would receive from Mark.

'Mel?' Dave spoke in a low voice. 'When we get there, I want you to go straight inside, okay? I'll bring the girls. Don't stop and talk in the doorway, just get inside, okay?'

Glancing over at her, he saw anger had well and truly replaced fear.

'What have you done to us?' she hissed.

Not having an answer, Dave was relieved to turn into the driveway. 'Okay,' he said, as the car came to a halt. 'Off you go. Be quick.'

He watched as Mel ran up the steps and banged on her parents' front door. Mark opened it, staring at her as she caught his arm and dragged him inside.

'Bec, can you undo your seatbelt and climb over the front seat to me, sweetie?'

'You don't like it when I do that. You get mad.' Bec crossed her arms and frowned at him.

Biting down agitation, Dave said, 'I know, princess, but I need you to do it for me today, okay? Come on.'

As if sensing the urgency, Bec unclipped her belt and clambered into the front.

'Good girl.' He gave her a kiss. 'Now, wait here for me. No moving.' He slid out the driver's door and felt for the gun at his waist as he looked around. The curtain moved inside the house and he saw Mark's face staring out.

Dave quickly unbuckled Alice and lifted her out of her capsule, then opened the front passenger door to help Bec from the car. He grabbed the car keys and Bec's hand, and ran with her up the steps.

Inside, he shut the door, locked it and breathed a sigh of relief. Bec let go of his hand as Mark's loud voice shattered the uneasy silence.

'What the hell is going on?'

'Hello, Granddad,' Bec said, running towards him with her arms outstretched. 'We're coming for a sleepover!'

Mark smiled and held out his arms towards Bec for a hug, just as Ellen appeared and offered to take Alice. 'Hello, Dave,' she said quietly. 'I'll take the littlies and leave you to talk to Mark.'

Dave smiled gratefully and handed Alice to her. Waiting until the passage was clear, he said, 'Can we go into your office to talk?'

'A different room isn't going to make any difference to what I have to say to you.'

'But it might to your safety,' Dave snapped back. He felt momentarily appeased when he saw Mark stop for a moment and glance at the front door, before storming off to the back of the house.

'Now, what's all this about?' Mark said as he sat behind the large wooden desk, putting distance between them. He poured himself a brandy but didn't offer one to Dave.

Giving the short version of the story, Dave finished with: 'But on questioning Mel, I believe him to be the suspect we know as Bulldust.'

'*On questioning Mel?* Do you realise you're talking about your wife?'

Dave stopped. Falling into police-speak wasn't the best idea when he was talking about his family. 'Of course I do. I'm relaying what's happened. Now I'm going to see Bob Holden at the stock squad and make sure you're all safe tonight. I have to get an investigation underway.'

Mark glared at his son-in-law. 'So, you've finally done it,' he spat, rising from his chair. 'Brought this filth—this, this *precious* work that you ignore your wife for—into *my* house, undermining the safety of *my* family.'

Drawing himself up and barely holding back his temper, Dave said, 'There's no time to argue about this now. The important thing is that I'm going to make sure you're all safe. If you hear, see or even *smell* anything suspicious, you have to ring triple zero. I'll make sure they have your address listed as priority.'

'Well, there you have it,' Mark scoffed. 'Going to do what you do best. You run off and play policeman while you leave your family in the lurch once again.' Mark put down his drink and walked to the office door, holding it open for Dave to leave.

Bristling, Dave fought his anger and fear. 'This is neither the time nor the place,' he answered, his tone clipped. 'I'll be back as soon as I can. You just need to remember that it's me they want, not Mel, or the children, or you and Ellen.'

'But if they need us to get to you, I don't suppose that'll stop them, will it?'

Dave had no answer as he walked out the door.

Chapter 2

The King's Arms was a dark, seedy pub around the corner from the stock squad headquarters, and was the most likely place to find Dave's partner, Bob Holden, enjoying an early lunch.

The paint was peeling from the door and the sign above it was faded. Bob could often be found here eating with another copper, retired or still in the job. They'd be sharing old war stories or speaking of good coppers who'd passed. There would be two schooner glasses in front of each, and the remnants of a chicken parmi or steak with gravy in front of Bob. He rarely deviated from his choice of food, or the amount of beer he drank.

When they'd first started working together, Dave had wondered how Bob got away with drinking on the job. Now he knew that the other members of the stock squad protected their boss. The older detective lived with the deaths of two innocent people on his conscience, and this was the way he coped. Spencer had always told Dave that the best therapy a copper could get was at the elbow of his colleague in a bar. They were the ones who understood because they'd been there.

Throwing open the door, Dave glanced at his watch and saw that it was approaching one o'clock. He would have to hurry if he wanted to catch Bob, whose lunch hour stretched from about eleven a.m. to just after one p.m.— unless there was a case pending, in which case he didn't drink and wasn't at the pub.

Things were quiet in the stock squad. Only two weeks before, they had closed an important case from the north of Western Australia, arresting two brothers for years of theft and sabotage on an Aboriginal cattle station. It had taken many weeks to close and Dave had missed the birth of Alice, which had put even more strain on his relationship with Mel. Mark had been none too pleased either. Ellen had tried to counsel both on Dave's regret, but her words had fallen on deaf ears.

Still, Dave had a feeling this could be the calm before the Bulldust storm.

'Bob,' he said, striding quickly up to Bob's usual table by the window. He observed his partner's red cheeks and glassy eyes. Maybe they'd had more than two beers today.

'Dave!' Bob threw out his arms in welcome. 'Pull up a pew. Grab a beer! Have you met Harry here? We used to work together back in—'

'We've got a problem,' Dave said sharply. 'Sorry, Harry,'

he said, turning to the elderly policeman, who looked like he was even more pissed than Bob.

Both men sat up quickly and Dave watched as they went from drunk to sober in seconds—an innate ability cops had in times of crisis.

'What's up?'

'The fuckers found Mel. In the supermarket.'

'Who? What?' Bob put down the beer he was holding and stood up. 'Not . . .'

Dave nodded. 'I reckon it was him, the bastard.'

'Bulldust?' Bob swayed a little, then signalled to the barman. 'I'll have a black coffee, mate. Takeaway.'

'I can't be a hundred percent sure from Mel's description, but my gut says yes.'

'Are you sure that you're not just overreacting? He's threatened you, which could make you a bit skittish.'

'No, I'm convinced it's him. Don't forget, the judge . . .'

Bob shook his head in disgust. 'Stupid prick.' He turned to Harry. 'Dave here was undercover and had to testify in a closed court. The judge let slip where he was from and the defendant was in the courtroom. We believe he's passed the information on to the blokes who're in the wind and looking for Dave.'

Harry got to his feet. 'I'd better let you get on with it. Judges don't think half the time, in my experience. There was this one case I had . . .'

'This one certainly didn't,' Dave agreed quickly before the war stories could start again.

'Stay safe, my friend,' Bob said and shook Harry's hand.

The barman put down a coffee in a takeaway cup. Dave dug into his pocket and handed over some loose change as Bob picked up the coffee and took a swig.

'Okay, tell me what you know while we walk,' Bob instructed.

'I've got my car,' Dave said as they walked out into the bitter cold.

The white fairy-floss clouds that had come in over the past hour raced across the sky, buffeted by the strong southerly that was supposed to bring rain over the next few days. Cars whizzed along, tossing up spray from the small puddles that already lay on the road.

Dave looked around, making sure the area was secure, before shepherding Bob quickly across the road. He unlocked the car and both men climbed in.

'So?' Bob said, as Dave pulled out into the traffic and headed towards their office.

Dave told him quickly what he knew. 'It's the slow drawl that makes me positive it's him,' he finished.

Bob was quiet as they drove through the next set of traffic lights.

'What's your description of this bloke?' he finally asked.

'He's not looking like the bloke I knew if he's shaved off his beard,' Dave said. 'But it sounds like he's still shaving his head—Mel said he didn't have any hair.' He paused as he flicked the blinker on and drove into the compound of the stock squad's offices. The familiar terrain, with the high wall around the sheds and houses, made him feel safe. 'His hands—fingers—are tattooed: *BULL* on the left hand and *DUST* on the right. He's about six foot five or six and built like a brick shithouse. But she didn't mention that. In fact, when I asked about tattoos, she said no.' He paused. 'I didn't want to put words in her mouth or sway her memory—she might have thought she'd seen something I mentioned when she didn't really.'

'Mmm.' Bob tapped his fingers on his knee. 'It mightn't be him?'

Dave shook his head. 'I'm sure it is. Mel's tired from being up at night feeding Alice, so she could easily have missed it.'

'I see. Solid build?'

'Like a freaking tank.'

Walking up the steps into the offices, Dave glanced around. He wanted to shut the gate and set the alarm, but that wasn't possible. Bulldust was a known entity but he was unpredictable—and dangerous. Everyone here was at risk.

At the end of Dave's undercover operation, Bulldust, along with his brother Scotty, had been unhinged. Without Dave knowing, the brothers had realised he was a copper and wanted to deal with him the only way they knew how—to murder him.

Scotty had been called in to help with Dave's demise; they'd set a trap. Dave only realised his true identity had been discovered when he'd walked into Bulldust's depot and saw the cable ties lying on the table. He'd run out into the darkness and tried to dodge the bullets that Scotty had been spraying out at anything that moved. Scotty had also been screaming at Bulldust that it was all his fault because he hadn't done a thorough background check on Dave before bringing him into the cattle-stealing operation.

In all the confusion, Bulldust had been pleading with his daughter; telling Shane that he'd done everything for her, and she'd reacted with disbelief and anger.

These men had killed before to keep people quiet, and Dave was convinced they wouldn't think twice about killing again. Even if it was a copper—or a copper's family. They were bushmen; they knew the outback well. They could do the job, then stay hidden for years, maybe forever.

The thought sent shivers through Dave. He turned slowly, looking around, making sure no one was following them. The door to the storage shed was open and Dave itched to go and peer inside.

'It'll be all right, mate.' Even though Bob hadn't been looking in Dave's direction, the detective had clocked his action.

Bob pushed open the door and indicated for Dave to go into his office, while he stopped to talk to Lorri Prior, one of the detectives, who was sitting behind the desk. Dave nodded at the other detectives, Parksey and Blake, who were on the phones, and passed Perry's desk.

'How goes it, Dave?' Parksey asked, looking up from the computer.

'Good,' Dave answered tightly, looking over Parksey's shoulder. 'What're you working on?'

Parksey stared at him for a moment. 'You're not looking so good.'

Dave shrugged. 'Got something on the go. Just not sure what. Will let you know when I do.'

The Detective gave a nod and turned back to his screen. 'Chasing a bloke who's stolen a heap of fencing gear from a couple of farms out in the wheatbelt.'

'Good luck.' Dave continued into Bob's office, but he wasn't able to sit still. He paced the perimeter of Bob's office, waiting for his partner, knowing Parksey was watching him curiously through the open door.

He kept going over Bulldust's words on that final day when the case imploded and everything went down: Dave's cover blown and the operation over. '*I don't like loose ends.*' Well, Dave knew he was one of those loose ends. He was in possession of enough information to put Scotty and Bulldust away for murder, the attempted murder of a policeman and cattle stealing. Probably worth more than one lifetime sentence. Unless they could silence him first.

Both Scotty and Bulldust had had a red-hot crack at trying to shoot him. One of them had succeeded—but the bullet had gone no further than his shoulder.

'Right,' Bob said shutting the door behind him and sitting at his desk. As Dave continued to wear a path in the carpet, Bob reached into his drawer and brought out a mouth-freshener spray, aimed it at his mouth and gave a couple of pumps. 'Here's how I see it,' he said, pulling the phone closer. 'If Bulldust had wanted to abduct Mel or hurt her, he would have done it right then and there. He would've made contact like he did, got the confirmation that she was your wife and then got her out in the car park.'

He paused as Dave passed the back of his chair again. 'For god's sake, son, sit down. Take a load off. Don't worry, we'll sort this out.'

'Sorry.'

'Remember who you are. I know this is your family, but you're a copper and a good one, son. Look at this like it's a normal case. Yeah?'

'I know, I know.' He finally sat in the chair opposite Bob, and put his fists heavily on the desk.

'Now, tell me: Mel and the kids, they're at your parents-in-law's?'

Dave told him what he'd done earlier, and of Mark's reaction, then finished by saying. 'We need to get their address to the triple-zero call centre for priority if something does happen.'

Bob made a note on his notebook and nodded, then leaned back in his chair. 'I'll call them. Okay, I think it's safe to agree the prick, whoever it was, was just sending you a message, you agree?'

Dave thought about that. 'I . . . Yeah, I guess so.' He put his hands back in his lap.

'Right. We'll have to look at that going forward. The bastard might want to keep frightening them to get at you. Unnerve you. Play with your mind.'

'I don't reckon,' Dave said. 'Bulldust isn't clever enough for that. He's calculating but impulsive. Scotty's the shrewd one. The older brother thinks things through and sees both the pros and cons of any situation. If they were going to play mind games, Scotty would be behind it and get Bulldust to do his dirty work. If this is a one-off, which you're beginning to convince me it is, it'll be Bulldust operating on his own. Like I said, he's the impulsive one. Scotty was the brains of the last operation, Bulldust was the brawn.' He paused. 'When I was undercover the fellas I worked with called him The Enforcer. They'd say if he turned up, there was going to be trouble.'

'Trouble as in . . .'

'As in, if something needed fixing, people disappearing—permanently.'

'Right.' Bob let out a heavy sigh through his nose. 'Now, I would also expect that he followed Mel to your house, and perhaps to your in-laws' place and here, so we need to assume these three locations have been compromised.'

'No,' Dave said, shaking his head. 'Not possible. At least not going to Mark's. I took every extra turn and drove down the side streets. I would have seen if he was tailing me.'

'Son, you're not thinking clearly. You're only talking about today when you realised he's around. He must've been watching the family for a few days to be able to work out where Mel goes so he could approach her. And what if he put a GPS tracker on Melinda's car? That's what you're driving now. He doesn't need to follow you.'

That gave Dave pause, before he said, 'That's unlikely.'

'I agree, but the technology is available, albeit expensive. I don't think we should discount anything at this stage, do you?'

'Jesus!' Dave let out a groan and slapped his hands on his thighs.

'Look, I think you're right: this action smells of impulsiveness, so we can surmise it's game-playing. That's all. Possibly nothing to worry about.'

Dave shot out of the chair, planted his fists on the desk and leaned towards his partner. 'He said he'd kill me, Bob! I believe him. I took everything from him—his daughter, his livelihood, the life he'd built over there in Nundrew. I'd bet my next pay cheque that Shane—that's the daughter—hasn't spoken to him since the night she overhead him confessing to the murder of at least two other employees! I heard her say how much she loved the blokes he'd got rid of. One of them used to read her stories. He drew a breath, then continued his rant. 'I saw the cable ties linked together on the kitchen table that night. They were meant for me.' His chest was heaving. 'He's found me and my family. I don't think that's game-playing!'

'Settle down, son.' Bob held his hands up in a calming manner. 'You're going to pop a valve. I know all this, okay? And I've got your back. I'm not playing this down, I understand the dangers. I just want you to know, now we've talked, that I don't think we'll see him again until he's ready to make a move on you. I'll get this sorted as quick as I can. The best thing to happen now is for you to go home and pack a bag. You can camp with me tonight. I'll send Parksey with you.'

'What are you going to do?'

'Get your in-laws' details to the triple-zero centre, then organise a static guard at their house. That'll make the family feel safe. Then we're going to go and visit them. Tell them all what's going on. We all know that Mark's a dick, but maybe this will make him realise that we're doing something to protect his family. You haven't said what happened there, but I'm guessing it wasn't good.'

'No.'

Bob stood up and clapped Dave on the shoulder. 'Son, we can't undo what's already been done, but we can put a plan in place to stop anything else from going wrong, and that's what I'm going to do. Meet me back here in about three hours.' He glanced at his watch. 'Yeah, that should give me enough time. It'll be nearly dark and we'll go to see your family then.'

Dave looked at his partner, who had become his friend over the time they'd been working together. Initially, Bob's insistence on calling Dave 'son' and the cliches that continually came out of his mouth had irked him no end. They'd had a couple of dust-ups over Bob's drinking, but in the end he'd come to understand that Bob's heart was bigger than the annoying things about him. 'Thanks, Bob.'

Bob smiled, but there was tension behind it. 'Remember, he's one bloke. A criminal. You've got the whole squad behind you. We'll get him.'

❧

Bob and Dave stopped at the static guard's vehicle, which was parked on the street outside Mark and Ellen's house.

'Quiet?' Bob asked the constable in uniform.

'Yes, sir. No movement.'

'Good lad, keep at it.' He gave the roof of the car a tap and walked on, Dave alongside him. Bob got out his breath freshener and squirted another few sprays into his mouth. 'Hope that lunchtime beer's gone,' he said quietly. 'Your father-in-law is just the sort of bloke to pick up on it.'

'I can't smell it,' Dave said.

They hit the stairs up to the house together and walked side by side onto the verandah. Dave noted the curtains were drawn tightly, but light still filtered from around the edge. The night was quiet save for the odd passing car and occasional raised voice from the next-door neighbours.

Dave could smell garlic and onions cooking on the night air and his stomach rumbled. He couldn't remember if he'd eaten today.

Bob rapped on the door and called out: 'Mark? Detective Sergeant Bob Holden here.'

Heavy footsteps sounded on wooden floorboards, then the clink of a chain being slid back and the door opened a crack. 'What do you want?'

Dave ground his teeth.

'Evening, sir. Could we come in for a minute?' Bob said.

The door swung open a little more and Mark let them both in. Dave could see the door into the kitchen was shut, so there was no chance that Bec would have known he was there. Even so, he was disappointed not to hear her call out, 'Daddy!'

'What can I do for you?' Mark asked, looking only at Bob.

24

'I thought we'd bring you up to speed about where we are at tonight. As you know, we believe Mel has been approached by a man who threatened Dave in an earlier investigation.'

Mark didn't say anything, but resentment radiated off him.

'I'm sure you've seen we've stationed a guard at the front of your house.'

'Yes, for all the neighbours to see.'

'A visual deterrent is always helpful when it comes to situations like these. And with all due respect, sir, I for one would rather that my family was safe, regardless of whether the neighbours spent their time wondering what I'd been doing to warrant a guard,' Bob said with a raised eyebrow, before continuing. 'As of this afternoon, we're in discussions with Major Crime, and they will come and interview your daughter tomorrow morning.'

Mark nodded, his eyes still on Bob. It took all Dave's self-control not to get in his father-in-law's face and remind him that he was here.

'Major Crime have advised us it wouldn't be safe to have Dave stay here tonight, so we'll put him up for the night.' He paused. 'If you don't have any questions, then I'll let Dave say his goodbyes.'

Mark shook his head. 'No. No questions. Thank you, though, Detective, for all your work on this. It's nice to know my family will be safe.' At that point he glanced across at Dave, an accusation clear on his face.

'Right.' Bob moved towards the door, but Mark was quicker. He opened it and let Bob outside. 'I'll be in the car, Dave.'

The door was shut gently behind Bob, and Mark dropped all pretence. Anger flashed through his eyes and he took a step towards Dave. 'Fantastic. Not only do I have a fuck-up for a son-in-law, he brings his drunken boss around here to tell me what he's going to do. Do you—'

'He's not drunk,' Dave interrupted.

'From what I hear, Bob Holden is permanently pickled. Long lunches at the King's Arms most days.'

Briefly, Dave wondered how much Mel had told her father about his work colleagues or if he'd researched them himself. It was all ammunition against him, he supposed. Instead of saying anything, he stood there and let Mark speak.

'Anyway, I could smell it on his breath. Beer. Mixed with breath freshener. As if I wouldn't notice. And don't bother denying it, because I'd be able to find out if he was at the pub today with one phone call. Let's not forget I have friends in high places.'

Dave didn't doubt that. His father-in-law had worked in finance before he'd made his millions and retired early. These days he spent hours at the Royal Golf Club, playing with the who's who of Western Australia.

He didn't rise to the bait. Dave knew that Mark was goading him. Trying to get him to react. Well, Dave had learned his lesson from the last time, when he'd given Mark a fat lip and bruised cheek. He wasn't going to assault him again.

'Look, Mark, we couldn't have foreseen that Bulldust would turn up here and approach Mel. What we have to do now is—'

Mark talked over the top of him. 'See, Dave, that's your problem. You don't think. That's why you'll never get anywhere in life.'

'I wish this hadn't happened as much as you do,' Dave pushed on. 'All we can do is our best to keep everyone safe, going forward.'

'If you want to run around playing boy scout and chasing this Bulldust, or whatever his name is, without any decent plan, putting your life and the life of my daughter and grandchildren at risk, then so be it. I—'

'Mark!' Ellen's voice sounded from the gloom of the passageway. 'Mark, be fair. Dave didn't intend this to happen. This is part of his job.'

Mark rounded on Ellen and pointed a finger at her. 'Which is why he should do as his wife asks and resign. And you stay out of this—you have no idea what you're talking about. He's a disgrace to the family. Everyone else thinks he's a hero because he got himself shot trying to track these men down—but all he's done is cause more problems!'

Ellen walked down the hall and put her hand on Mark's arm. 'This will be okay.'

Dave was grateful for Ellen's kindness but he couldn't stand being in Mark's vicinity any longer. 'You know what? I might just say goodnight to Mel and the kids and get out of your hair. If there's any trouble, please make sure you call triple zero first and then me.'

'Don't bank on it,' Mark said, giving him a cold stare.

Chapter 3

Bulldust changed down a gear as he entered Laverton and slowed to the required sixty kilometres an hour.

The place was caked in red dirt, and the buildings ached with the tiredness and heat of a goldfields mining town, despite the trees planted along most of the streets.

He took his foot off the accelerator as he approached the Desert Inn Hotel. Maybe he should pick up a carton for the rest of the drive. There was still another two hours to go until he reached the camp that he and Scotty had set up nearly six months before.

Mate, that could be a half-a-carton trip, he thought and pulled over in front of the hotel. The quietness of the town was broken only by a crow cawing overhead, and a gust of warm wind sent leaves scattering down the road.

Even at three in the afternoon, people were sitting at the bar in the pub. Some in high-vis shirts, mining companies' logos embroidered on the pocket. They'd finished their shifts and were having a pint before they headed to their accommodation to fall exhausted into bed, only to do it all again the next day. Others were tourists heading up the Great Central Road. He'd noticed two LandCruiser 200s in the car park, hauling caravans, along with three dusty four-wheel drives with either a camper or swags secured to the roof racks.

Nothing but a pain in the arse, he thought. *Go slow, and most of them know nothing about the bush. Just cause trouble. Flat tyres, branches up through the radiators. Then some poor bastard has to go and rescue them.*

The continual stream of caravans and camper trailers gave Bulldust the shits. One thing they'd learned since they'd been out there was that even though the area was isolated, there were always people around where you least expected them.

'Carton of draught stubbies, thanks, fella,' Bulldust said, his eyes combing the pub for any familiar faces—from his past life and any he needed to be aware of now. He was suspicious by nature and was relieved to see no one he knew drinking there.

Last time he'd been in, he'd seen a bloke he'd ridden in a rodeo with four years earlier. He'd got out of there pretty quickly when he'd seen the man sitting with his back to the wall, staring at the TV. He didn't want anyone eyeballing him in case the coppers turned up asking questions. Didn't matter if they were mates or enemies; he didn't want to be in the forefront of anyone's thoughts.

'Forty thanks, cob,' the barman said.

Bulldust threw over a fifty-dollar note, waited for his change and hoisted the carton into his arms. 'Cheers.'

Outside, he looked around again. Scotty had shown him the faces of the local police for Barrabine, but unless there was a gold theft, rollover or death, they rarely headed up this way. They had enough to keep them busy in the town and surrounding mines. And the copper he wanted was in Perth.

He rested the carton on the passenger's seat next to him and climbed into the dirty Toyota ute. Staring through the windscreen he had a fleeting thought that he should clean it before heading out. The splattered insects were making it difficult enough to see, but it would be worse when he got out a bit further with the dust.

Thankfully, the sun was behind him.

Instead, he shoved the LandCruiser into gear and pulled away from the kerb. As he hit the dirt road, the corrugations shook the ute, making the tray clatter loudly. The radio cut out as a wheel fell into a pothole full of dust. Reaching over, he opened the carton of beer and pulled out a can before giving the dash a bang in hope that the radio would work again.

It didn't.

With a half shrug, Bulldust thought back to meeting Melinda Burrows in the supermarket. He hadn't intended to approach her, just observe from a distance—he'd been watching Dave's house for the past three days, between being with Missy, the private detective who'd found Dave for him. He gave a chuckle as he thought about how close

Dave had come to him in the car two days earlier. Bulldust had been slumped down in Missy's car, watching the house, trying to get a bead on Dave's activities. What he'd come to understand was that there wasn't a routine. Dave came and went at strange times of the day and night.

But his wife had one. That's why Bulldust had decided to approach her.

The night Dave had pulled up in the driveway, Bulldust could have reached out and touched his arm, they'd been so close.

So much for being a detective, he thought.

His thoughts switched to Missy. Ah, Missy. He smiled, remembering her soft skin pressing against him and her silky hair trailing over his stomach as she moved lower and lower. He felt himself grow hard, just thinking about her.

'Better stop that, brother,' he said to himself, putting the cold can against his face. 'Be a while before you see her again.'

A movement on the side of the road caught his eye and he saw the familiar five emus, their long necks stretched up as if they were on high alert, watching the vehicle as it bumped down the track. The family were there most times that Bulldust drove by.

Concentrating on the road, now the sun was almost below the horizon, he thought back to Melinda. She'd opened up so easily, it had made him wonder if she even knew about him and Scotty. Surely Dave would have coached her not to give out personal details if he knew that Bulldust was looking for him. Perhaps that gave him the element of surprise.

Although maybe not now. She would have run home and told Dave everything. *Tell him Ashley said g'day and I'll catch up with him real soon*, he'd said. As soon as Dave heard the name Ashley, he would have known.

That perfect life Dave had set up with the little missus and couple of kids was just about to become not so perfect. A harsh chuckle escaped Bulldust's lips as he took another sip from the can.

'You'll know I'm coming now, won't you? Think you can take everything from me, without me returning the favour? I don't reckon.'

Out of habit, he picked up his phone from the dash and looked at it. No range. He still hoped one day he would see a message or missed call from Shane. It had been a year since he'd heard anything from her.

That fucked-up night when everything had gone wrong. They'd discovered that Dave was an undercover copper, and Shane had turned up in the middle of Bulldust's ramblings, which could've been a confession. She'd stared at him as if she'd never known him. Ever since, in the early morning hours when he couldn't sleep, he reheard her pleas: *Have you done it to others? What about old Hec? He used to read me stories when I was little, after Mum left . . . Did you do something to him too?*

Curling his fingers around the steering wheel a little harder, Bulldust gritted his teeth and, without meaning to, let a snarl escape his lips.

His mustering company had been lucrative, but stealing cattle had proven more so. He'd worked with a tightknit crew and made sure he had enough dirt on his employees to have a hold over them. To command their loyalty. But every so often, one would stray. Or say too much or put an operation at risk.

He'd had to make the call to kill off the blokes who'd opened their mouth too wide. Even if he'd liked them. And he'd liked Dave.

Dave's betrayal had hit harder than most. Dave had pretended to be a mate. A good worker. Weaselled his way into his business, his friendship and . . . Shane's heart.

Oh yeah, Shane had fallen for him. Bulldust had caught them kissing once. *Bet the little missus wouldn't like to know that,* he thought.

And all the while, he was a dirty, stinking copper; it had all been an act.

Bulldust tossed the empty bottle into the footwell of the ute and ripped another one from the carton as he stared moodily out the windscreen.

Only another hour and a half until he got back to camp.

❧

Lifting his foot from the accelerator, Bulldust searched the trees lit up in the spotlights, looking for the tiny piece of dark rag he'd tied onto the branch to indicate the entrance to their camp.

They'd set it up on Crown land, deep in the bush, and the little two-wheel track they'd pushed through was well hidden. Slowing to a stop, Bulldust got out and removed the tree branch from across the drive. A tingle of excitement rose in him as he replaced the branch and headed towards the camp.

Hopefully, the water was holding up for their crop.

Scotty was the brains behind the new venture. Once it became clear that Dave Burrows was going to take them in, Bulldust and Scotty had separated and disappeared deep into the bush. Bulldust had been hiding out in Lightning Ridge when Scotty had got in contact with him, with the new plan.

They would head west and set up out in the desert. He knew where there was underground water. They would grow marijuana, then dry and sell it. Bulldust could run it to Perth when the crops were ready. Scotty had a station out of Barrabine and was known around the area, but no one would recognise Bulldust; he'd always lived in Queensland. Scotty had contacts within bikie gangs who would take as much green as they could supply.

They had over an acre of land planted, each area at different growth stages. It wouldn't be long now.

This trip to Perth had been Bulldust's maiden run, which he'd combined with stalking Dave and reacquainting himself with Missy. Overall, it had been a successful trip. Although it had taken a while to convince Scotty to let him go. His brother liked to be in control of the transactions.

The lights powered by a small generator glowed in the distance. Reaching down, he clicked the two-way four short times to let Scotty know he was about to arrive.

Four flashes of the lights came a couple of moments later.

He eased the vehicle forward slowly, lights on high beam, as he navigated the rough two-wheel track until he saw the fire, another two utes and the camp.

With a sigh of relief, he grabbed the carton sitting next to him and heaved himself out of the driver's seat.

Scotty was sitting in a camp chair next to the fire, a two-way at his side. On his lap was a paper plate filled with camp-oven stew; a pannikin of scotch sat on the ground, at his feet.

'Okay?' Scotty asked, as he wiped his mouth with the sleeve of his jumper. He got up and grabbed the shovel and dug it into the coals of the fire, heaping a pile under his chair to act as a heater. The muscles in his arms rippled as he did so, reminding Bulldust that even though his brother was shorter than him, he was stronger.

They didn't look alike, the brothers. Half-brothers with different mothers, Bulldust had fiery red hair, which he shaved off, while Scotty was dark. Bulldust had vivid ice-blue eyes and Scotty had brown.

'I'll have one of them,' Bulldust answered as he put the carton down near his chair and went to the camp oven.

Without a word, Scotty shovelled another heap under Bulldust's camp chair on the other side of the fire.

'Got on, no worries,' Bulldust said as he piled his plate with beef and potato stew.

Scotty didn't answer, just nodded and sat down again.

'Okay here?'

'No problems.'

'Water holding up?'

'I've got the pump going. Was a bit short this arvie.'

Bulldust tucked into the stew. No matter how much of an arsehole his brother was, he could cook better than most stock-camp cooks . . . and he didn't get stuck into the cooking sherry to boot. Not that Bulldust would have ever complimented him. That wasn't how they worked.

'Nothing happened in Perth that I need to know about?' Scotty asked, lifting the pannikin to his mouth.

A flash of Melinda Burrow's smiling face hit his memory and he chuckled. 'Couldn't help myself. I had to work the detective's bitch while I was there.' He watched Scotty still and his eyes swing towards him.

'You did what?'

'Couldn't resist it. She was there, ripe for the picking.'

'What do you mean?' Scotty leaned forward and stared at Bulldust.

'In the shopping centre where I was. Had the new pica-ninny with her. She was all a bit lost in her own world. Thought I'd just get her to pass on my regards to her husband.'

Scotty put down his mug and stood up. 'What if they can identify you or your car?'

'Nah, caught a bus. Missy showed me how to.'

'There're security cameras in those big shopping centres, you dickhead. You'll be on one of them for sure.'

Bulldust paused. He hadn't thought about that.

Blustering on, he said, 'Nah, nah, she'll be right. They won't know who they're looking for.'

Making a disgusted noise, Scotty jabbed his finger towards Bulldust's chest. 'You're a fucking idiot. You'll want to hope that hasn't fucked us up again.'

'What do you mean by that?' Bulldust stood up, his heart thumping, anger pulsating through him. 'I'm sick to death of you treating me like I'm an imbecile. You're not perfect, you know.'

'You know that not following our own rules brought us undone last time. The buck stops with you. *You* caused it.'

'Don't worry about me, mate,' Bulldust answered. 'I know what I'm doing.'

Scotty turned and stalked off, but not before the words 'I highly doubt that' filtered through to Bulldust.

He clenched his fists but let his brother walk away. It would do no good to pick a fight now.

Ha. And Scotty thought he didn't have brains.

Chapter 4

'Get your lazy arse out of bed,' Scotty snarled as he kicked Bulldust's swag.

Bulldust's eyes opened and he saw stars. 'What's the time?' he muttered.

'Doesn't matter. We've got work to do.'

Bulldust rolled over and looked at his watch as he heard Scotty throw more wood on the fire. The sparks shot towards the stars, and then he heard the clink of the billy on the coals Scotty would've dragged out from the fire.

The glow of his watch showed four-thirty. His head thumped a little; the after-effects of last night's beer and whiskey.

Wriggling out of his swag, he reached for his boots and put them on, before heading to the part of the camp that doubled as a bathroom. There was cold water in a bowl, which he slapped onto his face and under his arms, before walking a little further away to relieve himself.

Looking at the night sky, he made out the Southern Cross, the Saucepan and the Seven Sisters. It would be a good hour and a half before the sun started to rise. Walking the boundary fence before daylight was a shit of a job, but he knew it had to be done.

There was no talking between the two men as they poured their cups of tea and ate the damper that Scotty had cooked the previous evening. Only as they were about to leave for their separate jobs did Scotty say, 'You right, then?'

'Done it before, reckon I can do it again today.'

'Had trouble with camels yesterday, so you'll have a bit of fencing to do when you get out there. They can smell the crop and think it's grass. Probably smell the water, too, so they're wanting to come in and graze it.'

'Doped-up camels. Could be interesting.'

'I chased out four. Three females and a calf. I reckon there'll be a bull around somewhere. Managed to shoot one of them, but they were in around the bush, so I didn't get them all.'

'Did you get rid of it?'

'Yeah. Don't want the dingoes coming around. Dragged it about five ks to the north. Can't go too much further, otherwise we'll end up on the Aboriginal land.' He paused. 'I had a dingo around the camp while you were away.'

'Bastard.'

'Never saw him. Just the tracks. Reckon it's a young one. Prints were small. We'll need to keep an eye out.'

'Will do. What are you going to do?'

Scotty's face glowed golden as the flames reflected off him. 'Check the pump again for the crop that's just beginning to bud, then start harvest on the next lot. You can come and help with that when you get back.'

Bulldust nodded. He grabbed the large torch and his .243 rifle and walked the two hundred metres to the fence line.

When they'd first decided on their plan, they'd spent many days in the Crown bushland off the Great Central Road heading out to the middle of Western Australia. They'd found this patch of country, with a dry creek bed running along the bottom of a high hill range. Then they'd found a couple of caves and knew that it was the perfect place. Scotty had been taught to water divine by an old Aboriginal man who worked for their father many years ago, and when he'd found the deep underground river it was if they'd been kissed on the dick. This was their space. Their land. Their new start.

They'd carted in rolls and rolls of six-foot ringlock fencing to keep the camels and any other wildlife out— roos didn't mind having a chew at the marijuana crop, and the sweet smell, when it started to bud up, attracted the animals. The water, too, brought unwanted pests that put pressure on the fence. Bulldust and Scotty had discovered that they had to walk it every day, often finding camels had pushed through and were happily munching on their profit.

'Nothing that a gun won't fix,' Scotty had grunted when he'd first come across them. So now Bulldust walked the fence every morning and shot the camels, roos or any other vermin that had got in overnight.

They'd brought in water pumps and fertiliser in drums. Stretched out netting as a camouflage across the tree tops and started to plant in an old water course so there wasn't anything symmetrical about the planting that could be seen from the sky, on the off-chance a plane flew over. They had about a thousand plants—four months' worth—in each planting.

Together, they had run the reticulation dripper system to each plant and had carted in a large tank and placed it up on a hill so the water would syphon down to the retic. One diesel pumped the water from underground to the tank.

Bulldust wasn't sure, but he thought it must be just about time to make a trip to one of the smaller settlements and refill their mobile fuel tanker. They chose a different place each time; you never knew who you'd run into.

It had been Scotty's idea to hang shade cloth from the trees, higher than the netting, in case someone flew over and noticed them. It would also help protect the smaller seedlings from the viciousness of the sun. The cloth hadn't taken long to absorb the colour of the ground—a vivid red. They were camouflaged well, as was their camp.

Bulldust was sure-footed as he followed the fence, stopping occasionally to test the tension. His daily walk had created a track and he knew most of the trouble spots.

The fence was cold to touch and as he bent down to check the bottom wires a spiky bush caught on his jeans and he felt the dew soak through them. He stumbled and fell to his knees, the torch falling from his grasp and the gun poking into his leg.

41

'Fuck it,' he muttered and got up, dusting his hands on his jeans. Then he stilled, his hand straying to the trigger of the rifle.

He wasn't sure what had caught his attention, but a sixth sense was making the hair stand up on his arms. Moving slowly, he reached for the torch and swung it around in an arc.

Nothing.

He repeated the action, this time seeing a movement in the long spinifex grass. He kept the light trained in the one spot, taking a step towards it.

Eyes suddenly reflected in the light.

Dingo.

Bulldust adjusted his gun and looked through the scope.

The grass moved again and a small paw came out, followed by another. A few seconds later, a brown pup emerged and sniffed the air. It took a couple of tentative steps towards him and then let out a short, high-pitched bark.

Bulldust lowered the gun. 'That's not a dingo bark,' he said.

The pup ran across, his tail wagging, and sniffed at the bottom of Bulldust's jeans and around his boots.

'What are you doing all the way out here without an owner?'

The pup flopped at his feet and stared up at him.

Fishing in his pocket, he took out a muesli bar and broke off a small piece, offering it to the pup, which wolfed it down quickly and looked up for more.

Bulldust's stomach dipped a little as he looked at the liquid brown eyes staring up at him. This pup was scruffy, scrawny and clearly unloved. How had he got to be out here? Maybe he'd fallen off the back of a station ute or someone had left him behind. Lucky not to have picked up a bait already. Or to have succumbed to the midday heat.

He'd had to leave his dogs when he and Scotty had run. They'd been good mustering dogs; knew how to ring a mob and bite the noses of the troublemakers. They had been like him: fearless and unrelenting. They'd rarely let a beast beat them.

When he'd gone to Lightning Ridge he'd missed his constant companions, and not knowing what happened to them had torn at his heart. His guess was they'd been taken to the pound and probably put down.

'Come on, then, let's have a look at you.'

The little body squirmed under his touch and just about disappeared inside his large hands. A tongue reached out and licked Bulldust on the nose.

'There'll be none of that going on,' Bulldust growled good-naturedly. 'What are we going to call you?'

He turned the pup over and inspected him. 'You're bloody lucky, that's what you are. Should call you that. But . . .' He saw light-tan fur on the pup's chest and realised he had light brown eyebrows, too. 'You're actually a proper kelpie.' He ran his hands roughly over his head and ears, then, putting the pup down, he called to it. 'Come on, follow me, Desert. Found you in the desert, so that's what you can be.'

❧

Walking back into camp, Bulldust reached into his pocket and pulled out Desert. He'd only walked half of the fence line before he'd stopped, curled into a ball and fallen asleep.

'Can't be sleeping on the job,' Bulldust had told him, picking him up, but the pup hadn't moved.

Scotty had just come out of one of the greenhouses and stopped.

'What is that?'

'Pup.' Bulldust took some sausages from the car fridge, cut them up and them put them in a bowl. The pup roused, sniffed around the camp, then padded across to Bulldust, before sitting and looking up at him. 'Got good manners already.'

'What are you doing with it?'

'What do you think? Can't stay out there by himself.'

Scotty walked over and looked down. 'He can't stay here either.'

'Yeah, he can. We'll train him as a guard dog.'

'Going to be a bloody long time before he's capable of that.'

Bulldust put the bowl down and Desert started to eat. Ignoring his brother, Bulldust poured himself a cup of tea, grabbed some biscuits and sat in front of the fire. The pup finished his breakfast and wandered over to Bulldust before curling up at his feet and going to sleep.

'He'll get in the way,' Scotty said, scratching his own stomach, before pouring himself a cup of tea as well.

Bulldust watched Scotty lean against a tree and bat flies away. He was still fit and strong, and would probably outrun most people if it came to a foot race. His hair was beginning to tinge with grey above his ears, and his neck and face were burnt a dull red. And he didn't like dogs. That pissed Bulldust off.

'Did you hear me?' Scotty snarled.

Looking over at the white-trunked gum trees that lined the creek, Bulldust again fought the urge to hit his brother. Instead, he focused on the soft red dirt at base of the trunk. The vibrancy of the colours always amazed him, and the green leaves contrasted vividly against the whiteness of the trunk.

Ignoring his brother had always been the way he coped with Scotty's constant belittling and commands. Their father had been the same, and Scotty had taken on his traits. With no mother—or mothers—to protect them, there had been little mollycoddling or affection in their lives. Scotty was older and had bullied Bulldust through most of his childhood.

When Bulldust had been small, he'd wished his mother would arrive and whisk him away. If he ever said anything about his mum, his father would tell him to take a teaspoon of cement and harden the fuck up. There wasn't any room for softness out in station country.

By the time he was five, he could ride motorbikes, horses and muster with the best of them, and he'd hardened up. But Scotty hadn't let up on him.

'Well, don't let him get in my way,' Scotty finally said. ''Cause I won't stop what I'm doing to make sure he's okay.'

'Wouldn't expect you to.'

'I need a hand to refuel the generators.' Scotty put down his cup and took off towards the greenhouses.

'Come on, Desert,' Bulldust said, and watched with pleasure as the little pup followed him.

Chapter 5

'We're looking for Melinda Burrows.'

Two men dressed in plain suits and shiny shoes stood in the doorway. The taller one spoke to Ellen when she answered the door.

'She's through here.' Ellen ushered the detectives into the lounge room, where Mel sat on the floor playing with Bec and Alice. She looked up, her face grim, just as Mark entered the room.

'I'm Mark Beattie, Melinda's father.' He held out his hand and both men shook it.

'Detective Senior Sergeants Carl Lemming and Ken Smith. Major Crime.' He turned to Mel, who was getting up from the floor. 'You must be Melinda?' He held out his hand to her.

She shook both of their hands and smiled. 'Yes, I'm Melinda. Thanks for coming, but I'm not sure how much more I can help. I told Dave everything I can remember.'

'Mummy?' Bec got up too and tugged at her sleeve. 'Who are those men?'

She squatted down and pulled Bec into a hug. 'Some people who have to ask me some questions. Policemen, like Daddy. Can you go with Granny and help her now?'

'But I want to stay.'

'No, sweetheart. This is grown-up talk.'

Bec pouted but left the room with Ellen, who had picked up Alice and was holding her hand out to her granddaughter.

Taking a breath, Melinda faced the detectives. 'How can I help you?'

'We've got some questions about the approach. Can we sit down? I'd like for you to tell us what happened.'

'Detectives, she's already been through this. She's told her husband, who also happens to be a detective.'

Mel frowned. 'Dad, I can handle this.'

Mark walked to her and put his hand on her shoulder. 'I know you can, darling, but this is going beyond a joke. You shouldn't have to keep answering the same questions over and over.'

Sighing, Melinda held out her hands. 'It's okay, Dad. The quicker they ask their questions, the quicker we can all go back to normal.'

Mark jerked his head at the detectives. 'I hope this is the last time.'

'I understand your frustration, but we're from a different squad, looking into Ashley and Scott Bennett's disappearance. We've heard what you told your husband, Mrs Burrows,

48

but we need to hear it from you. Are you happy to talk in front of your father, or would you like him to leave?'

'No, no, he can stay.' Mel sank down onto the couch and looked at both men. 'Ask your questions.'

'I'd appreciate it if you could tell us what happened in the supermarket, as best you remember.'

Mel started from the beginning, stopping occasionally to try to remember more, but nothing else came to her. 'It didn't occur to me that this person might be the man who wanted to hurt Dave.' She sighed. 'I feel like I'm living in a fog at the moment. The new baby and all.'

'Of course. And this supermarket. Do you regularly shop there?'

'Yes,' Mel nodded. 'It's my local supermarket, so I go there all the time.'

'How many times each week?' Carl asked the questions while Ken wrote down the answers.

Shifting on the couch, Mel watched her father pace the room. 'Probably twice a week. Sometimes more.'

'And does your husband ever go with you?'

Mark harrumphed. 'Not likely.'

Carl's eyes didn't even swing towards Mark, he just kept looking steadily at her.

'Um, no. He has done, but it would be unusual. You'd never be able to rely on him being there, if that's what you're asking.' The bitterness in her tone was clear.

'I see. And the times you go—would they be the same times each week?'

Mel stopped to think. 'Um, not really. Or maybe . . .' She paused. 'I usually drop Bec with Mum so she can take her to her swimming lessons while I head over to do the shopping. So yeah, I guess it would be normally within an hour or so.'

'What kind of car do you drive?'

'A blue Toyota Corolla.'

'And that's what you always drive?'

'Yes.'

'You never take your husband's car?'

Shaking her head, Melinda said, 'No, he has the stock squad four-wheel drive. His other car is a beat-up Toyota tray-back without power steering. I wouldn't drive it if you paid me to.'

'Where did you park the day the man approached you?' Carl leaned forward as he asked the question.

'In the car park off Ruhind Road.'

'Is that where you always park?'

Melinda frowned. 'What? Why does it matter? Yes, I always park there.' The frustration showed in her voice.

'I'm sorry, Mrs Burrows. We're trying to establish a pattern. I'm sure this is annoying for you, but if you could bear with us, we hope we might be able to find Ashley and make sure that you and your family are safe.'

Taking a few calming breaths, Melinda chastised herself. She knew they were only doing their job, but as her dad had pointed out, she'd been through this already.

'So, you always park in the same car park?'

'Yes.'

'Who was with you?'

'Just Alice. I had her strapped to my chest.'

'Where did you go when you left the car?'

This time it was Mark. 'What does that have to do with it?'

Carl turned to him. 'As I explained before, we're trying to establish a pattern. A routine. If Mrs Burrows is always using the same car, car park, timing and route, then the suspect will have found her easily. He would have only had to follow her a few times to know her schedule, and that would have made it easy to connect with her.'

'Followed?' Mel asked, a lump forming in her throat.

'Yes. That's how he would've known how to find you.' Ken spoke for the first time. 'And it sounds like you would have been simple to locate. You're a creature of habit.'

Silence hung in the room as the reality of the situation sank in.

Finally, Carl cleared his throat. 'Can you tell me what he looked like?'

Mel stood up and joined her father pacing the lounge-room floor. As she explained what she remembered, she stood in front of their wedding photo staring at their happy smiles. So different to now.

How could she have known that marrying Dave was going to put her and her children in so much danger? Would have she changed anything if she had known? That was an interesting question, and one for which she didn't have an immediate answer.

'Mrs Burrows?'

She turned and focused on the detective. 'Sorry. I missed that.'

'Can you think of any distinguishing features? Tattoos or the like?'

'I want to help you, I really do,' Mel said, 'but I don't remember. It was so quick, and I was tired and all I was trying to do was get in and out of the shops quickly so I could go home. It's hard shopping with a baby. You just never know when they're going to have had enough, so you have to do everything in a hurry.'

Carl nodded. 'Yes, I understand. You don't remember any tattoos, then?'

She shook her head. 'Dave has since told me this man has letters on his knuckles, but I didn't see them.' She gave a hard laugh. 'If I'd realised it was the same man I would've looked for sure.'

'Okay. How tall?'

She stood up and place her hand a few inches above her own height. 'About that.'

'Hair?'

'Bald. And he needed a shave.'

Carl nodded at Ken, who produced a manila folder.

'Do you think you'd recognise him again?'

Melinda shook her head helplessly. 'I really don't know.'

'In this folder we have twelve photos of men who are similar in appearance. We'd like you to look at them and see if you can pick him out. Take your time.'

Ken laid the photos out on the coffee table and Melinda walked over to look at them. Mark stood behind her and looked over her shoulder. She could hear his heavy breathing and knew how angry he was. The tension radiated from his body. Part of her wanted to rub his arm and tell him it would be all okay, but she couldn't do that. Nobody could do that because nobody knew if it would be.

Carefully, she picked up each photo and looked at the man in it. For the first three, she shook her head. When she picked up the fourth one, she stopped, unsure. She put it off to the side, before looking at the others. At the end of the twelve she had two photos that she went back to check.

Finally, she handed number eight to Carl. 'I'm not certain, but I think it's him.'

'What do you mean?'

Mel screwed up her nose as she tried to explain. 'It's my gut feeling.'

'Why a gut feeling?'

'I think it's the hardness in his face. His eyes; they're really cold, like ice. And . . .' She took a breath and walked away. 'When I think back, he seemed very hard. I'd almost say mean, but that's not what I remember thinking at the time. It was like when he was talking to me, he was trying to be extra nice and to do that was an effort for him. Does that make sense? Sorry, I'm probably talking in circles.'

'Not at all, that's really helpful. Is there anything else you want to add?'

She shook her head. 'No, I just want all of this to be over.'

Ken turned the photo over. 'Can you just sign here and date the photo, please?'

Melinda reached for the pen and scribbled her signature.

'Okay, we'll be in touch as soon as we know anything.' Both men stood up. 'Thanks for your time.'

'You'll be in touch with Melinda or with Dave?' Mark asked.

'Both,' Carl answered.

'Do you think this man is in town?' Mark asked, coming to stand alongside Melinda. He put his hand protectively on her shoulder.

'I can't answer that question,' Carl said. 'I need to be convinced this is the person we're being led to believe it is. However, I would advise you to continue to use all caution when you're going out, and the static guard will still be stationed at the front.' He nodded at them both. 'Thanks for your time.'

Mark walked them to the door and thanked them, while Melinda leaned against the door frame and watched them leave.

'God, that was exhausting,' she said when he had shut the door.

Mark walked quickly to her and took her hand. 'I understand, darling. It's a frightening thing to go through.' He stopped and took a breath. 'Melinda, I don't believe you're safe here. If you're not safe, then neither are the children nor your mother and me. I'd like to make arrangements for us to go somewhere away from here.'

'What? No, there's no need, Dad. You heard what he said. He's not even sure if it's this Bulldust guy or not. Let's just wait and see.' She glanced back up at the wedding photo, desperately hoping to feel something for the man staring back at her from the frame.

All she felt was resentment. 'Look, I understand you're concerned, Dad, and of course I am too. But I don't want to upset the kids' routines or leave Dave yet. He's in danger as well. And before you ask, yeah, I'm angry he's put us in this situation as much as you are. But can you slow down and—'

'How could you want to wait?' Mark leaned towards her, his eyes serious. 'Let me ask you this: is it worth the risk? If something were to happen to you or one of the children, how would you feel?'

'But Dave—'

'Is not going to be able to look after you,' Mark snapped. 'He'd be here if he was really concerned about your safety.'

'Which might mean he's not?' Her voice rose in question. 'Because there isn't a reason to be.'

'Melinda, you're being naive. Dave put a guard at the front, he brought his drunken boss here to tell us what was going on. He's worried, all right. Let me organise to take us somewhere safe.'

Mel chewed the inside of her cheek. She wanted to give Dave a chance. Time to show her that he would be the one who was going to protect them all. Protect his family. But she knew her father was right. She just didn't want to admit it.

'Let's just wait and see what Dave says when he comes back a bit later,' she hedged.

'I'll make some plans in case. Compromise?'

She paused.

Bec came running into the room. 'Mummy, can you come and play outside?'

She glanced at the covered windows and focused on the fear that filtered through her as she thought about taking her child outside. She looked back at her father. 'Okay.'

Chapter 6

Out of the corner of his eye, Dave saw Bob snatch up the phone on the first ring.

'Holden.' Listening to the voice on the other end, he dragged his pad towards him and jotted down a few notes. 'I see. Information is where?'

Dave glanced across, a knot of anxiety building in his throat.

Major Crime was on the phone, he had no doubt.

Bob turned to his computer and clicked on something. 'Oh yeah, I see it. Right. Thanks for letting us know. You'll notify them we'll attend—' He broke off as someone spoke over him.

Pause.

'Okay. Yep, I'll do my best. Cheers.'

Dave looked over expectantly at Bob, who continued to read something on the screen and make notes.

'So?' Dave couldn't contain himself anymore.

'Actually, it's another job. Good timing too, I reckon.'

Dave slumped a fraction. 'What? How long is it going to take them?'

Bob continued to talk as if he hadn't heard Dave's question. 'Back to your old stomping ground, by the sounds of it. New manager taken over at Nefer Station, north of Barrabine. Found some discrepancies in the numbers of cattle and money in the bank. Should be a pretty straightforward case. Be good to get you out and about while this shit is going down. Bulldust won't know where to find you out there. Lot of country and space.'

'What?' Dave looked at him incredulously. 'I can't leave. What about Mel and the kids?'

'They'll be okay, as you well know. Protected by the police force. We've still got to get—' His phone rang again. 'Holden,' he answered.

Pause.

This time he looked over at Dave and then down at his notebook, before picking up a pen. 'I see. Can you flick 'em through?'

Pause.

'Yeah. Yeah, he's here in the office with me.'

The door slammed behind them and Dave jumped as Parksey walked in holding his hand up in a wave, before pulling his chair out and sitting down heavily. He fiddled with the mouse to get his computer to come to life then leaned over to Dave.

'Bob filled us in last night. Any news?' he whispered.

Dave shrugged and pointed to Bob. 'He's talking to Major Crime now.'

'Did you want to come in and interview him yourself?' Bob asked as he tucked the phone in between his neck and shoulder and looked at Dave with raised eyebrows.

Dave nodded.

Pause.

'Uh-huh. No worries. See you in a while.' Bob put the phone down and turned to Dave.

'Mel identified the photo of Ashley Bennett, but they want your confirmation, too. You spent time with him up close and personal.'

'Shit!' Dave paused, then gathered himself. 'Okay. We need to tell Mel.' He got to his feet and reached for his keys.

'Hold your horses, son. They'll be here in ten minutes, then you can go over and see the wife.' He turned to Parksey. 'Mate, Dave and I caught a job this morning. Got to head to Barrabine and do a muster. What've you got on?'

Dave only half listened as Parksey detailed a theft of ten stud rams from a White Suffolk stud in the south-west and the case Lorri was investigating out of Northam.

'Okay, so you'll be out and about while we are, too,' Bob surmised.

'Right. Perry's shift starts again in two days, so Lorri can stay in the office until then. He can catch up on his paperwork while we're all away,' Parksey said. 'Blake's going to take a week off, so we won't be seeing him for a while.'

'Yeah, yeah. That's the way to play it,' Bob agreed. He turned to write the instructions up on the whiteboard behind him.

Heavy footsteps sounded on the wooden stairs outside and they all turned as the door swung open to reveal two men in suits.

Bob rose and extended his hand. 'Good to see you, boys,' he said. 'Bob Holden. This is Dave Burrows.'

Dave stood and held his hand out.

'And Toby Parke.'

'Detective Senior Sergeants Carl Lemming and Ken Smith.' The taller of the two men introduced them, shaking Dave's hand and nodding at Parksey.

'Just on my way out,' Parksey said, standing up. 'Catch you all later.'

'Come and sit down,' Bob offered, pulling up extra chairs to his desk.

Dave watched as Ken brought out a folder and waited for the go-ahead from Carl.

'Thanks very much,' Carl said. He sat down and turned to Dave. 'You'll know that we interviewed your wife today.'

'Yes.'

Carl nodded to Ken, who brought out a photo and slid it across the desk to Dave.

'This is the man your wife picked out, from twelve possibilities.'

Dave held up the photo and found himself staring into the ice-blue eyes of the man who was intent on killing him. Instead of the long beard he'd always sported, he had a three-day stubble. His head was still bald and his neck still red from the Queensland sun.

'That's him.' Dave put the picture back down, unable to look at Bulldust any longer. The thought that he could have hurt Mel or Alice, or broken into their house, made him furious. The urge to hurt him rose so quickly and sharply in his throat that he had to look down in case Bob saw it in his eyes.

'How different is he from when you saw him last?'

'He doesn't have the beard, so anything below the cheekbones is unfamiliar, but the eyes are the same. I'd know them anywhere.'

'So,' Carl leaned back in his chair and regarded Dave curiously, 'tell me how you can be one hundred percent positive if he always had a beard. You and I know we can walk past acquaintances in the street who have shaved, and not recognise them.'

Dave nodded in agreement. 'But the eyes,' he repeated. 'I'll never forget them. I'm sure that's him.'

'I'd prefer a reason other than "I'm sure."'

'If I could see his hands, I'd be able to tell you.' Dave paused. 'He was quite proud of that tattoo. Said he was known for knocking the bulldust out of people. In fact, if you get in contact with Spencer Brown at the Barrabine police station, he may even have the old brief and photos that he showed me when I was heading undercover to hook up with Bulldust.'

'These ones, you mean?' Ken slid a couple of images out and passed them across to Dave.

This time he was looking at Bulldust's green-inked knuckles, then, in the second photo, his face, complete with the red beard that had hung to his chest.

'That's him.'

'Take a look at these,' Carl said.

Another lot of pictures were given to him. They were CCTV images; black-and-white and grainy. To Dave the quality didn't matter.

He knew.

Bulldust was standing in front of Mel, Alice strapped to her front. He towered over her, all the while smiling down at her.

Dave swallowed hard, fury raging inside.

'Height is correct, stance is right, posture is how I remember. I'm certain that is Ashley Bennett.'

'Right, can you sign here?' Carl flipped the photo over and indicated where to write his name and the date.

Dave scribbled quickly and looked up. 'What's your plan?'

'We'll put out a BOLO on him and make some enquiries.'

'A Be On the Look Out means you've got nothing. You don't know where to start.'

'And that isn't for you to worry about,' Carl said. 'Leave us to do our job. We'll find him.'

'He had a pretty good crack at trying to kill me,' Dave said, breathing heavily. He felt Bob's hand on his shoulder, but he ignored it. 'Pretty sure he'd like another opportunity.'

'Detective Burrows, we're aware of your history with the Person of Interest. We'll be doing everything in our power to keep you and your family safe.'

'Is there any CCTV footage that shows he was in a vehicle?'

Bob intervened. 'Son, you know they're not going to answer your questions. They've had to identify him properly, which they've now done. There's still a bit of work to do.' He turned to Carl and Ken. 'Can you tell me what security measures you'll put in place for the family?'

'We'll keep the guard at the front, and Mrs Burrows can have a guard with her when she goes out. We're in discussions to have them all shifted to a safe house.'

The two men stood up.

'Look, Detective Burrows, you're the one Ashley Bennett is after. It would be in your best interest not to be with your family at this time. For their safety. That's our strongest piece of advice.'

Dave opened his mouth, but Bob got in first.

'Thanks very much, fellas. Your advice will be taken on board. Won't it, son?' He clapped Dave's shoulder. 'Just got a job out bush, so we'll be pretty safe out there.'

Unhappily, Dave nodded. He could already hear the conversation with Mel.

'We'll be in touch as soon as we know something. Shoot across and say goodbye to your family today and leave the rest to us, yeah?' Carl held out his hand. 'I understand more than you realise how difficult this will be for you and how worried you are. But you have our word as fellow coppers that we'll look after them.'

Dave waited until the men had left the office and then turned on Bob. 'I've had another thought and I don't agree.'

'Agree with what, son?' Bob asked, sitting down in his chair.

'That he's only after me. Has anyone thought he might want my family too? I bet Shane hasn't come running back to him in recent times. She was so shocked to find out her father was a murderer. He might want to take my daughters away from me as well.'

'Now, let's not shadow box, son. We can only deal with what we know as of now. Act on the information we have. Let Major Crime do their job.' He tapped the computer screen. 'Here, I'm going to print these details off about this case north of Barrabine, you're going to have a quick squiz and then you're off to say goodbye to your family and we're getting on the road.' Before Dave could argue, Bob finished firmly: 'Let's take the advice of those coppers and get you away from your family and out of Perth.'

Chapter 7

Dave saw the suitcases before he saw Mel. In fact, he tripped over the first one—a small purple bag, which he recognised as Bec's.

'What's going on here?' he asked as he grabbed the wall and righted himself.

Mark strode in and gave a smile. 'It seems like I'm a broken record, Dave. You can't look after your family, so I'm going to have to. We're leaving in—' he checked his watch '—five hours.'

Dave glanced at Mel, who stood in the doorway with her arms crossed. 'Right. And when were you planning on telling me about this?'

'I wasn't going to leave, Dave,' Melinda said. 'I wanted to wait for a while. But then Bec asked to go outside and play—' Her voice broke as she spoke.

With two quick steps, Dave had her in his arms. 'Why did that upset you so much?'

'Because I'm too scared to take her out there. He could be watching.'

Dave breathed in a little deeper as guilt shot through him. 'I'm sorry,' he whispered against her hair. Turning, he looked at Mark. 'You didn't think to ring and talk to me about this?'

'Really, Dave, you chide *us* about communication?' Mark said. 'It's been you who's kept us in the dark. We had to rely on a phone call from Detective Lemming to confirm that the . . .' He stopped and harrumphed. 'The *filth* who approached Melinda was this . . . this *Bulldust.*' He said the word as if he had just stepped in dog shit.

'I—'

'I also found out from the helpful detective that you're leaving on another case.'

Mel pulled away. 'Jesus, Dave, that's not true, is it? Please tell me it's not.'

Looking down at her, he brushed her hair back from her face. 'Yes, it is, but it's not the way your dad's making it sound. Major Crime don't want me near you at the moment. I'm more of a danger to you close by than not.'

'See?' Mark exclaimed. 'You've just proved my point. You can't protect them.'

Dave took a step forward and glared at Mark. 'You're twisting this into something it's not. Using it against me when I—'

'Oh, harsh words, Dave,' Mark said. '*Using your lack of policing against you?* Was that what you were about to say? This is just proving everything I've known about you. I counselled Melinda against marrying someone so weak and spineless.'

Looking at him steadily, Dave said in a quiet voice, 'I know you asked Mel not to marry me and I know you've never thought I was good enough for her. Your behaviour towards me for all of our married life has been aggressive and antagonistic. Rarely have I reacted. But you cannot take my wife and my children away from me without a discussion.'

Mark appeared unmoved. 'The fact that you've failed to lock up this bastard is the exact reason I can't trust you to look after my daughter and grandchildren, and the exact reason I *can* take them somewhere safe.'

'Fuck me!' Dave exploded. 'Who's the broken record? Have a listen to yourself.' He turned to Mel. 'Honey, Major Crime have said I shouldn't be around you at the moment, that's true. I'm a risk to you. And that I shouldn't be in the areas I usually am. They've explained to you about routine and how people are found. That's why I can't be here. A job came in this morning. I'm going to Barrabine.'

'You should be happy there,' Mel said, a hiccup in her voice. She shook her head and looked at him, her disappointment clear. 'Really, Dave?' she asked softly. 'Really?'

Dave took her hands and faced her. 'Listen to me, Mel. I'm only going because it's safest for you and the girls. You don't have to go anywhere. The police will make sure you're safe here.'

Withdrawing her hands, Mel looked at him unhappily. 'I'm not sure I trust them.' She gave a half shrug. 'I know I don't have a reason to say that, but I—'

Dave quickly spoke over the top of her, not wanting to hear her say what he thought she might. *I don't trust you to keep me safe, so how can I trust the police, who are just like you?*

'I promise the police will make sure you're looked after. They're talking about a safe house.'

'You just said we didn't need to go anywhere!' Mark interjected. 'A safe house will upset the girls' routine. Where I'm taking them—well, it's just going to be a fun holiday. They'll have no sense of anything being wrong.'

Opening his mouth, Dave was about to snap that keeping them away from their father was wrong, but then he realised he would be away from them anyway. This wasn't an argument he was going to win. Not that he won many against Mark these days anyway.

'You'll need to tell Lemming and Smith—' he started.

'Already done,' Mark smirked.

There was silence as all three looked at each other, wondering who was going to say something.

Ellen bustled in with another suitcase. She looked like she'd been crying. 'Sorry, Dave,' she said softly. 'I know this will be very hard for you. But even I think this is for the best.' Putting her hand on his arm, she squeezed then left the room.

Dave knew that if Ellen agreed with what was happening, there was nothing more to say. He looked at Mel, who was studying the floor, her arms crossed.

'I'll just say goodbye to the kids, then.' He moved towards the kitchen.

Mark blocked his way. 'I don't think that's a good idea. They'll just get upset. Better to see them when this is all over.'

As Dave started to object, Ellen's voice rose over his.

'Mark, you stop right now! You are being ridiculous.' She gave him a warning glare and stood back from the door. 'They're in the spare room watching TV.' Tipping her head towards the passageway, Ellen forced a smile, before glaring at her husband.

Dave kept a poker face as Mark rounded on his wife. 'Beg your pardon?'

'You heard me: stop being ridiculous.' She jerked her head for Dave to move. All three looked at her in shock. 'Go on, then.'

'Dad, you can't stop him from saying goodbye,' Mel said. She turned and left the room.

Well, well, there's a first time for everything, Dave thought. Ellen had stood up for herself and for Dave in one sentence. He wanted to laugh at Mark's face. The astonishment and disbelief had rendered him speechless.

Dave quietly stepped around his father-in-law, smiling at Ellen as he did. He quickly kissed her cheek. 'Thank you.'

'You know the way,' Ellen said gently.

Dave walked through the kitchen and towards the back of the house, where he could hear Bec's happy chatter.

'Alice, Granddad is taking us on a holiday! I've never been on one, have you?'

Dave peeked into the room and saw Bec standing at the side of the cot, in which Alice was sound asleep. He watched the baby for a moment, her rosebud mouth working as if she were at Mel's breast, suckling.

Bec was looking over the side, stroking her sister's head.

'Granddad said Daddy's not coming.' She was quiet for a moment and Dave's heart gave a thud. 'I wish he was.'

'Hello, princess,' Dave said quietly.

Bec looked over and gave a squeal. 'Daddy!'

Alice started at the high-pitched noise, her little arms flailing about, but didn't cry, while Bec ran across to him.

'We're going on a holiday,' she told him as he swung her into his arms.

He buried his nose into her neck and blew a raspberry. 'I know. Won't that be fun?'

'Why aren't you coming, Daddy?' Bec pulled away and looked at his face, putting her hands on his cheeks.

'It's a long story,' he said. 'When you're older, I'll tell you, but what I want you to know is that I love you very much. I always will. Don't ever forget that.'

'And Alice?'

'Yes, and Alice.'

'And Mummy?'

'Definitely Mummy.'

'And Gran—'

Dave swung her down again so he didn't have to answer the question she was about to ask. 'Now, Bec, will you promise me something?'

'Yes.' She looked at him solemnly.

He drew a small brown-and-black toy dog from his pocket. 'This is a Kelpie dog,' he said softly.

'What's a kelpie?'

'A loyal friend. Someone you can always talk to if you're sad or scared about something.' He made a *woof* sound and tapped the nose of the toy gently against her face. 'So, any time you want to talk to me and I'm not near you, I want you to talk to your friend here. What do you want to call him?'

'Is he like a policeman? Will he look after me too?'

Dave nodded. 'If you want him to, he'll protect you.'

'Then I'm going to call him Daddy, because you're a policeman and look after people, and if I get scared I talk to you.'

Dave swallowed hard before pulling her into a hug. He breathed in her kids' shampoo and felt her heartbeat. 'Love you, princess.' He held her to him until she started to wriggle. 'Be good for Mummy, okay?' He let her go and kissed her cheek.

'I love you, Daddy.' Bec was clutching the toy in her hand.

Dave stood and went to Alice, touching her soft cheek. He put his finger to his lips and kissed the tip before pressing it to Alice's mouth. She looked up at him with large blue eyes, reflecting his own.

Squeezing his eyes shut, he turned and patted Bec on the head before he quickly left the room. He didn't want either of his children to see him cry.

Mark and Ellen weren't around when he went into the kitchen, but the bags had been moved from the passageway.

71

He looked around for Mel. Surely she wouldn't let him go without saying goodbye.

'Hey.' Her soft voice came from behind him and he turned, his face serious.

'Mel.' He took a step towards her, but she shook her head and he stopped. 'You don't have to do this,' he said.

'Yes, I do. I really do.'

'I'd be able to come and see you if you went to the safe house.'

'No, you wouldn't, Dave. You'll be in Barrabine, and Dad won't be comfortable unless we're well away from Western Australia.'

'Bulldust has connections, you know. You might be followed.'

'I guess we'll have to take that chance, because I feel in danger here.' She paused. 'I've got to go somewhere that I feel like I can live a half-regular life and not look over my shoulder.' She stopped and took a breath and looked up at Dave. 'He came right up to me, Dave. He knew where I shopped and probably where we live! I just can't—' Tears threatened, but she rallied. 'He nearly killed you and now he's after us. Dad's organised this holiday because he knows we're going to be protected.'

'Okay, it'll be okay, honey,' Dave said softly. 'If this is what you want to do, then you do it. Where are you going?'

Mel shook her head. 'I don't know. Dad hasn't told me, but we're going for three weeks. Can you find him by then?'

'I don't know what Major Crime will be able to do, Mel,' he answered honestly. 'It'll depend on what information they can find quickly. If they can track him to a vehicle and follow him through the cameras on the highway, it might all happen pretty quickly. I think that's fairly unlikely, though.

'A wounded dog always goes to where he feels safe, and for Bulldust, that's the bush. I reckon he and Scotty'll be holed up somewhere an age from the city. Camped out in a creek or cave where there's no chance of anyone finding them.

'If he's in the city, then he won't be comfortable and will more than likely make a mistake. He'd be like a fish out of water, I reckon.

'Until they get something concrete on him . . . well, there's a lot of Australia to look through.' Dave shrugged. 'And I'm not out there looking for him, so I can't drive the investigation.' He ran his hands through his hair, discouraged. 'And I've got to stay away because Bulldust wants me. If I go out there, I'm bait. Jesus.' He wanted to pace, but he knew he had to keep close to Mel. She was like an animal waiting to flee.

Mel pursed her lips but nodded her understanding.

Dave opened his arms. She hesitated, then went to him.

'It'll be okay, sweetie,' Dave murmured. 'It *will* be.'

'Dave?' Mel pulled back and looked at him.

Dave let her go. 'Yeah?'

'There's one thing I know, and I won't change my mind on. When we come back, you'll have to make a decision. It's either me and the kids, or the police force. I can't do this ever again.'

Chapter 8

'Son, from what I'm hearing, they've got nothing.' Bob raised the schooner glass to his mouth and took a long swallow.

Dave didn't reply. Instead, he surveyed the pub for the hundredth time since they'd arrived. He wouldn't let Bob sit with his back to the main entry and he wouldn't either, so they were side by side at the bar, facing the door.

Dave nodded at the barman and picked through the coins sitting on the bar to find enough to pay for their next round.

'What do you mean nothing?' he finally asked as the drinks arrived.

'It's just like when they disappeared from Nundrew. Like they vanished. I know they've had the connies looking through the CCTV and all they found was Bulldust getting off a bus at the shopping centre. They couldn't find him leaving on another bus, or being picked up by someone.' He took a breath. 'He's just vanished again. No movement on the bank accounts—not that there has been for months now anyhow. They must've had a shitload of cash stashed somewhere.

'Coppers in Brisbane stationed a couple of blokes on the daughter for a few days, hoping he'd turn up, but zilch there either. They said she was real easy to find.' He scratched his chin. 'Bloody annoying that nothing's showing up, really.'

Dave harrumphed. 'You reckon?'

'I'm sure.' Bob winked. 'But, look, I don't think I'm being told everything either, son. They won't want someone close coming in and compromising the intel they have, so they're probably going to keep some things back until they've verified them.

'Still, never mind. We'll hear when we need to, and your family will be okay, wherever they've gone. Bulldust doesn't seem to be in the city—that's another good thing. And we're off tomorrow. All will be well.'

'I said to Mel that I reckon he's gone bush. He'd feel out of place and uncomfortable in the city.'

'Agreed.' Bob put his glasses on and dragged the menu closer to him. 'Feed time, hey? Then we'd better get home and have an early night. What is it, six-hour drive tomorrow? Seven?'

'All of the seven,' Dave said, looking over at the menu Bob was holding. 'I'm not hungry.'

'You'll have to eat something. The way you're downing those beers, you'll need something to soak up the alcohol.'

Not able to help it, Dave laughed. 'Fuck, the shoe's on the other foot now. Last case, when we were up north in

Boogarin helping young Kevin, it was me telling you to eat something. And here I am thinking you're an old soak when you really do care!'

It had taken Spencer, his old partner from Barrabine, to tell Dave the story of Bob and why he drank. Having two deaths on his conscience would be enough to drive any man to drink.

'Well, son, you're not an old soak, but you are giving the beer a hammering tonight. And I can say what I like to you, because I'm much older.' He ran his hand through his thinning grey hair and grinned. He turned to the barman, who was hovering. 'Mate, we'd like another two of these beers—pints, thanks—and two chicken parmis. Double the chips, eh?'

'What? I don't need the threat of a heart attack, too,' Dave said.

'You'll be doing enough in the next little while to sort that out. Now, did you end up finding out where the family was off to?'

Dave shook his head. 'Good thing there are mobiles.'

'They're very handy, but a bit too intrusive for an old bloke like me.'

Dave drained the last of the second drink, ignoring the look Bob gave him.

'So, how were the goodbyes?' Bob asked cautiously.

Dave dropped his head into his hands and was silent, but Bob waited him out.

'Got the ultimatum. She meant it this time.'

The noise of the bar seemed to rise up around Dave as he thought about leaving the house, about Mel's final words: *You'll have to make a decision. It's either me and the kids, or the police force.* The lump in his throat had seemed so large, he'd thought it might choke him. He could still feel Alice's soft skin under his fingers and hear Bec saying she was going to call the toy dog Daddy.

He felt his eyes grow hot and quickly grabbed at his beer. After a swig he cleared his throat and looked at Bob. 'It is what it is.'

'I'd ask if you've got any thoughts, but I guess you don't. It's an impossible choice.'

'Yeah. Let's talk about something else.'

'Well, you're driving tomorrow, son,' Bob said with a grin as he lifted his glass.

'When don't I?' Dave grunted.

'I've booked us a couple of rooms at the motel there. Thought we might catch up with Spencer tomorrow night for dinner.'

'Grub's up,' the barman said as he slid the dishes onto the bar. 'Refills?'

'Go on, then,' Bob said. 'You've twisted my arm.'

❧

'Well, well, well, Dave, how's things, my man?' Spencer asked over the phone. 'It's been a little while. What's going on?'

Dave could just imagine his old partner sitting at his desk, leaning back in his chair, feet raised. Spencer was so laid-back Dave had thought he was almost horizontal when they'd first met. But underneath the casual exterior was an exceptional detective, confidant and mentor.

'Not bad,' Dave lied. 'How're things with you?'

'Pretty quiet, really. Nothing too exciting here. You seem to forget that the thrill-seeking follows you, not me.'

'I'd rather it didn't.'

'How're Mel and the kids?'

Dave sighed heavily and wished he had another beer in his hand.

'The kids are great. Bec's a little ripper! And Alice, well, she sleeps pretty well. Doesn't cry a lot. But the rest of it is shit. I've been given an ultimatum: them or the job.'

'Ah.' Spencer's tone held meaning. It hadn't been long ago he'd told Dave that sometimes it didn't matter how many times the cop changed things for the wife, because more often than not it wasn't the job that the wife hated, it was the fact that the cop wasn't the person she wanted him to be. Dave was beginning to realise he was right.

'Yeah, this thing with Bulldust has really upset her. With good reason.' Dave fiddled with the phone cord and let out a sigh.

'What's Bob got to say about it all?'

Quickly filling Spencer in with the developments of the day, he added, 'Bob's on a pretty short leash. Major Crime is only filling him in on what they want passed on to me. I can't go anywhere near it—I'll get strung up if I do.'

'Bloody oath. Don't want to compromise the case.'

There was a pause, then Dave said, 'Do you remember that dead beast we found in the middle of the bush back just before I went undercover? Everyone was getting a bit touchy about cattle straying onto mining land.'

There was a silence before he answered. 'Yeah, yeah, I do.'

'So, that brand was SA and an upturned horseshoe.'

'That was traced back to Scott and Ashley Bennett, if I remember correctly.'

'Yep, you do. Were any more cattle ever found wandering around the mines or in country where they shouldn't have been, with that brand?'

'Hmm, not that I recall.' Pause. 'What are you thinking?'

'Just an idea, but if we've driven Bulldust out of his comfort zone in Queensland, they'll be looking for somewhere safe. If he's fronted up in Perth, there's every chance he's back here in WA. We know they've got history here.'

'Yeah,' Spencer drew out the word. 'Could be on the money, my man. We know where Scotty's station out of Barra is. He could easily have another piece of land we don't know about.'

'Yeah, and I visited it with the truckie when I was undercover.'

'Hmm, I could do a bit of a search around—talk to the stock agents and hit up the greasy spoons, flash their photos around, if you like? See if anyone recognises their dials.'

'Would you?'

'It's been a while since I've done a drop-in at the road-houses north of here. Give me an excuse to go for a run. I'll do it on the quiet, though. Won't put you in any danger.'

'That'd be great, if you don't mind.'

'There's nothing to lose, is there. No one seems to have any idea where they are. I'll be careful not to step on Major Crime's toes, though. Have you mentioned this to them?'

'Nope. Only thought of it this evening, since we're heading your way again.'

'Yeah, I heard that Tez had called the stockies in. You remember Tez?'

'Yeah, yeah, another detective from our time at Barrabine station. I remembered him the minute he called it in.'

'When're you getting here?'

'We're rolling in tomorrow, but we'll head straight to the station and start interviewing the manager to find out what's going on. How does tea at the pub in the next couple of nights sound?'

'Excellent to me.'

'Good. How's Kathy?'

Dave heard the smile in Spencer's voice as he answered. 'She's real good. You know we made the finals for the ballroom-dancing comp here?'

Dave chuckled. If there was ever a more unlikely dancer than Spencer, Dave was yet to meet him. His short, stocky frame did not look built for dancing, and the fact that Kathy was a few inches taller than her husband made them an unusual couple on the dance floor. But Spencer was surprisingly light on his feet once the music started.

'Congratulations! When's the grand final?'

'In a couple of weeks. Nervous as a cat on a hot tin roof, so I am. She's making me practise every evening. I'd rather just turn up on the night and have a crack at the trophy—not have to think too much about it all.'

'You know the saying, Spence: "Perfect preparation prevents piss-poor performance."'

'True enough, and there's not going to be any lack of preparation.'

'That'll mean no piss-poor performance, then.' He laughed. 'I'll look forward to catching up with her while I'm there. If Bob and I are still around when it's on, we'll come and cheer for you.'

'That won't be necessary, thanks. I'll be nervous enough without you two blokes taking a gander at me.'

'Don't be like that—after a few beers we'd be able to offer all the advice you need.'

'Can't wait to hear that shit dribbling from your lips. But not while I'm on the dance floor, thanks muchly. Anyway,' Spencer changed the subject, 'Kathy'll be sad to hear what Mel has said to you.'

'Can't be helped. Can try all I like, but I don't think I'll ever change her mind. Kathy was such a huge help while Mel was trying to settle in to Barrabine when we first moved there, but I guess you can only stave off the inevitable for so long.'

'Got a plan?'

'Not yet. I love Mel. And I adore the kids. I'd rather I didn't have to choose. I'm hoping I can work it so I don't have to.'

'Ain't that the truth? Now listen, can you email me some mug shots of Scotty? I've still got ones of Bulldust. Then I'll get on the road tomorrow, unless something urgent comes up.'

'Sure, I'll get them through to you now. We're getting on the road early, too, so I reckon we'll hit town mid-afternoonish.'

'Drive safe.'

Chapter 9

'What do you reckon we're getting? Close to a kilo per plant?' Bulldust asked Scotty as he twisted another head expertly off the marijuana plant and tossed it onto the drying racks.

They were standing under a large gum tree harvesting the next crop.

'Close enough, I'd think,' Scotty answered as he used his hand to spread out the heads. Better if they didn't touch. 'Need as much as we can produce. I've more bloody orders than I can fill.'

Bulldust picked a couple more and pushed the plump buds between his fingers before holding it to his nose. Moist, sticky and smelling exceptionally sweet. One thing about his brother, he knew how to grow good weed. Not that Bulldust smoked it. He was happy enough with a beer or whiskey in his hand. He didn't need anything stronger.

When he was a kid he'd experimented with weed. A girlfriend when he was eighteen had made brownies with the drug in them. When she'd offered them around at a party he'd thought it was weird; they were all drinking alcohol, so brownies would be a pretty strange snack. But she'd smiled at him, all coy. 'Think you'll like them,' she whispered in his ear, then put one in his mouth before he could stop her. The reaction hadn't taken long; the music had seemed louder, the colours brighter, everyone happier. He couldn't stop smiling or touching his girlfriend; he couldn't even remember her name, but he wanted to stroke her soft hair again and again. Before he knew it they were off in the bedroom . . . where there was already another couple.

After that night, he decided that alcohol was his drug of choice.

He did, however, know good weed. Both brothers hung around with people who had grown it, dealt in harder drugs and knew their way around the drug industry. Bulldust had learned from them.

Scotty had grown weed on and off his whole life. He'd started when he was in high school. One of his mates had a disused farmhouse and they'd filled the bathroom with plants, before drying them in there, too.

One weekend their father had decided to give them time off, and Bulldust had gone into town to the races. Scotty had started packing the drugs early that morning and hadn't made it home, passed out on the couch of his mate's farmhouse.

Then their father unexpectedly come home, having had a phone call from the stock agent wanting to shift cattle the next day. Bulldust had covered for Scotty, to keep his father's leather belt from his brother's ankles, saying he'd had a vomiting bug the night before and was sleeping it off.

'Didn't smoke any of it,' Scotty had said by way of explanation when he turned up the next morning. 'Just the bloody fumes as it's drying gets you.'

Now, Bulldust moved over to the next rack covered in dried pods. They were lying on fine chicken mesh, stretched over wooden racks. He picked up a handful and examined them closely.

Desert used that moment to jump on his owner's ankle and bark, causing Bulldust to jump then shake the dog loose.

'Fuck off, Desert,' he said not unkindly. Bulldust turned to Scotty, who was brushing his hands off. 'Ready to pack?'

'Yeah. We'll get onto it now. I want to head off tonight. Going to meet the bloke who's picking it all up and get the money.'

'Meeting where?' Bulldust bent down and patted the pup, who was now lying down and chewing on a stick.

'Back towards Leonora. Out on one of the back tracks. Take me a few hours to get there.'

'I thought we'd decided that it was only going to be me shifting the gear,' Bulldust frowned. 'You're known around here, or have you forgotten that?'

Scotty looked up and glared at him. 'But I won't take the sort of chances you've been taking, brother.' He continued with his work. 'This bloke will only meet with me, and like I said, back tracks.'

'How do you know he won't have someone with him?'

'I just do.'

'I want to send some money to Shane when you get it.'

Scotty looked up from what he was doing and gave him another hard stare. 'That would be stupid.'

'I don't reckon. Nothing to say where it came from.'

'Postmark on the envelope?'

'Nothing to say who it came from,' he repeated.

Scotty shook his head and grabbed the vacuum-sealing machine from the humpy they'd built out of tin and wire. 'You're a fuckwit. Of course they'll know. Shane has thirty grand turn up in the mail? That's if it even gets to her! Don't forget the post has X-ray machines. The coppers'll be watching her, I've got no doubt. Especially after that last stunt you pulled in the shopping centre. Just don't fucking do it. Get the scales and fill up the generator so we can get packing.'

The familiar surge of anger flared in Bulldust's chest. Scotty had been telling him he was stupid all his life.

Still he had to admit, when Scotty said it like that, Bulldust knew he was right.

With Desert following him, Bulldust grabbed the jerry can, carefully poured the diesel into the generator, and slipped the handle onto the crank shaft. It was an old engine, one with her own personality; he needed to slide the handle off quickly as it started, otherwise he'd have to run like buggery because the handle would be stuck on the shaft until it worked its way down the end and flew off. That had happened once when he was a kid, and the belting he copped from his father ensured he'd never repeated that mistake.

The slow and steady *thwump* of the engine sent a flock of corellas into the wide blue sky, before they settled again, tearing at the leaves on the gum trees.

Even if we didn't have to hide out here, Bulldust thought, *it'd be a good spot.* The creek bed was wide, full of soft sand and shade from the trees. It was protected by the mountain range that ran along the edge and surrounded by thick bush and spinifex. Camping out here in summer would be another matter; the heat and flies would be enough to drive any man to insanity. The middle of the day got warm enough as it was. They'd have to make sure they were finished by October at the latest. Still a few months to go.

Back at the table, he took up his usual position of taking the thick plastic bags that Scotty had packed and weighed and started to seal them.

The noise of the generator coupled with the vacuum-sealing machine didn't let them talk.

～

Scotty manoeuvred the forty-four-gallon drum against the back of the ute and tied it on with a heavy strap. To anyone driving behind or passing him, it would look like he had a drum of oil on the back. No one would know there was close to eighty kilos of marijuana inside the drum, held down by mesh in the middle.

Even if he was stopped, and a copper wanted to look in the drum, all he would see was sump oil.

Bulldust tugged at the strap and made sure it was connected to the rail under the tray and it was tight.

'I'll check the road,' Scotty said as he walked over to the motorbike and got on.

'Uh-huh.'

Bulldust threw another strap around the bottom of the drum and listened for the engine. When it became faint and Scotty was out of view, he went to the packing table and kicked back the leaves under the large gum tree. He reached down and grabbed the four packages he'd managed to lift when Scotty had gone to turn the generator off.

If he wasn't going to let Bulldust send money to Shane, he'd go another way about it.

'Look-ee here, Desert,' he said as the pup stuck close to his heels. 'We'll whack these in here.' He lifted a flat rock underneath which was a crevice just large enough to hold a carton of beer. Inside were the five packages of weed he'd taken last harvest. It was his insurance.

Brother or not, he didn't trust Scotty.

His time in Lightning Ridge, away from Scotty, had made him realise there was more to life than being in business with his brother, but at the same time the thought of not having his brother close by, concerned him. They had struggled through this love–hate relationship all their lives. One foot forward, then something would happen and they would take two steps back.

The constant teasing and put-downs from Scotty when they'd been kids had been horrible, but he'd always stuck up for him in the school yard. Until the morning a kid with scruffy hair and a dirty face accused Bulldust of taking his lunch money. Bulldust had been shocked and denied it straightaway, but he'd still been hauled out of the classroom, given the cane and sent to sit outside the school office until the bus went home that afternoon.

At lunchtime, Scotty had walked past him with a pastie and a large cream bun, and Bulldust had known who'd taken the money.

He'd never trusted Scotty again.

And Scotty had again proved that it wasn't one for all and all for one when things had blown up last time. No, big brother had pissed off in his ute, grabbed the gear he wanted from his station and then hidden for months. Bulldust, in the meanwhile, camped out at Lightning Ridge waiting for word from him, or from Shane. Oh, he'd had money and was safe, but it would've been nice to have a debrief over what had happened, not months of silence.

If Bulldust needed to run now, the pot he'd taken amounted to about a hundred and seventy grand of insurance money to help him start again. Without his brother.

Grinning to himself, he slid the rock back over and grabbed the dead branch nearby so he could wipe his footprints away and leave it over the rock. Scotty would know nothing.

'That's the way it should be,' he told Desert.

Hearing the motorbike's engine change up a gear, Bulldust hurried back over to the ute and drove it to the mobile fuel tanker to begin refuelling.

'All good?' Scotty asked when he got back and parked the bike.

'Yeah, good to go.'

'Try not to do anything stupid while I'm gone.'

Bulldust struggled to keep his mouth shut. Instead he picked up Desert. 'See you tomorrow, then. Grab some beer on your way back? We're running out.'

'I've got a food order to get, too. Should all be in that.'

'Catch ya. Don't want to be late.' Bulldust turned and went back over to the crop and started to clean up.

The ute's engine soon faded and Bulldust was on his own.

He loved the silence. The solitude. He knew he should be mixing the fertiliser and watering the seedlings, but he couldn't be stuffed right now. Just revelling in the silence and the campfire would be enough for him.

'Come on, Desert,' he said. 'Beer time.'

Flopping down in the camp chair, he grabbed a stick and stirred up the coals, then popped the top on the can before taking a long swallow.

'Those bastards in the city don't know what they're missing,' he said.

Desert sniffed at his boot, then let out a heavy sigh, curling up near the fire and shutting his eyes. Bulldust looked at the dog. Half smiling, he thought about the puppy he'd given Shane not long after her mother had left. She'd carried it everywhere with her; her constant companion.

They would curl up together and sleep on the trampoline out the back of the homestead, her face glowing in the moonlight when Bulldust went out to watch them. It had been the two of them since she was three.

Shane's mother had walked out without a second thought, just like his own mother had, leaving Bulldust's heart calloused and closed over, whereas Shane's had been broken.

He'd sworn to her that he would never leave her; that he would give her the best of everything. But a ringer without much of an education could only earn so much. When Scotty had come to him with the idea of stealing cattle he'd realised that was going to be the way he could give Shane everything he wanted to.

So he had and now . . . Well. Now. There was nothing.

The look of disbelief and repulsion on her face when she'd realised what he'd done still made him feel sick.

He had to get in contact with her somehow. Surely after all this time she would have forgiven him. She must have thought about it and realised that he'd done everything for her and her alone. The workmen who had been murdered were just business repercussions, because they'd stepped out of line, nothing to do with Shane.

Crunching the empty can in his hand, he tossed it towards the wool pack they had set up on a steel frame as a bin. It missed, so he got up and put it in before taking another one from the three-way caravan fridge they had hooked up to a car battery recharged by solar panels. If anyone stumbled on their camp, they'd know that whoever was here was set up for the long haul. The camp kitchen boasted a table and chairs, a fridge and a bowl for washing up. The camp beds were set up under a canvas strung between two gum trees, and if a stranger looked closely, they'd see a track going out into the bush where the brothers went every morning after waking up.

Bulldust knew their set-up worked well and they were producing the goods.

Sucking down more amber fluid, he grinned. 'You thought you'd fucked us, didn't you, Dave. But we're better than that. You won't find us out here, either. We're the bushman ghosts.' Laughing, Bulldust leaned against the tree and surveyed what they'd managed to create in a short time.

A noise filtered through his consciousness and he turned towards it.

'What?' He walked towards the two-wheel track Scotty had disappeared down earlier. 'Must've had trouble . . .' Then he realised the engine wasn't that of a ute.

It was a motorbike. And it was going slowly, the noise more growl than high rev.

Bulldust turned to Desert and gave a low whistle. 'Come're.'

He tied up the pup and told him to stay, before grabbing his binoculars and gun and walking down the track towards the Great Central Road.

It only took him a few minutes to walk to where the two roads met, but he was puffing by the time he got there. Bulldust wiped his brow, wishing he was still riding horses and motorbikes and walking behind cattle.

Positioning himself in the bush where he couldn't be seen, he crouched down and waited. The engine grew closer and closer until finally he saw a rider dressed in thick adventure-biking gear. His face was covered by riding goggles and his hands encased in gloves.

'Fuck,' Bulldust said when he realised the motorbike's front tyre was flat. He turned and headed back to camp, hoping the rider wouldn't see the junction.

Not so lucky. The bike slowed even further as he came closer and closer to the access road.

Then the engine stopped.

Bulldust merged further into the bush and made his way towards the back of the crop. His brain was fuzzy from the few beers he'd had in the sun, but he knew he had to protect the crop.

'Shit, shit, shit,' he muttered.

'Hello?' he heard a voice call out.

Staying silent, he watched the rider, who had removed his helmet and goggles. Desert set up a round of barking; high-pitched puppy barking that wasn't going to do anything except make the bloke realise there was someone not far away. He should have brought the dog with him. He could hear Scotty's accusations already.

See? I leave you alone for a few hours and you still fuck things up.

'Hello? Anyone around? I've had some trouble with my bike. Could do with a hand.'

Fucking adventure riders, Bulldust thought. *Fucking tourists, just make a nuisance of themselves.*

'Hey there, pup. Where's your owner?' Bulldust watched the rider walk over to Desert, who growled and pulled at the lightweight chain.

Bulldust stayed still as the rider caught sight of the drying racks and walked towards them.

'Well, well, well, what have we here?' he said aloud as he pulled off his gloves and leaned over.

Bulldust watched, knowing there was only one thing to do. He had to stop the man from leaving, even though he could hear Scotty's voice in his head: *Don't be reactive!*

Still, what was the option? There wasn't one.

Clutching the rifle tightly, he held the butt in front of him and crept out from the bush and made his way behind the man, who was now inspecting the hundreds of seed-lings they had in pots.

The sound of Desert's high-pitched bark made the biker turn around and search the campsite. Obviously happy no one was around, he went back to investigating the growing area.

A little closer, closer, closer. Bulldust was only feet away from him now; so close he could smell the man's sweat. He raised the butt of the gun and brought it down on his neck.

The man didn't make a sound. He fell forward onto the ground and lay there motionless.

Chapter 10

'Fuck it all,' Bulldust snarled as he dragged the man by his jacket towards the ute, his bouncing feet leaving gouges in the dirt behind him.

Grunting with the effort, Bulldust managed to lift him into the tray inch by inch. Grabbing the cable ties from the glovebox, he quickly bound the hands and feet of the unconscious man.

'Couldn't keep your nose out of it,' he grumbled as he ripped a piece of tape from the roll and pushed it over the man's mouth.

Standing back up, he aimed a sharp kick at the man's ribs. 'Bastard! I'm not supposed to leave the camp and now I have to. That's our rule! The one rule neither of us ever breaks. We need to know if someone has come here. Fuck it all.'

He wiped the sweat away from his brow and shook his head, before glancing around. The man had to disappear.

But to where? Should he just kill him? That would be the easiest option. Dead men don't talk. Scotty's motto.

The man's breathing was shallow. 'How about I just dump you and the fucking bike out in the middle of the bush. You'll either make it or you won't.'

Jumping down from the ute, Bulldust untied Desert and put him in the front, before climbing into the driver's seat.

Shoving the ute into gear, the wheels spun as he took off. He looked in the rear-vision, dust hanging in the still air. Taking a corner at speed, he followed the track to the road and pulled up next to the motorbike. Loading that onto the back of the ute was going to take some doing.

Getting out, he walked around the bike, kicking in tyres. Not a bad-looking Triumph Tiger 800. Pity he couldn't keep it and sell it off to top up his insurance money.

Bulldust rifled through the saddle bags and found the man's wallet. From it, he pocketed the four hundred in cash and inspected the licence: Victor Richardson, lived in Perth, forty-nine years old. He tucked the licence back in the wallet after committing the details to memory. There was a photo of three small children and a pretty blonde woman, sitting on a lawn outside a brick and tin house. A Visa and ANZ bank cards were in the sleeve of the wallet and the rest was empty.

Good to know.

Flicking his hand over his face to brush a small black bush fly away, he grabbed the handlebars and wheeled it over. He released the tail gate, sliding the ramp out from the tray, before riding it up onto the back of the ute.

The man didn't move.

Bulldust bent over to check his breathing; he still was.

Letting the bike fall, he jumped off, fixed everything securely and loaded the ramp back up.

'Let's head north,' he said to Desert as he got back into the driver's seat. Desert looked at him, his tongue hanging out and Bulldust reached over to give him a heavy pat.

'Dunno why people can't mind their own business,' he told Desert. 'Still, they don't and now here we are. This one? He's in strife, real strife, Desert.'

The ute clattered as it bumped down the corrugated road, Bulldust heading towards a ravine where he could push the bike down into the scrubby bush.

A glance at his watch showed that there was a good five or so hours before Scotty was due back. Bulldust had no plans to tell his brother what had happened today. Scotty would just say he was being reactive. But there hadn't seemed to be another choice.

'Nothing,' he said aloud. 'He would've grassed us up to the coppers and then where would we fucking be?'

Desert let out a sharp bark as if in agreement.

The range of hills were coming closer as Bulldust drove. The rocky ridge was reflected in the setting sun, causing the hills to glow with colour. A large flock of budgies swooped and soared as they looked for water before the darkness came, and out of the corner of his eye Bulldust saw a kangaroo disappear into the bush at the sound of his ute.

Ten minutes later, he pulled off to the side of the road and turned the key.

The tick of the engine as it cooled was the only sound, and the moon, which had just started to rise across the silent land, bathed the ravine in a mix of cool white light and shadows.

'Stay,' he told the dog as he got out and slammed the door, the noise echoing off the ranges. He went to the edge and looked down. The cliff face was deep enough to cause the bike and the rider some damage, but perhaps not kill him.

Bulldust tossed up driving a bit further north where there might be a deeper gully. He really should; here was a little too close. Then he realised he probably didn't have time— he had to get back to camp to water the seedlings. Even though the days were cool and nights cold, the seedlings dried out quickly and twice-daily watering was important.

Turning back to the unconscious rider, Bulldust started to unload the bike, before dragging him from the ute. He took a thick strap from the toolbox and wound it around the rider's legs, under the fuel tank and through the engine, strapping him onto the seat of the bike. He worked quickly but was hampered by the heaviness of the body and the bike.

Finally, he drew the last strap tight and heaved the bike up. He turned the key and was rewarded after a few attempts when the engine roared to life. Wheeling them both to the edge of the road, Bulldust stood looking down. In the moonlight, he could see bushes and small trees growing out from the side of the cliff. There were large rocks with tufts of golden-coloured grasses in between, and a sandy creek at the bottom.

A sound and movement from the man almost made Bulldust drop the bike.

'Ah, ah, ah,' the man grunted, his eyes wide, as he stared down the deep gully. Bulldust grinned and moved so he was up close to his face.

'This is just your unlucky day, Victor,' he said quietly. 'Such an unlucky day.' He watched as the man's eyes widened at the mention of his name. 'Finding my camp and coming in there. Seeing what you did.' He tutted and smiled unpleasantly. 'I'm real sorry I have to do this, but I can't have any loose ends.' He grabbed hold of the accelerator and revved it a couple of times. 'If you survive, and you speak to anyone about this, I promise you I'll find you and kill you.' He leaned in close to the man's face. 'I know your address.' He said it aloud. 'You've got a very pretty wife and kids, haven't you? And so you know,' he paused for effect. 'I never go back on my promises.'

This time, when he revved the engine he clicked the bike into gear and let the clutch out. The bike roared away over the edge.

The screeching of twisted metal rang out across the land amid the sound of breaking branches and then a long, low wail was cut short as the bike came to a stop many, many metres below the road.

Bulldust looked over the edge. Nothing moved. There wasn't a sound.

Once down the embankment, Bulldust could see the man was still breathing but only slightly. Blood poured from a gash on his head, and his arm was thrown out at a painfully strange angle.

The wheel of the bike spun silently and then stilled. Nothing else moved.

He quickly released the strap and rolled it up, glancing once more at the unconscious man, before leaning forward.

'Just another reminder, in case you can hear me. Don't speak of this. If you do, I will find you and kill you. I promise.'

From above, he could hear Desert barking and knew he had to get away from the scene quickly.

Using the tree branches and thick grasses as hand holds, he pulled himself up and dusted his palms off when he reached the top.

He looked over the edge again and nodded with satisfaction.

Bulldust pulled up at the camp in a cloud of dust. He'd flogged the ute heading back in his haste to get away from the scene. The trouble was, out here on the main roads—if you could call them that—you never knew when you might run into someone. Could be a family taking a year off to complete the great Australian lap; a grey nomad couple in a caravan; or even a truckie carting fuel to the settlements out on the border.

He lifted Desert out of the ute and put him on the ground before walking around the camp, as he did every time he came back, looking carefully for any other signs of intrusion.

By leaving, Bulldust had broken the one rule neither of them was allowed to break. He had to make sure that nothing had been compromised and wipe away the tracks Victor and he had made, so Scotty didn't know anything was amiss.

A quick check showed no extra footprints or plants that had been shifted. Nothing was out of place, and he began to relax. He reached down to pat Desert, who was at his heels, then picked up the little animal, putting his face against the soft cheek. Giving a wiggle, Desert managed to get his head around and lick Bulldust's cheek.

'Get away with you,' he said quietly, putting the dog down. 'Good thing I've got you. Trust a dog more than any human I know. Other than Shane. You're my mate, Desert.'

He went to the shed to get out the trace elements and fertiliser, and to start the pump.

Carefully measuring everything into the venturi, he put the hose on and listened with satisfaction as it started to draw the mixture into the water and run it through the reticulation pipes set out across the ground to the plantation.

The pump thumped in time with his thoughts about Victor and the other men he'd helped bring to their demise.

It made him even keener to find Dave and bring him to his knees as well.

A flash of the motorbike going over the side of the ravine and Victor's eyes full of fear came to him and he shook his head. 'Enough.'

Bulldust blocked the image of the motorcyclist from his mind. Collateral damage. Nothing more.

Chapter 11

'Turn here,' Bob instructed as Dave saw a gateway come into his line of sight. A sign proclaimed the driveway to be Nefer Station, owned by the Windy Family.

'How much land do they own?' Dave asked, flicking on his indicator and driving over the cattle grid next to the forty-four-gallon drum mailbox.

'Thousands of hectares through Queensland, Northern Territory and Western Australia, but they don't own the land. All pastoral leases,' Bob said, referring to the sheet of paper in his hand. 'Originally run by three brothers, Willy, Matthew and Craig, but the sons have taken over now and run them all remotely. They live in the city and this is more of an investment for them than the mainstay of their business. Now there are eight cousins on the board.' He listed each name and location. 'None of them have worked the station, but they have degrees in agribusiness or something relating to agriculture. Never actually got their hands dirty, though.' Bob took a breath. 'And George is the Chair. And sounds like the boss. Comes with being the oldest of all the cousins, I guess.'

'We'll be dealing with the manager, then?'

Bob nodded as they drove towards the house. Dave took in the wide open landscape. Very few trees but scrubby bushland and swaths of native grasses covered the land, a sea of gold waving in the gentle breeze.

'John McDougal. He's taken over from the previous manager, Dunstan Kendal. Now, this is where it gets interesting, son. Kendal just walked off. When I was talking to the sarge in Wallina, he said that no one realised the bloke had gone. No jackaroos or jillaroos out there at the moment, you see. Just the manager. The sarge called in on a routine drive, and there was no one around.'

Dave nodded. He was beginning to see where this was going.

'Note on the table saying things hadn't gone the way he'd planned so he and the missus had headed off. Crew at head office didn't know anything about it either, so they sent another fella over to see what was going on.'

'Dead stock?' Dave swung the steering wheel to follow the sharp bend in the road.

'Nope, thankfully, no animal welfare issue here. Kendal couldn't have been gone that long. Few days at the most. Anyhow, this John McDougal has found the numbers for the cattle don't add up and seems a bit clueless as to what's happened. Ah, here we are.'

Dave brought the LandCruiser troopy to a standstill and looked around. The homestead was a stone-walled building, painted white but covered in the red dirt that seemed to infiltrate everything out here. The wooden fence had a couple of railings missing and the plants in pots on the verandah were crisp and in need of water, while the lawn had bare brown spots throughout.

It was so different to the farm he'd grown up on, where his mother made sure the homestead was tidy and the yard spotless. Even though Dave had spent his formative years on a property much smaller than this and in a higher rainfall area, he understood the people out here; they were like the environment: hard and unrelenting, practical and unhurried.

The workshop was about fifty metres away from the house, and the large tin door was flung open to reveal a tractor with the bonnet up, over the pit, while the horse yards were empty, though Dave could see hay piled up in a corner.

'Can't have been too long since there were nags in there,' he said to Bob.

'Howdy, I'm John.'

Dave and Bob turned at the sound of a lethargic drawl and saw an older man, bow-legged, wearing a large Stetson hat. His jeans were dusty, and he had a twig in one side of his mouth. It seemed he spoke around it.

'G'day, John. Bob Holden and Dave Burrows, stock squad. You're expecting us.'

'Sure am. Come inside for a cuppa?' Without waiting for an answer, the man turned and walked slowly towards the house. 'Sorry things are a bit untidy. Last bloke didn't do a real good job.'

'Been here long?' Dave asked as he fell into step beside him. He noticed Bob looking around and knew he was committing the whole place to memory.

'Got here about ten days back. Somethin' real strange about what's gone on here.'

'Like what?'

'Come on in and get yourselves settled first.'

Dave grinned. John was an old-school stockman. Didn't hurry anything.

'Worked for the family long, John?' Bob asked.

'Yeah. All of me working life. Came to them as a young ringer out of Katherine in the Territory. Never left. George sent me here to find out what's going on.'

'And what do you think is going on?' Bob asked as he sat at the table and took out his notebook.

The screen door slammed behind them and Dave took a moment as his eyes adjusted to the dim room.

'Reckon the bloke before me was a thief, that's what I reckon.' His work-hardened hands lit the gas stove and he put the kettle on the burner.

'Why do you say that?'

'Well . . .' He drew the word out. 'There're s'posed to be two and a half thousand cattle over three hundred and fifty thousand hectares. I've been over the whole place since I got here and there'd be lucky to be one thousand.' John got out the cups and tea bags and waited until the kettle had boiled before pouring the boiling water and dumping the cups on the table. There was no offer of milk or sugar.

Stockman's brand of tea—black with nothing. In the past they couldn't have sugar in the stock camp—it would bring the ants in—and the milk wouldn't last a day before curdling. Of course, it was different now. Stock camps were much more comfortably set up with caravans or huts pulled by trucks. Generators ran all day to keep the food and milk cold. Plus the beer. Almost luxury compared to the way John would have grown up in the camps, Dave knew. Thirty or forty years ago, the food would have been bully beef, damper, water and tea. And not much else. Maybe a tin of braised steak and onions if the cook was feeling adventurous. He knew all this from the times he'd spent in the north as a young copper.

'Pretty serious accusations,' Bob said as he pulled the tea bag out, squeezed it and left it on the table. Dave did the same.

'You tell me where the cattle have gone, then. Dingoes aren't going to be killing the old girls. Might have a go at the young 'uns, but not the wily old dames.' John took a sip of his tea, smacked his lips as if the liquid were the best thing he'd tasted all day, then leaned back in his chair. 'Can take yer both for a gander if yer want. From the air.'

'You've got your pilot's licence?' Dave asked, surprised.

'Bloody oath I do. I'm too old to be bumping around those rough paddocks out there. Buggered hip and knee from falls off horses when I was a nipper. Boss got me a plane about ten years ago.'

'Can't say no to that, can we, son?' Bob said to Dave and grinned over his cup. 'Now, tell us, is there any paperwork we can collect while we're here? You know, weigh bills, trading accounts with the stock agents, bills of sale. That type of thing. We'll certainly need the 30 June figures for the past three years. Natural increase and all that.'

'You'll have it before you go. But, here, look at this first.' John left the kitchen and Dave half stood to follow him, until Bob shook his head.

'He'll be back, you'll see.'

'Mustering wide?' Dave said quietly, meaning perhaps the neighbours had mustered up Nefer cattle and Kendal hadn't realised until much later.

'Now, son, you're assuming things again. What about the charge "stealing as a servant"? There're always plenty of employees who steal from their employers. Surely in the time we've been working together I've taught you not to assume.'

Dave flushed as he realised Bob was right. Spencer had also cautioned him against thinking that way.

John came back into the room, with three photos in his hand and a pair of silver-rimmed glasses perched on the end of his nose. 'These are the cattle you'll need to look for. Herefords. Not Shorthorns or Brahmans or any other breed. Good old-fashioned Herefords.'

'No trouble with eye cancers here?' Bob asked as he reached out for the photos. Herefords were notorious for it because of the white skin around their eyes.

'All you gotta do is keep on top of 'em, for sure. See 'em start early and cut 'em out or burn 'em off.'

Bob nodded. 'Ear mark and brand?'

John slid another piece of paper across. A shaky hand had drawn an ear with the ear mark in it and written down a brand. As in Western Australia, it started with a number and was followed by two letters. Dave jotted it down in his book and made a note to ring the local stock agents in the sale yards and see if any Herefords had been through recently.

'And what stock agent do you use?' he asked.

'The ones with the green shirts. Always found them to be the best.'

Bob drained his cup and got up to rinse it out at the sink. 'Right, well, shall we go for a stickybeak and see what we can see?'

❧

John handled the plane smoothly, seeming as comfortable in the four-seater Cessna as Dave would guess he was on the back of a horse.

'We'll stay at one thousand feet so you can get an idea of the land,' he said through the headphones both Bob and Dave were wearing.

Dave looked out across the red and khaki landscape. Even though the country was undulating, from the air it looked flat and unyielding. Summertime out here would be hard for any animal. The lack of trees and shade made Dave shiver, but he knew the stock were accustomed to this environment. Stations out of Alice Springs in the harshest of climates ran Herefords without losses from heat stroke.

They followed the road from the homestead, heading west.

'Down here was where I found the first mob,' John muttered into the microphone. 'Tank and windmill all in good nick. About fifty on that bore.'

Taking out his binoculars, Dave saw a small mob of cattle camped under the bushes and around the bore. Their tails were swishing and ears twitching; obviously the flies were feeling friendly today. A calf stood off to the side and although he couldn't hear it, Dave could see its mouth open and the stomach contracting in and out as it called for its mother.

Finally, a large cow got to her feet and went to it, sniffing down its body, while the calf quickly put its head under her rear end and found her udder.

'See, here's the boundary,' John told them about ten minutes later. He angled the plane to fly along the fence line.

Again, through the binoculars, Dave could see the fence was well maintained. Shouldn't be any problems there.

'How do you get along with the neighbours?' he asked.

'I haven't met them yet,' John said. 'But George tells me there's never been any trouble.'

'And this Kendal fella, how long did he work here?'

'Couple of years, I'm told. Plucked him out of a group of two. No other applications for the job. Hard to get good stockmen these days and there're not too many who are happy to give up the comforts of farms closer to a town, or the air-conditioned tractor cabs. Told George when I heard about him that he wouldn't last long, and now I'm here cleaning up his bloody mess.'

Dave caught sight of the frown that crossed his face.

'Why is it you who has to tidy this up?' he asked.

'I'm the go-to bloke. Been with George the longest. He trusts me.'

Dave nodded and made another note in the book he had resting on his leg.

Another long run down a boundary and a visit to three more bores and Bob indicated they'd seen enough.

The landing was smooth despite the potholes in the strip. As they taxied to a stop, Dave put his binoculars away and notebook back in his pocket.

'We'll just grab that paperwork from you, John,' Bob said as they got out and helped tie the plane down. 'Then we'd better get back and have a yarn to some of the stockies.'

'I've got it all in a box for you.'

'Could we get the contact details for George, too?'

'Yeah, I'll write his phone number down. He's got a . . . Whatcha call it? One of the computer thingies you can write to him.'

'Email address,' Dave said.

'Don't know why people want to do that. Better just to ring someone up and ask the question,' John grumbled. 'Won't be long and no one will be talking to each other if they keep communicatin' like that.'

Dave hid a grin.

'I know what you mean,' Bob sympathised. 'All the younger generation are in such a hurry. Don't realise you catch more flies with honey than vinegar. Eyeballing people is a real good thing to do when you want to know something. You can read 'em that way. Can't do that over the phone or by writing them an email.' He looked at John as they walked across the stony ground towards the ute. 'Don't know about you, but it takes me an age to find the letters on the keyboard. I can ask more questions a lot quicker if I am talking to them and writing down the answers by hand rather than typing.'

John laughed. 'I don't even try. See these?' He held up his hand to show two crooked fingers, while the others had skin knocked off the knuckles and grease ingrained in them. 'Don't reckon they'd even fit on the keys, from what I've seen in the boss's office.'

This time Dave couldn't help himself. He laughed aloud. 'I don't like them much myself. I always said I'd never let technology get in front of me, but unfortunately I think it has.'

'You're too young to let that happen, son,' Bob chided.

They clattered back to the homestead, where John passed them a large box. Dave could see invoices and tax returns inside.

'Right, so we need to verify the stock existed, which hopefully all this paperwork will do. I can see that the place is pretty tired, but that doesn't mean there's been poor management. However, we have to negate that option, too. Really, for us it's going to be about trawling through this information and coming back to you with any questions. So, we'll be in touch.'

John nodded.

'Have you got any questions for us?'

'Nah, just get in touch when you know something. I've got enough to do here for a few weeks.'

'You'll be the first to know,' Dave said and held out his hand. 'Good to meet you, John.'

'Likewise.'

Chapter 12

Dave threw his bag on the bed of the motel and opened the fridge door in hope of a mini bar.

'That'd be right,' he muttered. Empty.

The paint was peeling in one corner of the ceiling and the middle of the bed sagged. Still, the room was clean and warm, and for the next few nights it would be home.

The pipes in the ceiling creaked and groaned as another visitor turned on the shower.

Letting out a sigh, Dave collapsed on the bed, thinking he should have a shower, too—that it might wash away his anxiety about Mel and the kids.

He'd been trying to talk to Mel for the past two days. His calls had gone straight through to voicemail, and he wasn't sure if it was because she had the phone turned off, because she was avoiding him, or because they were in a remote out-of-range spot.

The need to hear her voice was strong.

He pulled his mobile from his top pocket and flipped it open to scroll for Mel's number. His fingers were hovering over the keys, when he paused. Then, without thinking much more, he hit dial.

Silence. Not even her voicemail this time. He took the phone away from his ear and looked at the service. Three bars. Should be enough to ring out.

Dialling again, he finally heard it connect. Jerking upright, he took a breath and paced to the window to look out. The ring tone seemed to go for an age and he was sure the voicemail would kick in once more.

'Hello?'

Suddenly he felt as nervous as a high-school boy asking a girl out on a date for the first time. 'Mel, hi. It's me.'

In the silence that stretched between them, Dave could hear seagulls screech and wind blow, muffled against the phone.

'Where are you?' he finally asked.

The pause went on so long, he was about to ask if she was still there, when she said, 'I can't tell you, Dave. Dad's asked me not to.'

Volcanic rage coursed through Dave and before he could help himself, he spat out, 'For god's sake, Mel! It's not me you have to be worried about. I'm still your husband. You don't have to listen to everything your father says.'

'Well, I've missed you too, Dave.' Her words dripped with sarcasm and Dave silently cursed himself for losing his temper. 'For your information, we've been on Dad's friend's yacht.'

He paused as he took in the news and the white-hot rage that he felt evaporated to a burn. 'Okay,' he said carefully. 'That's good. You'll see people coming if you're out on the water. Whereabouts are you?' He had to give it to Mark: that was a clever move.

'I'm not to tell you, Dave. Dad has asked me not to tell anyone, I just said that.'

He took a breath and silently exhaled. 'Can you just tell me if you're in Western Australia?'

He could sense her relenting. 'Yeah. We are.'

'North?'

'Yeah, up north.'

'Well, sweetie, if I can't find you, then no one else will.' He paced the floor, ending back at the window. 'If I had my way, I'd be there with you.'

Outside, a dusty LandCruiser ute pulled up at the IGA supermarket and a tall well-built man got out. Dave paused for a moment, squinting at him, but he was distracted by Mel's sad tone.

'No, you wouldn't. You won't stop until you've found this bloke. Anyway, I said "we've been", not "we are". I was seasick; couldn't bear the rocking and being tossed about.'

'So, you're not on the yacht now?'

'I had to get somewhere that didn't move. We're in a resort now.'

'And the kids?'

'Are fine. Bec is enjoying the beach and sand. And Alice, well . . .' Her voice trailed off and Dave could imagine her looking at the baby in the cot, stroking her hair. The pang of separation hurt so much he closed his eyes.

Her voice brought him back. 'She's okay now that I'm not seasick. I didn't have a lot of milk for a little while because I was vomiting. But that's better now I'm on terra firma.'

'Mel, I can't help you unless you let me.'

'You're never home, so how would you help now? We're managing.' She sounded bemused.

'I wanted to be with you, Mel. Surely you know that,' he repeated. 'I would be helping you with the kids if I could.'

Mel scoffed quietly. 'No, Dave, you're in Barrabine, solving another crime. And if you weren't there, Bob would have rung you, given you another case and you'd still have left. I've seen it all before.'

'That's unfair,' Dave said, but the words sounded hollow even to him. She was right. He had done that. Every time Bob had called, he'd gone.

But with good reason, Spencer's voice came to him. *Victims rely on the coppers they make contact with. That's part of your job. And I've told you before about coppers' wives and them trying to make us change.*

'Unfair?' Mel countered. 'Do you really think so? I asked you to leave the job when we moved to Barrabine and then again just recently. Our marriage has been about what you want rather than what we want, surely you have to see that, Dave? If you can't . . .' Mel let out a heavy breath.

'Mel—'

She interrupted him, her voice terse. 'I meant what I said when I left, Dave. You have to make a choice when all this is over.'

'Do you really think it's fair to ask me to give up something I've worked for since I was kicked off the farm? Mel, Jesus, have you forgotten what it was like for me? To be told there wasn't room for me on my own family's property? I've explained all of this to you before! You know the stock squad is the perfect thing for me. I've wanted this for so long and you've always supported that. Well, I thought you did.' He ran his hand through his hair and shook his head in disbelief. 'And now you're saying you're not going to.'

'But I didn't know it was going to involve this sort of thing, Dave.' Her voice was pleading. 'Surely you can understand that I didn't put my hand up for anything like this? I didn't know that we'd be scared and having to hide away because of your work. And it's not just that! Is it really fair for me and the children not to have you in our lives because you're off busy saving someone else's family . . . or someone has killed you? What about putting us first?'

'For god's sake,' Dave muttered under his breath, but his words didn't stop the pang of guilt that shot through his stomach.

'You know, Dave, if I can't have you, at least I've got your children. I've got a part of you that you can't take away from me.'

Dave shut his eyes as too many thoughts crowded in. *Is that a threat? Do you want to take the kids away from me?*

You can't do that! I have as much right to see them as you do, he thought.

But really, he argued with himself, *how do you think you're going to manage looking after them with your work? Mel is their mother. You can't take them away from her.*

Silence dragged out between them.

'Yeah, I thought as much,' Mel said eventually. 'You've got nothing to say because you know I'm right. Go back and be the policeman and I'll look after our children, and Dad will look after me.' Mel hung up.

Looking at the dead phone incredulously, Dave hit the button to call her back, but this time it went straight to voicemail.

'Fuck!' Dave let the word rip from deep inside him. He pushed the chair and it toppled backwards, hitting the desk. White-hot fury was exploding from him as he swiped at the desk, knocking the phone, pen and notebook to the floor. 'You've got to be fucking joking.'

The door opened after a brisk knock, and Dave ripped around, ready to tear whomever it was limb from limb. 'Don't fucking come in here without—'

Bob stood in the doorway. 'Didn't go well, son?' He eyed the damage. 'You might want to calm down.'

'I don't want to talk about it,' Dave snapped, looking at the mess he'd made.

Raising his eyebrows, Bob said, 'Really? Again?' He was referring to a time when Dave refused to open up and talk about the troubles he had.

Snatching up his wallet, Dave stormed past him. 'Let's get a beer and a feed. Spencer is supposed to be here tonight.'

'Whatever you think you need, son,' Bob said as he went inside, scooped Dave's mobile from the floor and stood the chair up. He picked up the key to Dave's room from the bed and pulled the door closed, making sure it was locked. 'You might want this,' he said, handing the key to Dave, who was standing under a tree with his arms folded, still breathing heavily.

'Where does she get the right to issue ultimatums?'

Bob started walking towards the pub.

Dave caught up with him. 'She knew. The whole time she's known me, she knew that I wanted to be a copper on the stock squad. Now she's saying that it's either her or the police. I mean, where—'

Bob stopped and put his hand on Dave's shoulder. 'There isn't anything I can say that's going to make this better, son. Plenty of us have been on the same island you're on now. It's isolating, frightening and unfair. And sometimes those women play mean. But you're not Robinson Crusoe.'

'You're telling me! She threw in a comment about "I've got your children"! What the fuck is that all about? Has she already decided she's leaving? That she's going to shut me out and apply for full custody? Well, if that's the case she'll have another thing coming—I've got the right to have my children too.'

Bob was quiet for a few moments, then he said, 'It sounds like you've made your decision.'

Dave swung around and looked at him. 'What? What do you mean by that?'

'Well . . .' Bob kicked at the dust. 'Well, son, you're talking custody. That usually means a marriage break-up.'

'I . . . ah . . .' Dave frowned. 'Nooo.' He drew the word out as he thought. 'No, it was just what she said. I was only reacting to that.' He fell silent, then shook his head. 'No, I haven't made a decision. She might've, but I haven't. I don't want to have to. What I *do* want to do is to find Bulldust and eliminate his threat. Once that's happened and she feels safe again, Mel mightn't think this way anymore.'

'Hmm, maybe.'

'You don't agree?'

'No, son, I don't. I am one hundred percent sure you're going to have to make a choice. Mel won't give you another option.' He slapped Dave's back sympathetically. 'Rock and a hard place and all that.'

Dave stared at him, willing him to say something different. But nothing came.

'Look, here's Spencer. Let's get a beer.'

Bob set off towards the short, stocky man in shorts and a shirt who was leaning against the door of the pub.

'Good to see you, Spencer. How're things?' Bob said.

'Excellent, excellent,' Spencer replied before turning to Dave. 'It's good to see you, fella. You're looking a bit wound-up there.' He took off his hat and grinned at them both. 'By god, it's great to see you.'

'Ah, he needs to get a few drinks into him,' Bob said, taking out his wallet. 'Bad phone call with the missus. Needs a distraction. Beer?'

'Never say no to one of them,' Spencer answered as they walked in. 'Here, we'll grab a table.'

Dave and Spencer sat down while Bob ordered at the bar.

'Not good?' Spencer asked.

Through the red mist of anger Dave saw Spencer look around and check out who was in the pub.

'No. And I don't want to talk about it now. I should calm the fuck down. It's all fucked.'

Spencer nodded. 'Yeah, it is. Anyway, mate, you know where I am when you need me.'

'Cheers.' Dave looked down and took a few more deep breaths before Bob put the beers on the table and threw down a laminated menu.

'What's good to eat here, Spencer?' he asked, sitting down and letting out a huge sigh. 'Well, cheers, boys. Here's to solving our case.'

Clinking glasses, Dave swallowed the beer like he might never get another one.

'Hear, hear,' Spencer answered. He looked at the menu. 'Haven't been here for a while. You might have to make your own choice or ask the girl at the bar over there.'

Bob leaned forward. 'So, what's new in your neck of the woods, huh, Spencer? Who're you chasing?'

'It's real quiet,' he answered. 'You know, since Dave here left, there's not been too much other than the usual B-and-Es. DUIs. Nothing. I think the excitement follows him. Not even anything going on with prospectors stealing gold.' He glanced over his shoulder. 'And let me tell you, that's just not normal! Not that I should speak too loudly. Saying something like that is usually enough to make it happen.'

Bob gave a bark of laughter. 'You're right there. We had an interesting yarn with an old fella out at Nefer Station today. Bit of a fly around.' He told Spencer briefly about the case. 'You know anything about that place?'

Spencer shook his head. 'Nope. The closest I've come to looking into any type of stock theft is those brands Dave and I were talking about.'

'Yeah, yeah, that's right. The brand that Scotty and Bulldust use.'

Dave put down his empty glass. ''Nother round?' he asked, not waiting for their reply as he got up and went to the bar. His heart was still beating too fast and he was having trouble concentrating on what his friends were talking about. All he could hear was Mel's voice in his mind.

I've got your children.

Was the threat of not having his girls near him enough to make him give up policing? He thought back over the past four years—three of them married. When had everything started to change? It wasn't a hard question: during his first posting to Barrabine. They'd only been married a few weeks when they moved there, and the change from Perth and Bunbury to the red soils and heat of Barrabine had been confronting for Mel.

She'd struggled to find her identity after giving up her job as a paediatric nurse to follow Dave to his new posting.

She'd become sullen, uncommunicative and angry, and Dave had found it easy to go work and not come home. An escapism that worked—that still worked.

He had tried in the beginning; tried to help her fit in, help her find a job. Kathy and Spencer had as well, and there had been a lovely few months when she found a job as a community nurse, but then she'd fallen pregnant and stayed at home. Her frustration had built, her sharp tongue becoming malicious at times.

Dave had fallen head over heels in love with Bec the minute she was born but his tentativeness towards his wife had lingered. Some of her stinging words had left their mark on his soul, and as much as he wanted to try with Mel, he had started to protect himself.

Mark hadn't helped. He never had. Right from before they got married when Mark had tried to convince Mel not to go ahead with the marriage. Told her that Dave would never be able to provide what she was accustomed to. His arrogance and interference had ended up pushing Dave to his limit, at which point he'd thrown a punch. Mel had left Barrabine and taken Bec back to Bunbury. And Dave had gone undercover.

Reflecting on his relationship with Mark, he wondered not where it had all gone wrong but whether it had ever been right? Probably not. The first time Mel had introduced them had been at the prestigious Perth Golf Club. He should have seen the writing on the wall about Mark's personality then. He'd been loud, big-noting his latest shares success and had called the Premier and many other politicians by their first names when he'd walked in. Dave was never going to, nor did he want to, fit into that world.

'Three pints, thanks, mate,' Dave said as the barman walked past and pointed at him.

'What are you coppers doing so far from home?' he asked as he pulled the beers.

'How'd you clock us as coppers?'

'I know one of your lot when I see one.' The barman winked. 'Not that I've had too much to do with any of you.'

'Good to know,' Dave said, willing him to hurry up.

'You up here for that motorbike crash that happened last week?'

'Don't know anything about it, mate,' Dave replied, placing cash on the bar.

'Bad news, that. I heard that it might not have been an accident.'

'Like I said, I don't anything about it.'

The barman cocked his head towards the table where Bob and Spencer were leaned in close, talking. 'Maybe not, but your mate does.' He placed the first beer in front of Dave. 'So, if you're not here for that, then what are you here for?'

'Can't really discuss that with you.'

'Well, you've certainly caused some interest around the place.'

'Really? We only got here yesterday.'

'Doesn't take long out here. Strangers stick out.'

Dave pushed Mel to the back of his mind and focused on the bartender. 'You been here long?'

'Since I was a whipper-snapper. Dad owned this place and left it to me. Don't know anything else.'

'Get many people in?'

'Yeah, 'specially during winter and spring. Tourists and the like.'

'And locals?' Dave picked up the newly poured second beer and took a sip.

'Plenty of them from the surrounding stations come in on the weekends.'

'Run cattle up here mostly, do they?' He watched as the barman set the third beer on the bar and then put the money in the till, handing him a few coins in change.

'Wild dogs don't let them run anything else.'

'Cheers for the drinks.' Dave raised his glass and went back to the table.

'Yeah, the boys thought it was real strange,' Spencer was saying. He looked up at Dave and took the beer he was handed. 'Cheers, mate.'

'Thanks, son,' Bob said as Dave put the other two drinks down in front of them.

'What was strange?' Dave asked.

'Motorbike accident. Up on the Great Central Road. Fuel-tanker driver found this bloke who'd driven down a cliff off the road.'

'Oh yeah, Curious Cat up there just mentioned something about it,' Dave nodded towards the bar. 'Said he didn't think it was an accident.'

'Yeah, well, funny he should say that, 'cause the boys have asked me to go and take a look at the crash site. The bloke's been airlifted to Perth, and Major Crash have tried to talk to him, but he's out to it still. Doc is saying he's got severe head injuries, but Major Crash says the helmet isn't damaged. They're not convinced the injuries are consistent with a motorbike crash.'

'Sounds interesting.'

Spencer shrugged. 'Who knows. I'll have a look when I get out there, see what I reckon. It'll give me an opportunity to call in at some of the stations along the way and show the pics of our friends.' He turned to Dave. 'And speaking of friends, what's the latest on our friend Bulldust?'

Chapter 13

'It's Detective Dave Burrows here.' Dave sat at the table in the motel room, a notebook and pen in front of him.

Spencer's question about Bulldust had set something off inside him. He hated not being the lead detective on the case. Being in the dark. He needed to find out what Major Crime had discovered and what they were doing to catch the bastard. Then he could make a plan to get his family back.

The only way he was going to be able to change Mel's mind was to talk to her. He wanted—needed—to see her, to start the conversation, to try to save what they had. He couldn't lose his children. Mel . . . well, his protection measures were still in place, but the kids? They took up so much of his heart. His fingers closed tightly around the pen; he felt helpless, but he had to do something.

'How can I help you?' Carl Lemming made it clear that Dave was the last person he wanted to hear from.

'I'm sure you know why I'm calling.'

Carl didn't rise to the bait.

'I want to know how you're getting on.'

He heard Carl shift and the loud creak of a chair reached him.

'Look, Dave, I've already told you: if I've got something to tell you, I'll ring you. I've got your number and trust me, I will ring. We understand how important this is to you.'

The familiar flare of anger was there as Carl spoke. Dave had often used a similar calming voice when speaking to families of crime victims who were calling for the fifth time that week.

'Will you ring? I'm not sure. Anyway, that doesn't matter. I need to know what you've found out since you interviewed Mel,' Dave insisted. He gripped the pen, poised to take notes.

'Hold for one moment, will you?'

Dave didn't get to answer, he heard the phone being placed heavily on the desk and papers rustling before it was picked up again.

'Right, we put the composite drawing out to the media the day your family left town. You know what it's like: every Tom, Dick and Harry has dobbed in their ex-partner, neighbours and people who owe them money. So far nothing has checked out. We have three sightings that we need to do a little more follow-up on.'

'Where?'

'Around here in Perth.'

'He won't be in Perth.'

Silence. The chair creaked again.

'Why do you think that?' Carl asked.

'Because he's a bushie. He won't have hung around.'

'Well, we can take that into consideration, but I haven't had any leads come in from the bush.'

'Has anyone checked Scotty's station out of Barrabine? I've got this feeling . . .'

'Detective Burrows.' Carl's voice hardened. 'As you well know, we can't operate on feelings. And I'll thank you for not questioning how I do my job. I've been in this game longer than you. I'm aware of what an investigation entails. However, for your information, yes, the station has been visited.'

Dropping the pen, Dave tapped his fist on the table before he pushed himself up from the chair and started to pace the room. It was repetitive and dizzying, being such a small room, but he had to move, otherwise he was going to say something to this pompous prick at the end of the phone that he couldn't take back.

'And what did you find?'

'Nothing, Detective Burrows. Nothing. Now, you know I don't *have* to tell you anything. This is our investigation. You'll know something when we do.'

'Mate, I didn't know you'd been to the station and that's information I should have. So, you keep on telling me what you've got.'

Silence hummed down the line and when Carl spoke, it was clear his patience was waning. 'I'll make this clear: what I'm about to tell you is purely because we're in the same job. Out of respect for the same badge we carry. The station has been taken back by the Pastoral Lands Board. There's a caretaker out there, keeping an eye on things.'

'What about the cattle?'

'Cattle have been sold. They've been gone since it was clear that Bulldust and Scotty were in the wind. Proceeds of Crime have put frozen notes on everything there. The equipment and so on. Sold all the cattle off and the lease has been resumed. They're not there.'

'Have you got anyone keeping an eye out? Have you driven all over the place?'

'There are people watching for anything suspicious and if they report something it's directed straight to us. So far, everything has been a negative. Bulldust and Scotty are clever.'

Dave blew out a breath in frustration.

'I can tell you, Lemming, those two blokes will be out bush somewhere. You need to focus on station country. That's where they'll be most at home. God, I can't work out why you blokes can't see that!'

'Burrows, you're out of line,' Carl snapped. 'I've given you my time and I've been patient. Told you more than I should have, out of respect. But, mate, you just crossed over to somewhere you shouldn't go. This isn't your investigation; it's Major Crime's. The powers that be have warned you off. I'm telling you now: fuck off and let us do our job. Do not interfere. Do not have your partner ring us up and call in favours from some of his old pals. Oh yeah, I know Holden has been doing that. Both of you need to run along and chase your sheep and cattle and leave the real crime to us. Because let's face it, Burrows, if you were a great detective, you would have had these two arseholes locked up before they knew what was happening and saved everyone a lot of trouble.'

Dave opened his mouth, but nothing could get past the ferocious rage circling inside him.

'Cat got your tongue? Good. Been nice talking to you.'

Dave sat stock still, his mind racing, before he slammed the phone down on the table. 'Fuck!'

He wanted to kick something, but instead he opened his kit bag and threw his clothes on the bed. 'Prick. Wouldn't know if those two bit him on the dick.' He found his sneakers and shorts and changed into them. He had to move. To run. Something hard and physical. Something to take away the ache in his chest.

Yanking the door open, he found Bob with a raised fist to the door.

'Going somewhere, son?'

'You know what those fucking dickheads in Major Crime just told us both to do?'

'I wouldn't know what bullshit could come out of their mouths.'

'They won't focus. Won't listen. I told them Bulldust and Scotty would've gone bush again. Even explained why. But they won't listen. Told us . . . both of us to chase sheep and cattle and leave the real crime to them. Jesus, Bob!' Dave ran his fingers through his hair. 'This is my family they're playing with!'

'Son, those fuckwits couldn't track an elephant through custard. I'll make some calls to try to see where it's going. I know a bloke who isn't in the investigation but close enough to it.' He put a calming hand on Dave's shoulder. 'We'll get these buggers. You and I will make sure it happens.'

'Ha, they know you've been making calls. Said for you not to bother making more.'

'They can get stuffed. I'll ring who I want, and about what I want. Look, Dave, these guys, they're detectives, and they solve some big crimes, and usually they're very good at it. But they'll find it hard to understand what goes on out here in the bush. How can you expect a city bloke to get inside the mind of someone like Bulldust? And as detectives, that's what we have to do: think like the crims. Some blokes are good at it and some aren't.'

'It frustrates me that they put on a suit and tie and cufflinks and think they're a great copper. Being a decent detective's about more than looking good.'

'Now, listen, don't go picking on the way the look. If you've got something constructive to say, sure, but don't just pull the piss about their clothes. Reckon this will all go a lot smoother if we keep on the right side of them, okay?'

Dave stepped back into the room and sat at the table, putting his head in his hands. 'There's no way Mark will bring Mel and the girls back until after we've got them. And I know those two blokes are back out bush somewhere. I said this to Mel and Major Crime and I'll say it to you: they'll be like wounded dogs. They'll go somewhere familiar, where they know it's safe.'

'I agree, but this is a big country, son. They could be twenty kilometres away from us or two thousand.' He spread his arms out, indicating the space. 'They've been on the go for twelve months and no one can find them. Clever buggers to be able to hide their trail as well as they do.'

'You're not telling me anything I don't know.' Nervous energy was circling inside Dave, making his body hum.

Bob was watching him. 'Maybe we'll have a word to Spencer and see if his boys at the station can keep an eye out, too,' he said calmly, then paused. 'See, the trouble is, as you well know, we can't be seen to be interfering with Major Crime. And I know the need to find the brothers is overpowering. There's a whole lot of fear, adrenalin and even revenge involved in your thought process.'

'Revenge?' Dave frowned at him.

'Ah now, son, don't tell me you haven't thought about stringing Bulldust up by his dick one dark night. I know I would've.'

Dave stayed silent, not willing to admit he'd murdered Bulldust and Scotty more than once in his dreams.

'Maybe you need to cool your heels, yeah? I've told you before, you need to stay calm and think things through. You're a hot-head and it'll get you into trouble one day.'

Dave got up and pushed past him. 'I gotta get out and go for a run.'

'You do that. Calm yourself down. Then you need to put this to the back of your mind and remember the job we're here to do.'

When Dave returned, Bob had the paperwork spread out on the table in his motel room.

'Better?' he asked without looking up.

'Maybe,' Dave said as he sat on the bed and pulled his sneakers off, then went into the bathroom.

Splashing water on his face, he looked at his reflection in the mirror, water still dripping from him. His eyes were a deep blue and his hair a dark brown. There were a few fine lines beginning at the sides of his eyes and he could do with a good shave.

What did Mel see in me? he wondered. Did she see the young, enthusiastic sergeant she'd met on the beach all those years ago? Or did she see a driven detective who always wanted to do what was right?

Or worse, did she not see him at all? Maybe their relationship had gone past her even thinking about him. She certainly wasn't trying to call him. And his children? Did she talk to them about him? Did they miss him? Would baby Alice forget him before he had the chance to see her again? Was Bec keeping Daddy close?

He pushed away the tears that threatened to form at the image of his daughters' faces, and forced his thoughts to Bulldust. His eyes narrowed. Funny word, revenge. Oh, he'd like it all right. But not because he wanted to change the previous investigation—because he didn't get to arrest him. Carl Lemming was right. If he'd done his job properly, neither of the men would've been in the wind right now. They'd be rotting in prison.

Was it revenge or was it making sure the job was done right? It had certainly got personal, but revenge? What he wanted was to make sure they were arrested and tried properly. To serve the sentence they deserved.

And that's what makes you a copper and nothing else, he thought. *If only Mel could understand that.*

'Son, as hard as you try, you're not going to make yourself good lookin'. How about you get your arse out here and start helping me?' Bob called.

Dave smirked, his heart lighter. He was a copper, and coppers tracked down crims. That was his job. He rubbed the towel over his hair and patted his face before getting dressed. 'You should try it some time,' he said, going back out into the room.

Bob looked at him over the top of his glasses. 'Try to be good lookin'? Nah, I'll leave that to the likes of you. Now, see here.' He pushed a piece of paper towards him. 'These are the opening and closing figures for the financial year 1999/2000. Opening being the stock they had on hand at 1 July 1999 and closing what they had on hand, including all the natural increase, on 30 June 2000. Understand?'

Dave threw Bob a look. 'I know this. Farmer from way back, remember? Natural increase is all the calves that have been born on the place.'

Bob ignored him and tapped the paper. 'You'll see here that there were fifteen hundred breeders and the natural increase was twelve hundred. That's eighty percent increase—about twelve hundred calves. You're never going to get a hundred percent natural increase out here.'

'No,' Dave agreed as he took the pages. 'Dingoes, mum has calving trouble, no milk, calf dies. Whatever. Got live ones, you've got dead ones.'

'True enough.'

Dave looked through the figures. 'Says here there're three hundred steers.'

'Well, from the figures from the muster that John's done, there's only a thousand all up and the breakdown of that is five hundred cows, four hundred calves, a few bulls and fifty steers.'

Silence stretched out between them.

'We're missing a few, then,' Dave finally said.

'You're Einstein.'

'Are there any dollar amounts that could be sales in the bank account? You know, that we can link back to sales of the missing stock.'

'Well, son, since you've been out getting rid of your anger and I've been here covering your arse, that's what *you're* going to work out.' Bob smiled and indicated a pile of bank statements on the other side of the table. 'Have fun!'

Chapter 14

Work backwards—that was what Bob had always told Dave to do.

Backwards from the bank statements. As Dave looked, he realised the statements weren't for Nefer Station, they were for Dunstan Kendal.

'How'd you get these so quickly?' Dave asked Bob, who was immersed in another trail of figures and brands.

'Fax.'

'I mean, how'd you get a warrant?'

'Talked to the sarge at Wallina while you were having your tanty yesterday. He's friendly with the local judge. All happened pretty suddenly. Course, there's not much going on out here with these types of things, like there is in the city.'

Dave eyed the statements, then picked up a ruler and started to study the transactions. The dates spanned back over the previous twelve months. Blacking out the transactions clearly unrelated to sold stock, he quickly eliminated cash, groceries and day-to-day living expenses. That didn't leave a lot.

'Can't see anything obvious here,' he said as he flicked. 'Lot of transactions at the pub and cash.'

Bob nodded. 'I thought the same. Reckon we need to go and have a yarn to the local stock agent.' He tapped a piece of paper. 'This is a transaction put through the Nefer Station account, but I can't find where the money has come into the bank account.'

Reaching for it, Dave checked the dates against the statements he had in front of him. 'There's nothing for that amount on here either.'

'Hmm, so where's that money gone?'

'Another account somewhere?'

'Most likely. Pretty sure that twenty grand won't have been handed out in cash.'

'The stock agent should have details of who the money was paid to.'

'My thoughts exactly. Come on.' Bob stood up and took his coat from the back of the chair.

Dave followed him out to the vehicle and climbed into the driver's seat.

'Hey,' Bob said as Dave turned the key in the ignition. 'Here comes your mate.'

Dave looked up and saw Spencer walking towards them, his hand held up to try to get their attention.

'What's going on?' Dave asked as he switched off the engine and wound down the window.

'Morning, fellas. Off somewhere?'

'Introducing ourselves to the local stock agent.'

'Ah, Peter William. Good bloke. You might have to make an appointment with him. He's often on the road. Takes a while to get around to all the stations with the distances between them up here.'

Bob nodded. 'We thought we'd hit the office and see what we found.'

'You not heading home yet?' Dave asked.

'Kathy's going to kill me. It's the second dance practice I've missed this week. The finals aren't that far away.'

'I'd offer to be your practice partner,' Dave said with a shrug, a grin on his face, 'but I think you value your toes. Why're you staying out a bit longer? What's the go?'

'Well, that's what I've come to talk to you about. I've been speaking to Major Crash. You remember the motorbike accident I told you about?'

'Hmm. You said they weren't sure it was an accident?'

'Yeah, that's the one. The vic's come around and he's got no recollection of what happened. The guys have tried to talk to him a few times, but he just says he can't remember.' He stopped and tapped on the bonnet of the troopy. 'Or if he does, he's not saying.'

'Such a suspicious mind,' Dave said.

'Funny, that's what I'm paid to have. But listen to this. I'll be interested to see what your take on it all is.' He held up his pointer finger. 'Number one, severe head injury.'

Dave nodded.

'Two, there wasn't any damage to the helmet.'

'Yeah?'

'Three, the helmet was on his head when he was found.'

Dave frowned. 'That can't be right. If he's got a head injury, the helmet has to be damaged in some way. That's the first thing that's going to hit anything.'

'That's why no one is sure this is just an accident. I'm going back to the crash site to have a look around.' He stopped and looked at Dave. 'This is why I needed to tell you this. Dave, the medical report said this bloke had lineal bruising on his wrists that they're not able to explain.'

There was a pause as Dave processed what Spencer had just told them. 'His hands were bound?' he finally asked.

Spencer nodded. 'In a way we've seen before.'

Bob shifted next to Dave and leaned across the gear stick to look Spencer in the face. 'Before?' he asked, just as Dave said, 'As in cable ties?'

'Well, I think we need to keep an open mind but, yes, that was my thought. That's the way these two blokes like to operate, and I haven't seen anything like that in my area in years. Reckon it's worth mentioning since we know Bulldust has been in WA.'

'Interesting. And concerning,' Bob said.

'We have to let Major Crime know,' Dave said.

'Hold your horses there, cowboy.' Spencer gave Dave a grin. 'I've got some work to do on that first.'

'You going out to the scene?' Bob asked.

'Yeah, the boys asked me to head out there, see what I can find. I've got the GPS coordinates. Only said a couple of days ago that I was looking for something to do, didn't I?'

'Where was the incident?' Dave asked. His heart was pounding and, right now, all he wanted to do was get in the vehicle with Spencer and help him investigate the scene.

'Up on one of the tracks that runs off the Great Central Road. Towards the Gun Barrel Highway. Fuel-truck driver saw tracks in the dirt and stopped for a squiz. That's how they found him in the first place. Still breathing but unconscious. RFDS was brought in and they got him to Perth quick smart. He'd been there for only a few hours by the sounds of it. One lucky boy, if you ask me.'

'And who is he?'

'Bloke by the name of Victor Richardson. He was out on an adventure ride.' Spencer shook his head. 'Why the fuck people feel the need to do these types of holidays by themselves I've got no idea. Better off going in a group when you're headed out bush away from any type of civilisation.'

'Agreed,' Bob said. 'The number of times I've come across tourists with a flat tyre and no idea how to change it, out in the middle of the bush somewhere, defies belief.'

Dave asked, 'Has anyone run a check to see if this bloke has links to Bulldust and Scotty?'

'Got the fellas on that now,' Spencer said.

'Don't you reckon you should wait until you get the answer?'

Spencer stared at Dave in amazement. 'What, and let the scene be even more compromised than it is now?'

'I don't think another twenty-four hours will make much difference.'

Spencer leaned forward and poked Dave in the chest. 'You've made him soft, Bob.'

'I can't claim that, Spencer. He came that way,' Bob chortled.

'Dave, have I taught you nothing? Another twenty-four hours and a crow might pick up something shiny, or the wind might blow away an important piece of evidence.'

Dave fiddled with the gear stick. 'Maybe just make sure . . . Who's going with you? I could come.'

'No, mate. You've got to stay away—and you've got another job to do, in case you'd forgotten. I'll head out there by myself. Doubt I'll see anyone. Plus, I've got a sat phone and the Glock in my gun safe in the car. She'll be right.'

'Mate, these guys are dangerous.'

'You think I haven't worked that out? Don't forget I was your handler when you were undercover. I was the one who briefed you on Bulldust. I'm more than aware of what he's capable of. And let's be clear, there's no clear evidence that they're around here.'

'If you do come across them, don't tell them who you are, just back away. Get in the car and drive out of there as quickly as you can.'

'Dave, I didn't come down in the last shower. And to come across them will be highly unlikely. I'll ring you when I get back.'

'When will that be?'

'Tomorrow night at the latest. It'll take me a good three or four hours to get out there, process it, then drive back again. I'll probably camp out there the night.' He tapped the bonnet again. 'Right-oh, chaps. I'll be getting on. See you on the flip side.'

Dave watched his old partner walk away.

'Someone should be going with him.' Dave turned to look at Bob, whose apprehensive face matched Dave's unease. 'He shouldn't be sniffing around out there by himself. I'm not happy.'

Bob shifted back in his seat and indicated for Dave to start the engine. 'Not your call, son. He's a smart man. Been in the job a long time.'

'I realise that, but you know, these two aren't playing. I've looked in their eyes and seen how cruel they can be. They won't think twice about getting rid of Spencer if they come across him.'

Twisting in his seat, Bob looked at Dave. 'Can I reiterate to you again what your old partner said? That at this stage, there is nothing linking Bulldust and Scotty to this scene? There's some minor evidence that a motorbike rider had cable ties around his wrists. Now, you're a detective. How circumstantial is that evidence? Spencer will know if something's not right and won't go near it. Don't worry about him. He'll be okay.' Bob nodded. 'Come on, get that engine going and let's go to see this Peter William.' Bob sat back in his seat. 'Take your mind off this shadow-boxing you keep insisting on.'

'I'll just say this,' Dave said, his hand going to the key, 'cable ties is their modus operandi. I can list four people they've used them on—'

'In Queensland,' Bob interrupted.

'Yes, but we know Bulldust is in WA.'

'Do we?'

'Fuck!' Dave frowned heavily, knowing Bob was right. Irritation coursed through him. 'Okay, okay.' He held his hands up in defeat. 'Let's get on with our investigation.'

Chapter 15

As Dave opened the car door, a whirly-whirly of dust blew across the yard and a chain banged against the steel gate.

'Looks deserted,' he said, taking in the peeling sign that announced Wallina Stock and Station Agents. The sign was attached to a large tin shed surrounded by a tarmac pad and a high wire-netting fence.

'Seen better days, that's for sure,' Bob said, hitching his jeans up as he got out. 'Spencer did say we might need to make an appointment.'

A dog barked in the distance as Dave went to the glass door that looked like it had been inserted in the wall of tin without much thought. He pushed, but it stayed firmly shut.

Cupping his hands around his eyes, he peered through the glass and saw in the dim light a large bench holding a few brochures and an empty coffee cup. Twenty-litre drums lined the wall and a few lick blocks were on top of them.

'No one here,' he called. He glanced up at the sign, hoping to see a phone number they could call, but there was nothing. From the pocket in his blue stock squad-issued shirt, he took out his notebook and wrote a couple of sentences describing what he could see, then wiped his hands on his dark denim jeans to get rid of the sweat on his palms. The sun was high and the wind was warm.

'How do station owners pick up their gear?' he wondered aloud. 'You'd think there'd be a merchandise guy or someone floating around.'

'Probably not that surprising. They wouldn't get a huge amount of business this time of year. Mustering time would be busier.'

As he spoke, they heard the crunch of tyres on dirt and turned to watch a Toyota Prado drive in and park next to the tin shed. A tall man with a wide girth and a red face got out with a smile. Dressed in moleskin jeans and a light green shirt, with a large Stetson hat, Dave thought he looked just like a station ringer.

'G'day, didn't know I was going to be having visitors otherwise I would have been here earlier. Sorry to keep you waiting.' He held out his hand. 'Peter William. What can I do you for?'

Bob introduced them and handed him a card.

'Stock squad, huh? Perth? You're a long way from home.' He unlocked the glass door and reached in to turn on the lights. 'Come in. I'll put the kettle on.'

'We're here making some enquiries about Nefer Station,' Bob said as they followed him in. 'Is it only you here?'

'Nah, my missus helps out but she's crook today. She usually mans the phones and loads up the orders when they come in. It's a quiet time of the year, so I didn't come racing in this morning. Tea?'

'Cheers,' Bob said, and Dave nodded.

'So, how can I help? I assume this isn't a social call if you're talking about Nefer Station. Heard there's a new manager out there.'

'Yeah, seems they're missing a few cattle. You deal with them?'

'Sure did. That Dunstan Kendal, he was a good guy. I was a bit surprised when he shot through the way he did.'

'You knew him, then?' Bob sat at the wobbly Laminex table and nodded for Dave to get out his notebook.

'Yeah, like I said, a good guy. Battled a bit with the owners, I think, but he was a good manager, so I don't really know what's happened out there.'

'Tell me a little about Kendal.'

Peter placed mugs of steaming tea on the table before grabbing the milk and sugar out of the fridge and setting them down.

'I'm not sure what to tell you. He'd been there for a while. I don't know how long—couple years, maybe?'

'And you've been the stock agent all that time?'

'I surely have.' Peter nodded, spooning three sugars into his tea.

'And Kendal, he was a good manager?'

'From what I saw, that would be right. Trouble was, his bosses weren't as easy to get along with. He used to tell me about fences they wouldn't fix and cattle straying.' He leaned forward. 'See, that's where I'd assume the cattle have gone—across to the neighbour's joint. Kendal used to say that they'd expect him to fix everything on a lick and a promise, and you can't do that out here. Fences have to be good quality. Tight, you know?'

'Good fences make good neighbours,' Dave agreed.

'And that's the truth of it.' Peter nodded. 'I think it's pretty unfair that the owners are trying to pin this on him, if I'm honest about it.'

'What makes you say that?'

'Well,' he spread his hands out in disbelief, 'isn't that why you're here? They think the cattle have been stolen.'

'Not necessarily. We get called in to find where the cattle have gone. Now, yes, sometimes that might mean they've been stolen. Other times they could've wandered next door to the neighbours' place because the fences are bad, just as you've said.'

'And what do you think has happened here?'

'At this point we're still investigating.'

'Kendal was trying hard, but not getting any support from his bosses.' Peter put down his mug and leaned back in the chair. 'And I'd see it, you know? He'd come in and book up some fencing gear, then they'd make him return it. I'd have to hand out credits. You can see it on their accounts.'

'How many times did that happen?'

'I'd have to look it up, but at least three that I can think of quickly.'

Dave jotted down some notes. 'We'd like to see that paperwork.'

'Sure, no problem.'

'And the cattle, did they have good breeding?'

'Yeah, they were pretty good. Genetically solid for here.'

'Where did you sell the calves?'

'Used to put them on a truck and send them north. They'd end up on the boats going to the Middle East. That's where most of them went. If there was a demand, I could send them west and put them through the sale yards, but freight is cheaper across to the coast from here and the prices wouldn't be too much different for the type of cattle I was selling.'

Bob nodded. 'I see.'

'Have you met the owners?' Dave asked.

Peter nodded. 'Yeah, once, not long after Kendal started. Got an invite out to a meet-and-greet.'

'And?'

Peter shrugged. 'Seemed normal enough to me. Can't remember which one I met—the Chair of the board, maybe? Anyhow, whoever it was, they didn't seem to know their way around a set of cattle yards, if you get my meaning.'

Bob and Dave waited, until eventually Peter continued. 'He knew nothing about station country. Or breeding cattle. Seems to me that the board haven't spent time on the land.'

'Right. And what about other stations around here—any talk of missing cattle?'

'No.' Peter spoke slowly, squinting as if in deep thought. 'No, I don't reckon I've heard anything. And I would. Bush telegraph and all that.'

A thought flashed into Dave's mind and he spoke up. 'The brand SA in an upside-down horseshoe, have you sold any cattle with that brand recently?'

'I don't think I even know that brand. It's not a WA brand because I'd remember that.'

Dave nodded as his heart sank a little. He'd hoped Peter might say he'd sold some just last week, and they might have got a lead on Bulldust and Scotty. Still, he persisted. 'Do you recognise the names Ashley Bennett or Scott Bennett?'

'Hmm, doesn't ring a bell.' He repeated their names, then took out his mobile phone. 'I'll just check and see . . . Nope, doesn't look like I have them listed in here. Where are they from?'

'We're not really sure,' Bob said as he glared at Dave. 'Dave's just information gathering. Now, Peter, can you remember the last time you sold cattle for Nefer Station?'

'I can look it up, no worries. Don't reckon it's been this year, though.' Peter went to stand.

'What we'd really like is to see their sale accounts as well as their merch account, if you wouldn't mind. Could we see all the transactions from the end of the 1999/2000 financial year up until now?'

Peter paused. 'Do you need a warrant for that?'

'Not if you willingly show us.'

Frowning, Peter looked at them. 'I reckon I might need to speak to the boss about that.'

Dave glanced around. 'You're not the boss?'

'Nah, I just work here. It's a multinational, you know, and I'm employed by them.'

'Sure, give your boss a call and let us know.' Bob stood up. 'But if you could just give us the last date you sold cattle, that'd be much appreciated. If you're more comfortable with us getting a warrant, I'm happy enough to come back with one this afternoon.'

Bob's words were a bluff, Dave knew. To get a warrant would usually take much longer, but this always seemed to work.

'Take me a couple of minutes to get the computers running.'

'We've got time,' Bob smiled.

'Right.' Peter went into another office and started a computer, while Dave stood and read the posters on the wall. Adverts for stations up for lease lined the pinboard near the door.

'Lots of places for lease,' Dave said.

Peter's voice filtered back through the open door. 'There sure are. The high interest rates of the eighties hurt a lot of families, and I know it's a while on since then, but many of them have been hit with bad seasons, and interest piling up on interest has caused a lot of pain to so many owners. Some haven't been able to hang on.

'Can you see that ad for Jacaranda Downs? Family-owned place. Been in the same hands for eighty years. They just had to walk off. Bank wouldn't back them anymore. Criminal. That land is just sitting there with no one on it. Banks haven't got their money because the family has declared bankruptcy and yet if they'd let the family stay there, they would've had a chance of getting some repayments back. I don't understand how the bigwigs in the city make their decisions, do you?'

Dave gave a mirthless laugh. 'I know what you mean.'

'Right, here it is. I sold a hundred steers back on 10 June in 2000.'

'Where to?'

'These went across to go on the boat. Live export.'

'Great. Well, thanks for your time, Peter. If I haven't heard from you later, I'll be back with a warrant to grab that other information we need.'

'No worries. Anything I can do to help.'

'Oh well, there is one other thing. Do you know where Dunstan Kendal is now?'

Shaking his head, Peter gave a half laugh. 'Nah. Wish I did. I liked the fella. Good to have a beer with.'

Dave narrowed his eyes. 'So, you socialised with him?'

'Ah, well, not a lot. We used to have a beer together when we were in the pub at the same time. But we weren't glued at the hip or anything. Kendal was just a great bloke to be around, you know.'

The men got back into the troopy and looked at each other.

'Different story there to what John told us,' Dave said, glancing back at his notes.

'And that surprises you because . . .'

'Not surprised, but it *is* different.'

Bob took out his mobile phone, dialled and then listened. 'Yeah, Holden here. Can you do a check on Peter William, lives in Wallina.' Pause. 'Nope, don't have a DOB. But the numberplate on his vehicle is . . . 9JJ-714. Might be a company vehicle, though.'

He lowered the phone and glanced over at Dave. 'Come on, let's get going out to Nefer Station. Yeah, yeah, I'm still here. Uh-huh. Right. Address?' Bob wrote with the phone tucked between his ear and shoulder. 'Good, right. Cheers for that.'

Putting the phone back in his pocket, he turned to Dave. 'Just go for a swing by 18 Norwood Street.'

Dave looked across at him curiously but flicked on the indicator in the direction of the main street. 'William's house?'

'Yeah, let's just get a bit of a feel for him.'

'Did you pick up on something?'

'No, no, just crossing the t's and dotting the i's.' Bob turned to the window. 'Reckon I saw that street on the way into town.'

'We need a map.'

'Just read the street signs, son! That's the best way to get a feel for a town. And it's not like there're too many of them in Wallina. Here we go, Jackson Street, and the next one is . . .'

Dave looked as he drove past. 'Hunter Road.'

'And . . . ah, here we are, do a U-turn. It's that one we just passed.' Bob jerked his thumb back over his shoulder.

'I'll do a lap of the block,' Dave said as he turned down the next street. 'Built in squares, these towns.'

They were both silent as they watched out for number 18.

The houses on Norwood Street were like the others Dave had seen in Wallina. Mostly weatherboard and looking in need of some TLC. Occasionally, there would be a brick house with a nice garden at the front, but he knew the cost of getting the bricks from Perth would be prohibitive.

'Here we go,' Bob said. 'Sixteen, ah. Oh.' Bob fell silent as number 18 came into view. 'Well, bugger me dead.'

It was clear that a woman lived in the weatherboard house. The lawn, though dry in some spots, was neatly trimmed, and a few tough flowers bloomed bravely in the garden beds that lined the length of the walls. On the verandah was an outdoor setting with cut flowers in the middle. A reading chair swinging from the ceiling and as it swung in the wind, Dave caught sight of a book on a brightly coloured cushion.

In the driveway was a silver BMW X5.

Dave whistled. 'Whoa, that's an expensive four-wheel drive.'

'Pretty flash. Guess the wife drives it.'

Dave slowed right down and they crawled by. Curtains hung in the windows and fairy lights ran the length of the railing.

'Nice place, though. Better than some of the other shit-boxes around here.'

'Mmm,' Bob said.

'Any priors?'

'On who? Peter? No.'

'What are you thinking?'

'The question should be, what are *you* thinking, son? You're a detective, too.' He turned to Dave and gave a wink. 'Just saying.'

His face serious, Dave said, 'He liked Kendal a lot. The only person we've found so far who has anything good to say about him. And sometimes we know that the best place to hide is in plain sight.'

Chapter 16

Spencer stepped out of the car and looked around. The sun was high in the sky and yet the heat, which he should have been able to feel, was negated by the cold desert wind blowing from the north.

A drought wind, his mother used to say.

He stared across the land stretched out before him, taking in the red dirt, the mulga scrub and the golden spinifex swaying in the breeze. The sky was a vivid blue, devoid of clouds, and in the distance he could see a cluster of large gum trees. His guess was, if he drove towards it he would find a stony outcrop waterhole. There were plenty around here—that's why the station country had been able to survive. Even though the land was dry and feed was often short, there was water.

He walked to edge of the road and looked down. This was the third place he'd stopped in the last kilometre. The accident site had to be close to where he was now.

He shrugged his CamelBak onto his back and put on his hat, complete with fly net. The flies out here, especially in the middle of summer, could carry you away. He reached for his belt, on which hung a pair of binoculars, a camera and a notebook, and clipped it around his waist.

Walking the road, he knew he was close; the satellite phone was in his hand and he kept referring back to it to check the GPS coordinates.

With the sun on his back, he revelled in the quiet. If he didn't know the bush, he would have found the silence unnerving; instead, he found it peaceful. His eyes combed the ground as he walked, looking for anything that had been disturbed that might indicate a crash site.

Because the truck driver who found Victor pulled him to safety and then loaded him in the truck, there wouldn't be the usual vehicle tracks to help indicate where it had happened but there might still be some broken branches where the bike had hit going down.

The caw of a crow reached him, and he stopped, shading his eyes from the sun as he looked skywards for the bird. Sometimes birds were the best type of clue: they were where water was, where dead animals were, and their alarm calls could alert you to danger.

Spencer had learned early in his career that it served him well to observe the native animals—they knew the land best.

Glancing back, he judged he was about fifty metres from his four-wheel drive. In front of him was a corner to the right. Slowly and steadily, he kept his pace even and his senses sharp as he searched.

Flies buzzed at the edge of his ears, outside the flynet and when he rounded the corner, he stopped for a drink and looked out over the land. High above, a wedge-tailed eagle was circling, looking for prey.

Kicking the stones at the edge of the road, Spencer walked over and looked down the ravine. It was about a ten-foot drop, but there didn't seem to be anything out of place.

No broken branches. No scuff marks.

'Bloody hell, shouldn't be that hard to find,' he muttered as he took a sip of water. A flash down below road level caught his eye.

He stopped and looked again, but it had disappeared. Slowly moving his body to try to recreate what he had seen, he swayed from side to side, slowly.

Stop. No. There!

Spencer squinted then took the binoculars from his waist.

Amber plastic on the ground.

Putting his foot over the rocky embankment, he clambered down among the rocks, using the bushes as a hand hold. Rocks scattered beneath his feet and tumbled down to the bottom. Securing his footing, Spencer was able to look carefully, before leaning in and picking up what looked like a piece from a vehicle's indicator.

He placed it back where he found it and took a couple of photos before carefully and slowly turning around, searching for something else that would indicate this was the crash site.

'Nothing,' he muttered, batting a few flies away from his net. 'And it doesn't look like the bike hit too hard.' Silence. 'Either this isn't the site, or—' He broke off as a shadow passed overhead.

Circling above him, the wedge-tailed eagle swooped and soared on the thermals, all the while keeping his eyes trained on Spencer.

'I'm still moving, mate, so don't bother.' He turned his attention back to the ground.

After ten minutes of examining the area, he decided it couldn't be the site and grabbed hold of a bush to help him back up the steep hill. Just as he stepped up, the rock he used as a foot hold gave way and skittered down below him. His feet slipped out from underneath and he landed heavily on his stomach.

'Oomph!' The air left his lungs and he lay frozen for a second, gathering himself. He lay his head on the rough ground and closed his eyes.

'Fuck,' he muttered, testing his ankles and hands. Kathy would have a fit if he wasn't able to dance in the grand final. It took a moment before he realised everything was okay, and after a few deep breaths he gingerly got to his feet.

'I'm getting too old for this shit,' he said to the ground as he put his hands on his waist to check that his binoculars and camera were still there, intact.

Glancing up, he reached to grab the trunk of another bush, when he stopped.

'What the . . . ?' Spencer reached up under the bush before stopping himself and grabbing out a pair of latex gloves from his pocket. Carefully he drew out a cable tie. There were two linked together but they had been sliced open to release whatever they'd been holding.

A shiver of adrenalin ran through Spencer.

'Now we're getting somewhere,' he said. He put the cable tie back where he found it and took his camera out again. After capturing four photos in situ he reached for his notebook to record the time, GPS coordinates and his observations.

Standing up and balancing on the rocky terrain, he walked a few metres from where he was, then started to circle the area, moving further and further outwards.

He saw nothing but stones, branches, grass and bushes.

'Come on,' he urged the country. 'Give me a bit more!'

The ground revealed nothing.

Finally, he went back to where he'd slipped. He placed the cable tie and the part of the plastic indicator casing into an evidence bag, then he started back up to his car.

Up on the road, he stowed the plastic bag in the gun safe, which was bolted to the floor behind the driver's seat, and started the vehicle.

Slowly he drove, watching either side of the track for any indication that someone had left the road. He noted there were fresh vehicle tracks—the wind had only blown the tips of the imprints off.

Stopping on the crest of the hill, he hit the steering wheel in frustration. 'There's got to be more.' He grabbed the report the coppers in Perth had sent to him and read the interview with Victor Richardson.

Richardson: The sun was in my eyes and I couldn't see the road. The next thing I knew I was over the edge of the road and careering down the side of the hill.

SS Grant: What time of the day was this?

Richardson: I'm not sure. My bike had a flat tyre and I was limping along trying to reach the closest settlement to get help. It must have been afternoon, though.

SS Grant: Your helmet isn't damaged, while you have a head injury. This raises some concerns for us.

Richardson: I can't help that. I can only tell you what happened.

SS Grant: Was there anyone else involved in the accident?

Richardson: No.

SS Grant: We're here to help you, but we can't do that unless you give us all the information.

Richardson: There's nothing more to give. Now my head's hurting again. Could you leave?

End of interview.

Spencer looked into the distance, letting things play out in his mind.

Afternoon? If Richardson's story was right, it couldn't have been in the afternoon, he would have been travelling away from the sun.

Spencer scratched a note in his book: *Get SS Grant to ask Richardson which direction he was travelling in.*

There had to be more to it.

He stood still and continued looking towards the horizon, trying to work out what he was seeing. What he was missing.

A way from the road, to the left, the sun was reflecting off something shiny.

Slowly putting the interview report down, his eyes never leaving the glint, he put the car into gear and drove forward. If he lost sight of it, with the sun setting, he mightn't find it again.

What have we got here? he thought. *Probably a prospector's camp.*

It took minutes of searching, then he saw it.

A branch—not quite dead, but the leaves beginning to turn up from the heat of the day—dragged across a two-wheel track.

Spencer sat for a moment observing the scene in front of him, then he switched off the engine. Getting out, he noted tracks turning across the edge of the road, which looked like they'd been brushed away with a bunch of leaves. If he looked hard enough he could see the tracks disappearing under the branch. Camera in hand, he snapped a few photos and then walked around the branch and into the bush, following the track.

The low growl of an engine reached his ears and he stopped, his copper's intuition on high alert. Turning back to the car, he picked up the satellite phone and tried to call the station, but the line wouldn't connect.

'Fuck,' he whispered, looking towards what he knew now to be a campsite. 'Bloody sat phones.'

Sitting in the driver's seat, he chewed his nail. The sensible thing would be to camp for the night, try to get in contact with the station and get them to send back-up. If the people who were in there didn't know he was around, he'd be fine overnight, sleeping a distance away from here.

But there was nothing to say this wasn't just what he'd first thought—a prospector's camp. Chiding himself for being jittery because he thought that Bulldust and Scotty could be here, he gave a half laugh. If it had been two weeks ago, he wouldn't have considered calling the station, he would have wandered in and had a yarn to whoever was in there.

The branch across the roadway was concerning. That looked like the people were trying to hide the track.

He glanced up into the trees looking for game cameras, but couldn't see anything.

Yes, his plan was the right one. He could go in, with back-up, when the sun was high in the morning. The pinks and purples of the sunset and long shadows thrust across the land told him he had only about twenty minutes more of light.

The need to know what—who—was in there was too strong. To him, it seemed the perfect hiding spot for Bulldust and Scotty. The cable ties, even though circumstantial, made him believe they were close by. His gut told him he was on the right track. The link to Richardson and the two fugitives wasn't clear, but maybe there didn't have to be one. Maybe

Richardson had done the same as Spencer—just stumbled over their camp.

If it was them.

Making a decision, Spencer grabbed his gun out of the safe and leaned on the door so it clicked quietly shut. He locked the vehicle, pocketing the keys.

With adrenalin coursing through him, he tucked the firearm carefully into the back of his waistband and quietly made his way back into the bush, following the noise, until he could see the soft glow of lights and campfire.

The fire was burning brightly enough to show the outline of a man sitting, his legs stretched out in front of him. To his right was a table, with spotlights next to it. Further away, a camp bed was set up under a tarp. There appeared to be only one bed, one chair, one person.

If there was only one, it couldn't be Bulldust and Scotty. He was convinced that, wherever they were, they would be together. Relaxing a little, he continued to watch.

His heart, which had been thumping hard, slowed a little.

A high-pitched puppy bark sounded and Spencer froze, wondering if the dog could smell his scent on the wind.

'Shut up!' a male voice yelled.

Spencer kept moving, slowly inching forward.

The man got up from the chair and hurled a stone towards a black-and-tan pup. He was only a little thing—not more than three months old, Spencer judged—and he was tied on a long chain, and staring straight at Spencer. That dog wasn't going to cause him any problems.

He barked again.

'Shut the fuck up!'

Narrowing his eyes, Spencer tried to work out if the voice was different to the one he had just heard. How many people were in the camp? But no, he was still convinced there was only one.

Now that the man was standing, Spencer could see he was tall and stocky, dressed in jeans and a heavy jumper. He started to peer into the bush, just as the pup let off another round of growling and barking, still looking towards where Spencer was hidden.

'What's wrong, you dickhead? Roo lurking about, is there?'

The man started to walk towards Spencer and suddenly there wasn't a choice.

Spencer stepped forward into the light of the fire. 'G'day. Sorry, mate. Got a bit of trouble.'

Chapter 17

Spencer saw the man's hand go straight behind his back and knew he was reaching for a gun.

'Whoa, steady there, fella,' Spencer said, his hands coming up in a calming gesture. He couldn't reach for his weapon without starting something he didn't want to start. 'I don't want to cause you any trouble.'

'Who the fuck are you?' the man asked.

Spencer knew this man wasn't Bulldust. But could it be his brother? When Spencer had briefed Dave about the stock-stealing mustering business in order to send him undercover, they hadn't known Scotty existed. He wasn't on their records, and all they had was a composite drawing from the description and information Dave had given them after he'd come out of hospital.

Was it him?

This man standing before him had a long black beard and an earring. Under the heavy jumper, Spencer could tell he was well built and strong. Agile. His eyes held an iciness to them. Whoever he was, he was evil and cruel. Spencer had been around long enough to be able to make a call on people easily.

'Name's Spencer.' He took another couple of steps forward.

'Stay where you are.' The man looked him up and down. 'You a copper? You smell like a copper.'

'Know a bit about coppers, do you?'

The man stayed silent, his hand stilled, so Spencer continued. 'Yeah, I'm from the gold squad. Just doing a little run around to see what's going on out here in this neck of the woods. Going okay for you, is it?'

Crossing his arms, the man shook his head. 'Mate, got no time for coppers. Just fuck off.'

'That's not very polite. What's the problem?'

'Got nothing to say to you.' The man turned his back towards Spencer. 'You'd better get on your way.'

'Is this your lease? Looks like you've been out here for a while. Got a good set-up.' Spencer carefully watched the man's eyes, noting they were flickering towards the creek. Was there someone else out there?

For the first time, he felt a sliver of fear work its way into his stomach. The gun at his back suddenly felt heavy.

'What's it to you?'

'Listen, fella, I'm just out here working out who's in my district. I keep a fairly close eye on these sorts of things, you know.'

'Good for you.'

'I actually came out to check out the site of a motorbike accident, just down the road. Know anything about that, do you?'

A look of surprise lit up the man's eyes. 'Why would I know anything about that?'

Spencer shrugged. 'Only that you're not too far from the crash site. Thought you might have heard something.'

'When did it happen?'

'About a week ago.'

'Well, I know fuck-all.'

'Bloke came off his bike and had a pretty bad head injury. Been trying to understand what happened. He's okay but can't remember exactly how he ran off the road.'

'Can't help you.'

Spencer noted his jaw was clenched and flinching slightly, and the surprise he'd initially displayed had been replaced by a deadpan expression.

'Okay. Just thought I'd ask. Be great to have an eye-witness.' Spencer looked around. The pup was straining at the chain and the spotlights were bathing the gum trees in an eerie glow now that the sun had slipped below the horizon. He tried a different tact. 'So, what's your name? Like I said, I'm Spencer. Spencer Brown.'

'Look, Spencer Brown, I'm not doing anything wrong. I'm out here minding my own business, keeping out of trouble. So, just fuck off and leave me alone. I don't like people, and usually people don't like me. That's why I'm out here.'

'I can see why people don't like you. You're not the friendliest type. Still, it takes all people to make the world go round.' He shrugged, feigning being relaxed. 'And I'm not here to cause you any trouble, but it's my job to check things out. If you'd just give me your name and tell me why you're out here, I'll head off.'

The man took another step towards Spencer, his eyes narrowed. 'Well, now that you've *checked things out*, you can go. If you don't, I'll set my dog onto you. This is private property.'

Calmly, Spencer raised his hands again. 'Cute pup. Private, is it? I could've sworn this was Crown land.' He shifted his body so he was angled away from the man's line of sight and reached behind his back, his fingers touching the gun. As his hands closed around it, his fear mixed with confidence. He would be back in control once he could bring the Glock out into the open.

The man noticed the movement and took a couple of steps towards Spencer, then one back. 'What are you doing?'

Spencer watched the man's face as he brought the gun out and let his arm dangle beside him in the least threatening manner he could manage. 'Gotta tell you, fella, all your aggro is making me feel a little uncomfortable. Like there's something else going on here. Something you don't want me to see. So, how about you take a seat over there next to your dog and take a breather?'

The man's arm went to his back again, and Spencer tensed, but his hand came away empty. His fists were curled up in a ball, anger radiating from him.

'You got anyone else out here with you?' Spencer asked, moving towards the man and indicating for him to sit in the camp chair.

'No.'

'Hands behind your back.'

'You can't cuff me, I've done fuck-all wrong! I keep telling you, I'm just out here minding my own business.'

'If you haven't done anything wrong, you won't mind me taking a look around. I'm going to ask you again, what's your name?'

A long silence was broken only by the crackle of the fire and a mopoke's call.

'Scott.'

A trickle of anticipation ran through Spencer. 'First or last?'

'Whatever you want it to be.'

Letting out a sigh, Spencer grabbed one of the man's hands and quickly cuffed him to the chair, his gun aimed at Scott's thigh. 'This isn't *Pretty Woman*.'

'Scott Bennett.'

'Is it really?' Spencer made sure the man was secure before he stood in front of him. 'I think we might be looking for you. Where's your brother?'

'Dunno, he fucked off about a month ago. Went to Perth.'

'What, and left you out here by yourself?'

'We don't get on.'

'With your attitude, I'm not surprised.' Spencer squatted in front of Scotty and looked him in the eye. 'So, tell me, where've you been all this time, while we've been looking for you?'

'Here and there.'

'And what am I going to find when I head over towards the creek there?'

Scotty didn't say anything, just stared straight ahead.

The pup began to whine, and Spencer turned to look at it, hoping it might give him a clue about whether someone else was here. Handcuffing Scotty to the chair had been too easy. From the stories Dave had told him, he'd expected Scotty to put up a fight, throw a punch, try to disarm him.

Either Bulldust was still around or . . .

He glanced around, remembering the words of his first sergeant at the academy.

Be aware of your surroundings.

The back of Spencer's neck prickled and he stilled.

Scotty sat, staring straight ahead. There wasn't a sound. Even the fire's flames burned silently.

Slowly, Spencer started to turn around to see what was behind him and squinted into the dim light of the fire. Was that the outline of another swag or was it a lump of wood?

Nothing.

His eyes flicked from side to side. No movement.

Keeping his gun in his hand and glancing around, he walked towards the creek, following the sound of the generator and the light.

He wished he had a torch with him, but it was back in the vehicle, sitting on the dash. And that was a rookie mistake.

As he rounded the container at the generator, he saw large tubs of trace elements and fertiliser stacked under a tree, the large drying racks in a line, the shade cloth hung to hide it all from aerial surveillance.

'Reckon I know why you didn't want to talk to me, Scotty,' he called out. 'Got a real little business going on here.'

What an operation, he thought. *No wonder they've been off the radar for so long. They'll have all the money they'd need by selling this.*

He considered his next move. He needed to get Scotty to the car and make a phone call. Had to let Dave know that he had one of the brothers, but Bulldust was still in the wind.

Turning around, he reassessed the camp, his eyes falling on the dark shape he'd thought had been a swag. He still could only see one chair and one camp bed. He realised another chair and camp bed could be packed away as it would have been during the day so creepy-crawlies didn't get in there. Maybe Scotty was telling the truth when he said that Bulldust had taken off . . .

The back of his neck prickled again and this time Spencer turned quickly, but as he brought the gun up there was a whirl of movement, then he felt a stinging blow and crumpled to the ground, the Glock tumbling from his hand.

❧

'Jesus Christ, you took your time,' Scotty said. 'Get me out of here.'

Bulldust felt around in Spencer's pockets and found the key to the handcuffs. Unlocking them, he released Scotty, who shot up from the chair and rubbed his wrists.

'Fucker,' Scotty spat. 'How the hell did he get in here? And what was he talking about with the motorbike accident? Know anything about that, do you?'

'What?' Bulldust half turned and looked at Spencer on the ground before swinging back to his brother. He drew himself up and looked him in the eye.

'He said he was out here looking into a motorbike accident,' Scotty said, moving over to where the man lay. 'If you did anything to bring him out . . .'

'Don't know what you're talking about,' Bulldust lied, following him over.

'You'd better not.' Scotty looked down at the motionless body. 'Shit,' he muttered, and squatted down, putting his hand on the man's neck and waiting a few long moments. Looking up at Bulldust, he said, 'He's dead.'

Bulldust stared at the dirt, which was turning dark from blood seeping out of the wound on the back of Spencer's head. He bent down quickly and, mimicking Scotty, searched frantically for a pulse.

There was nothing. 'Fuck, I didn't mean to kill him.'

'Jesus, Ash. You've killed him. A copper! What the hell have I told you before about being reactive. You do this every time!' Scotty bounced up and started to pace, every so often looking back at the dead man.

'Must've had a soft skull. What are we going to do with him?' Bulldust walked nonchalantly back to the fire and

174

threw the piece of wood into the flames. 'Easy enough to get rid of the murder weapon.' He gave a laugh.

Scotty was silent as he paced.

'Guess we don't have a choice,' he said finally. 'It's bloody déjà vu from when Burrows made us, except he got away. We'll put him back in his vehicle, leave him on the side of the road. Someone will find him but hopefully he'll be decomposed a bit by then and they won't be able to tell he's had a whack to the back of the head.'

Bulldust went over and yanked the man's arm over and stared in his face. 'Don't reckon I've seen him before. You sure he's a copper?'

'That's what he said.'

Bulldust reached into his pocket and found his identification. 'Spencer Brown. Barrabine. That's a fair way from here.'

'And we're going to have to get him a fucking long way away from the camp. We can't have coppers anywhere out near here—'cause they *will* come looking for him. We've still got too much of the crop left to pack up and go now.' The agitation in his voice was obvious. 'Fuck it all, I don't mind having to kill normal people, but murdering a cop is a different matter.'

'Didn't matter when we were trying to get at Burrows.'

Scotty's face hardened. 'That's different and you know it. Come on, get him in the back of the ute and we'll get him out of here. Bet his car is back out on the road. We'll have to take that, too. There's an access road about a hundred ks from here. That's where we'll take him.'

❧

Two hours later, Bulldust was puffing as he struggled to lift Spencer into his car. Finally heaving Spencer's legs inside the vehicle, he pulled the seatbelt over the body but didn't fasten it properly. Bulldust arranged the feet on the accelerator and used a cable tie to fasten the right foot, then found a stick to jam the accelerator down.

He turned the key and the car's engine roared to life, revving high and loud. Gingerly, he leaned over to put the car in gear, before jumping out of the way as the car shot off down the road, gently pulling to one side.

Bulldust grinned as the car hit the grader drain and flew into the air, before landing on its side. The car flipped once, twice, three times, the engine still revving noisily.

The car landed heavily amid the sound of tearing metal, the window shattering in the quiet of the night. Smelling diesel, Bulldust smiled. At least this had gone perfectly to plan.

Waiting until it was quiet again, he approached the vehicle and removed all evidence they'd been there. He glanced at his watch, quickly broke off a branch from the tree and used the leaves to sweep away his footprints, just as Scotty pulled up beside him.

'Come on, let's get the fuck out of here.'

Bulldust climbed in, feeling the butt of Spencer's Glock sticking into his side.

'We're going to have to shut down the access road. We don't want anyone driving or walking into our camp like that again. When we get back, you need to get out there and dust off all the tracks—the utes and our footprints. Find out where he was walking on the side of the road looking for the accident site and get rid of tracks there, too.

'And here's what we're going to do once all that is done. We'll stay here until this last crop has finished drying. Only got another couple of days before it'll be ready and neither of us is going anywhere until we've harvested the last of it. The buyers are just going to have to wait.'

Bulldust only half listened while he stroked Spencer's gun. He was thinking about how there was going to be nothing better than killing that lowlife copper Burrows with another copper's gun.

'You listening?'

'We're still going to get Burrows,' Bulldust said, ignoring the question. He gave a smile that was more like a snarl as he thought, *Bet the dumb coppers won't realise the gun is missing when they do find him.*

'I've told you before about doing things personally and jeopardising our business. That's what got us into this mess in the first place.' Scotty glared at him, but Bulldust didn't care. He had one aim, and that was getting to that mongrel prick Dave Burrows.

'Once the crop is over you can fuck off and do what you want to,' Scotty said. 'I'm done with you. For good this time. You're a liability.'

That was the best thing Bulldust had heard in months. Years, maybe. He smiled, feeling the cold metal touch his fingers.

Chapter 18

Dave slammed the door of the troopy and waited for Bob to climb out.

The drive to Nefer Station had been long and they'd had to stop once to change a tyre that had blown out because of the rough corrugations.

John was waiting for them.

'Got the ute ready,' he said without preamble. 'Ready to go when you are.'

'Thanks, John,' Bob said. 'Yeah, if we could go for a run around the place for a look, we'd appreciate it.'

'Hop in.'

Dave got into the back of the dual cab and grabbed out his notebook and pen. The camera was resting alongside him, on the seat. He brushed a couple of pesky flies away and wound down the window, trying to encourage them outside.

Bob started the conversation. 'Can you tell me a bit more about the family and how they like to run their business?'

Clearing his throat, John rested his arm on the window. 'The best they can,' he said. 'If there's no money, then they don't start a job until it can be done properly. They take pride in what they do and how the stations look.' He reached into his pocket and fished out a box of matches before putting one in his mouth and chewing on the end. 'Trying to give up the baccy,' he said.

'Geez, that's hard. Did it myself a few years back,' Bob said. 'Just about climbed the walls with the cravings. Managed it somehow.'

'Haven't had one for nearly a year now. Still want one, though.'

'Close enough to five years for me. It gets easier with time, but occasionally the need takes me by surprise.'

'Mmm. Got any up-to-date info on the cattle?'

'We've established the cattle were definitely on the station. The numbers haven't been mucked around with.' Bob paused. 'But some of the information we're getting is that this Kendal was fighting a bit of an uphill battle with the bosses. Couldn't get the work done on the fences or things that needed to be maintained.'

John's glance slid across to Bob and he harrumphed, but didn't say anything. Instead, he swung the ute around a corner and kept driving.

'You don't agree?' Dave asked.

John didn't answer but pulled the ute in alongside a fence and kept driving next to it.

Dave could see the fence was new and the wires tightly strained. He looked down at the statement, which said there had been four thousand dollars' worth of fencing gear returned, then back at the fence.

'Boundary fence,' John said, nodding towards it.

There was nothing about the fence that suggested the job had been skimped on. Post every twenty metres or so, and the wire looked like a sturdy brand, rather than cheap wire that was made overseas.

'Got a set of cattle yards just up here.' John turned the ute in another direction and they bumped over the clumps of grasses and wound their way around the trees that towered above the landscape.

Red-and-white cattle grazed contentedly on the wheat-coloured grass, only a few taking notice of the clattering ute driving by them.

'Now, see here,' John said, pointing out the window. 'These yards, they are state-of-the-art. That platform up the top there, that's where whoever is drafting stands. See them levers? They pull on them to open the gates and let the cattle through. Not a lot of stations have the platform, see? Sorta got to get in the yards with the cattle. Not always the safest when these animals don't see humans from one month to the next and they get 'emselves all a bit worked up when they're contained.'

'These don't look that old, John. When were they built?' Bob asked as Dave snapped a photo.

'About three years ago. The yards that were here before were okay, nothing really wrong with 'em, but the bosses knew they could be improved, so that's what they did. Over all the stations, they built this design of yards.'

Bob nodded.

'Now look here, I dunno who's given you that info saying Kendal had a battle with the bosses. This is a family who have the money and the land they have because they run a good show. They don't skimp on fixing stuff with baling twine and barbed wire. Reckon you can see that's not the case.'

'Well, mate, in the two hours we've spent with you here, I can't see anything that isn't top shelf. And we get to see a lot of stations,' Bob agreed.

'What happens now?'

'I think we'll head back to Barrabine. There's really not too much more we can do here for the time being. We need some more information on bank accounts and such, but we'll sort that from the offices.'

'Can I give you anything more? The bosses are good people. I don't like the thought of some little shit stirrer causing 'em grief.'

'You've been really helpful, thanks, John. We've got everything we need from you.'

'Right-oh, you've got a long drive back, so I'll take you to the homestead.' He drove the ute around the yards and headed back.

'How long are you here for?' Dave asked.

'As long as the bosses need me here. That's what I do; I go where there's a problem, get it fixed and wait for the next job.'

Dave frowned. 'A professional fixer?'

John gave a bark of dry laughter. 'If that's what you want to call me, then yeah, that's what I do.'

'Do you have to fix things a lot?' Dave wanted to know.

'Not like this! Nah, this is way over the top to what I normally do. Last thing I helped fix was when some cattle got into some poison. Heap of them died and we had trouble with the RSPCA. Fair call, too. No one wants animals suffering. We didn't know it was there. I went in and fenced off the affected areas and all was good. Took a bit to appease the animal-rights people, but I did. Mostly what I do, though, is go from station to station and make sure everything is running smoothly. That's my job.'

Dave jotted a couple of sentences down and closed his notebook, thinking hard.

A fixer.

❧

'What do you think about the term "fixer"?' Dave asked as he and Bob left Nefer Station.

'Just a bad choice of words, I think. I knew you'd picked up on that, son, but I think you're barking up the wrong tree.'

'Hmm, I'm not so sure. Why would a business with integrity need a fixer?'

'I know what you mean, but you heard him. He goes to the stations and makes sure things are running smoothly. I reckon he's like the manager of all of the stations. Every different one would have their own manager, but he oversees the whole lot together.'

'I understand that, but there's something . . . I don't know. Just a feeling in my gut there's more to him.'

Bob was silent as the troopy ate up the white lines on their way back to Barrabine.

'Well, son, I've always said you should never discount a gut feeling, so let's keep that in the mix but not focus on it too much.'

Dave nodded. 'What now?'

Bob took out his notebook. 'I'm going to write a list of things for you to do when we get back to Barrabine. Make some calls, camp the night then head back to Perth tomorrow. You're going to do a Request For Information from Major Fraud so we can look into any bank accounts and businesses that Kendal's linked to. I want to track him down. He's the main POI at this stage, but who's to say he was even involved? We've got to make that connection— which we haven't yet—back to him. If we do, well, we might have a yarn with him.' Bob tapped the pen against his lips. 'Let's look into Peter William while we're at it. Maybe we haven't got enough probable cause to get a warrant on his bank accounts, but let's give it a crack. That four-wheel drive is showy.'

'The information William gave us bothers me. It's contra-dictory to what we saw out at the station. There wasn't anything that looked like it was second-rate quality to me. The feed was good, not overstocked—'

Bob gave a snort. 'It's not going to be overstocked if they're missing nearly fifteen hundred head of cattle!'

Dave threw Bob a look and kept talking. 'Fences were first-rate and the cattle were in good condition. Roads were smooth. Someone's had a grader there recently. I don't think I've ever been on a private access road that was as good as that one.'

'Good for getting the trucks in and out, that's for sure.' Bob stretched out his legs and sighed. 'It's certainly worth keeping an eye on Peter William. A good stocky always knows his client's business back to front, and either he hasn't been out to Nefer Station at all, or he was fed a heap of bullshit by Kendal. Either way, something's not right.'

❧

As they walked into the Barrabine police station they were tired, dirty and in desperate need of a cold beer to wash the dust from their throats—but they stopped short when they saw Tez came out of the detectives' office, his face ashen.

'Dave, you'd better come in here for a minute,' he said, ushering both men inside.

'What's wrong?' Dave asked, instantly on alert. 'What is it? Mel? The kids?'

Tez shut the door and shook his head. 'No, mate, it's not them. God, I can't . . .' He shook his head and ran his hand over his face.

'Who is it, son?' Bob said quietly.

'It's . . . it's Spencer.'

'What?' Dave reared back. 'What do you mean?'

'Up on the Great Central Road. Tourist came across him. Looks like he hit a culvert. The car's flipped.'

184

'He's dead?' Dave couldn't believe what he was hearing. Tez nodded.

'Jesus.' He stood there staring at Tez. His words didn't compute.

'We're just about to head up there. The guys from Wallina are out there. They called it in.' He took a couple of steps towards Dave. 'I'm sorry, mate. I know how close the two of you were.'

'Are you sure it was an accident?'

Tez blinked. 'Meaning?'

'What if he ran into Bulldust and Scotty?' Dave asked.

A look of realisation crossed Tez's face. 'I'll make sure everything's looked at. You have my word.'

'What about his wife?' Bob asked. 'Has anyone gone to her yet?'

'The Inspector's telling her now. Look, I've got to get on the road. I'll be in touch as soon as I know anything.' He clapped Dave on the shoulder and walked past him.

'You be safe,' Dave said, turning to Tez. 'He was your mate, too.'

Tez nodded, his face still grey.

'I've got to go and see Kathy,' Dave said, his voice tight. 'Fuck! What is this? How could he have made a mistake like this? He's driven hundreds of thousands of ks. He knows dirt roads.' Dave felt like his heart was going to burst out of his chest. 'Nah, he didn't just have an accident.'

Bob stepped over and clamped a hand on Dave's shoulder. 'Leave it to the boys for the moment, son. We don't know anything yet. Let's wait until we hear more before jumping to conclusions. But you need to get to Kathy now. She's going to need you.'

❧

Spencer's house looked exactly as it always had. The geraniums were in pots at the front door and Kathy's car was parked in the driveway. But nothing was the same and it never would again—for Kathy, for the people who loved Spencer.

On the street, Dave saw an unmarked police car.

'Inspector's still here,' he muttered, nodding towards the vehicle.

'Looks that way,' Bob replied, then the two men lapsed into silence as they stared at the house, knowing what was inside: a broken woman, the Inspector with soft, calming words that couldn't undo the damage.

'I don't want to do this,' Dave said quietly.

'Who does?'

Staring at the pathway, Dave shook his head. He couldn't find any words. Clenching his jaw, he snarled, 'I'll get those bastards if they've killed him.'

'We'll get to the bottom of it. Come on, son. Spencer was one of us. He'd do it for you. Let's go.' He clapped Dave on the shoulder.

Feeling like he was sleepwalking, Dave walked up the path, with Bob behind him.

The front door was open and Kathy was standing in the entrance hall, her face pale, her hands clasped in front of her mouth as the Inspector and a female constable stood facing her.

'If you need anything. Anything at all,' Dave heard the Inspector say.

Kathy shook her head and closed her eyes, as she slumped against the wall.

'Can I get you a glass of water?' the female constable asked.

Breathing in deeply, Dave thought about his grandfather and what he would have said in this moment. Although he was a farmer, he'd always had the right words for any situation.

There's nothing you can say, you can only be there.

Dave cleared his throat and stepped into the doorway, aware that Bob was close behind him.

Kathy looked up and seemingly more tears filled her eyes. 'Dave.' Her voice broke. 'Dave, it's not true, is it?'

'I'm so sorry, Kathy,' he replied, wishing he was anywhere but here.

'Oh, not my Spencer.' The tears came thick and fast and she threw herself towards Dave, her arms around his neck.

Dave felt the heat of her tears soaking through his shirt and he clenched his teeth. Putting his arms around her, he gently patted her back, waiting for her to let go.

She didn't. She continued to sob and hold on tight.

Dave sought Bob's eyes as he stepped alongside them, and raised his eyebrows, silently asking what to do.

Shaking his head, Bob turned away. They both knew there was nothing that could be done.

The Inspector cleared his throat, clearly uncomfortable.

'Mrs Brown, obviously you have someone here who can care for you. I'll get out of your way. You've got our contact details if you need anything, and I do mean that. Please use those numbers I've given you. Detective Brown was highly regarded by us all and he'll be sorely missed.' The Inspector put his hat back on and nodded. 'I'll touch base in the morning and see how you're travelling. Someone from Health and Welfare will be in touch soon to talk about matters going forward.' He looked at the woman in uniform and inclined his head towards the door. 'Goodbye, Mrs Brown.'

The constable followed him out, along with Bob, and Dave heard them talking quietly on the front porch.

Dave let Kathy go and led her down the hallway into the kitchen, where he helped her sit at the table. 'What can I do for you, Kathy?' he asked.

She stared at the table, tears falling onto the wood. Not trying to stop them, she shrugged. 'It can't be true,' she whispered. 'He's going to walk through the door any moment now. He promised me.'

Holding her hand, Dave stayed silent. He knew full well Spencer never would have promised Kathy that he would come home every night. Coppers didn't make those kinds of assurances—they couldn't. That's why he himself had never promised Mel.

Looking at Kathy now, he finally understood the fear his own wife would hold every time he walked out the door.

The ache in his chest made it hard to breathe. What type of hell did all coppers' partners live when the person they loved went to work, until they came home?

He pushed the thought aside; he knew had to stay strong for Spencer's widow.

What a god-awful word. Widow.

Chapter 19

'I just can't believe it,' Dave said to Bob over the table in the pub. 'He was . . .' He blew out a breath. 'Are there any words?'

'No, son, there aren't.' Bob signalled to the waitress for another two beers while Dave continued to talk.

'Have you . . . How . . .'

'Listen to me, son. Yeah, I've lost mates in the line of duty. We don't put our hand up for that, but every day when we wear that uniform or put our ID in our pocket, we know there's a chance we won't come home that night. You, more than anyone, know that; you've got the scars to prove it. But we don't think about it. We don't let that thought rule us, do we?'

Dave shook his head. 'But how do you come to terms with it?'

'Nothing but time. We know the risks.' He paused. 'We *accept* the risks. Spencer knew all of this. But, you know, dying in the line of duty isn't the biggest danger we face.

Certainly, it's a hazard of the job. But think about all of the good coppers who take their own life because they've seen something they can't move on from.' He paused again. 'Our mental health is the biggest chance we take. Like we willingly play Russian roulette with ourselves.'

There was nothing to say to that, because it was exactly true.

'Doesn't take away that we've lost one of our own while on duty,' Bob clarified.

'No, I know what you're saying.' Dave thought about Mel again. 'I guess that's what Mel is on about all the time, isn't it? Not coming home. She's frightened I won't, and I gave her a scare when I got shot. I can sort of understand. Especially now I've seen Kathy. I wouldn't like it much if she was going to work every day and the underlying thought was, she might not come home.'

'You know, that's a discussion I never had with my ex-wife. We never once talked about it. Some people have the ability to understand what could happen but not let it bother them until it comes about. There's no point in worrying about something that hasn't happened.'

'Until it does.'

'Yeah,' Bob said quietly. 'Until it does.' He paused. 'I always had everything up to date, though. You know, will, life insurance, all that sort of thing. Have you done that?'

'Yeah, I did it after I was shot. Mel won't have to worry.' He paused. 'She wouldn't have to, anyway.'

Bob harrumphed. 'No, you're right there. Daddy would make sure she was taken care of.' He stretched his legs out and leaned back in the chair. 'One of the blokes I went through the academy with was killed on his third shift.'

Dave grimaced.

'Yeah, he'd pulled over a car that was suspected of having been used in a ram raid. He and his partner got out and went over to speak to the driver. Damo never even got to the driver's-side. There was a shot through the back window, and he went down.' Bob unconsciously rubbed the burn scars on his hands. 'And my old partner, JD. That accident I was involved in.' He sighed heavily. 'Every copper's got a scar.

'And look, that was tough. To lose someone out of our year within the first week of all of us starting. Certainly made us aware that what we do is risky and that life is fragile. But I'll tell you one thing: an incident like that could've been enough for some of us to get cold feet about being a cop, but none of us did. We became more determined to get the riff-raff off the streets and keep the community safe. That's why most of us become cops. That and we want to help people. And the only thing that gets us through these times is just that: time.'

'Time?'

'Yeah. Time. Tuck their memories away in a box and put it to the back of your mind. That way you'll always have them close with you but the grief won't overtake you.'

Dave nodded and looked up as the waitress put down their drinks.

'You coppers?' she asked with a toss of her head.

'Listen, love,' Bob started, 'we're not—'

'Nah, I'm not hittin' on ya or nothing, but that bloke who was killed in the car accident today. Spencer. He was good to me, yeah? I liked him. One of the nice coppers. Unlike some.' She looked around, as if losing her nerve about talking to them. 'He helped me get this job here after he'd given me a bit of a talking to. Got me thinking in the right way, you know. I'm . . . I don't like what happened today.'

Bob nodded. 'That's a great story. He was one of the good ones. And we don't either, love. But there's nothing that can be done now.'

Swallowing hard, Dave looked down. He could almost hear the conversation with Spencer in his head.

She just needs a bit of guidance. Bit of help. And I'm the one for the job.

'I'm glad he helped you,' Dave said.

'Yeah, well, he did. Just thought you should know.' She ducked her head and gave the table a quick wipe with the tea-towel that was over her shoulder and then went back to the bar.

Bob watched her thoughtfully. 'Wonder how many stories there are like that out there.'

'Hundreds,' Dave said. 'You know he'd always have a word of advice. There was a bloke that had gone bush—we found his car out on a back track to the north of here a few years back. This fella, he'd had enough, needed to get out of the house, two young kids from memory and there was a problem with the wife. It's all a bit hazy. Anyhow, this guy had some serious mental-health issues. Spencer went and saw him a couple of days later to make sure he was okay and told him how there wasn't any shame in getting a bit of help. Gave him the address and phone number of a counsellor and just talked man-to-man with him. I often used to see that bloke around Barrabine afterwards. He always came up and talked to Spencer every time he saw him.

'And he had projects, like that girl.' Dave nodded towards the bar. 'I was one of them. Used to round me up and point me in the right direction, but he'd never tell me what he wanted me to do. He'd just sort of lead me to where he thought I should be and before you know it you're doing exactly what he wanted.'

'He didn't manage to beat that hot-headedness out of you though, did he? Still, if he had I wouldn't have anything to do.'

Dave smiled. 'He rounded off the edges.' He took a sip of his beer. 'Listen, if it's okay with you, I'm going to go back to the room. I want to ring Mel and let her know what's happened.'

Bob nodded. 'You do that. You know where I am. Solidarity at the elbows of your colleagues, son.'

The phone rang and rang and Dave thought it was about to go through to voicemail when he finally heard Mel's voice.

Suddenly his throat closed over and he couldn't speak.

'Dave?' she asked into the silence. 'Is that you?' Her voice held fear.

'Yeah, sweetie, it's me,' he finally managed. 'How are you? The kids?'

'We're all fine.'

'Where are you?'

'Come on, Dave,' she said quietly. 'Are we going to have this conversation every time? I'm safe.'

'Mel, I'm sick of this shit. Just tell me where you are.' He felt like kicking the door in, but he was too tired and too sad.

Sighing, she answered, 'We're still in the same spot.'

'And you've not had anything go wrong, anyone suspicious around?'

'Not that I've seen. Dad's got a private security guard here now. He watches everything.'

'Good.'

'You don't sound right. Are you okay?'

Dave was silent, forming his words. God, how to do this? He'd notified people of a death on many occasions. This wasn't the first time. He should know how to do it.

But it was the first time he'd known both the victim and the people around them.

'It's been a really tough day.'

'I guess that's part of your job, isn't it?'

Dave closed his eyes. Rip the bandaid off. 'Mel, sweetie. Spencer . . . ah, he was involved in a rollover today. He . . . he didn't make it.'

There was a heartbeat of silence, then: 'You're kidding?'

Dave wanted to scream down the phone, *Do you think I'd joke about something like this?* But he didn't. 'I wish I was.'

'Where?'

'Out on the Great Central Road. He was out investigating a scene—' He didn't get to finish his sentence.

'Oh my god, Dave, this is what I'm talking about! The job's killed him, and I don't want it to kill you.'

For a moment Dave couldn't speak. The fury in her voice took him aback. There wasn't sympathy or concern, just anger.

'Mel, it was a car accident. It could've happened to anyone.'

'How do they know? It could have been something else, couldn't it? What I mean, though, is that he wouldn't have been out there if it wasn't for the job. You said he was investigating a scene, so he was out there *for the job*.' Her repetition and emphasis were clear. 'If he'd been down the main street of Barrabine, going to the office, it wouldn't have happened. This could have been you. You're always out doing long days and lots of kilometres on lonely roads. You're not going to roll your car in the back blocks if you're working in the city. At least I'd know you're going to come home every night.'

She paused. 'Still, that's not true either, is it? You could get shot in the city just as easily as in the country.' She sounded tired and defeated, as if she knew there wasn't a unit that he could transfer to that would make her happy. 'You know, accountancy is a pretty safe career.'

'Just stop it,' Dave snapped, getting to his feet. 'This isn't a murder.' As the words came from him, he knew he still didn't believe them, but he couldn't let Mel know; it would only make the situation so much worse. 'Don't make this about the job; it's about Spencer and Kathy. You haven't even asked about Kathy, how she is.' *Are you that shallow?* flitted through his mind.

'Don't you understand that Spencer and Kathy *are* the job? If you can't see that, it's obvious I'm wasting my time.'

'Mel—'

There was a click in his ear.

'Mel?' He pulled the phone away and looked at the screen. She'd hung up.

Dave stood there for a moment, unable to believe what had just happened, then he gently put the phone down and went to the bathroom.

Stripping off, he turned on the hot tap and let the water run until it was so hot he could barely stand under it. He let the jets hit his back and the steam swirl around him.

The sob that ripped from his throat was loud, and raw. He couldn't feel the tears on his cheeks, but he knew they were there. Was he crying for Spencer or for his marriage? Probably both. All he knew was that he felt like his heart was breaking in half and there was nothing he could do to stop it.

Chapter 20

Dave sat opposite Kathy in her kitchen, a cup of tea in front of him. Three days had passed since Spencer died, and now grief was replacing shock.

For the first two days, Dave had expected Spencer to ring, or walk through the door of the police station, hitching up his shorts, with his booming laugh and his large smile. To tell Dave about the ballroom-dancing grand final and whatever new case he was working on. But his office desk remained untouched.

Dave had been surprised by the numbness—he'd walked around in a fog, not really understanding what had happened—but as he'd woken up this morning and stared at the ceiling as he lay in bed, he began to realise that Spencer wasn't coming back.

He didn't know how to make his heart accept what his brain already knew.

His fingers had ached to dial Mel, to talk to her, to hear her voice and understanding, but that wasn't possible. Her dismissiveness and lack of compassion had left him breathless.

Looking at Kathy, he surmised she hadn't slept much since the news had come through. The dark shadows and red-rimmed eyes, along with her pale face, told a story of intense anguish and loss. It was as if she had aged twenty years in the past three days.

The change in her had made Dave think about how he would feel if he lost Mel; or if she lost him. He'd come to the conclusion that losing him might well be a relief rather than any great loss. In fact, it would take away the anxiety and anger she'd been feeling towards him since they'd first moved to Barrabine three years ago.

As for how he felt? He wasn't prepared to admit to himself what he thought he knew.

He picked up a sympathy card from the middle of the table and read it.

Dear Kathy,
Spencer was an exceptional detective and lived a remarkable life. We are sharing your sadness.
Grace and Terry

'There are lots of lovely tributes here, Kathy,' he said, placing the card back.

'It's nice that people have thought about me,' she said, clasping her hands tightly in front of her.

'The neighbours have been busy,' he said, nodding towards the kitchen bench, which was littered with Tupperware containers.

'That's what people do when they don't know what to do,' Kathy said with a wan smile. 'They cook. They feel like they're doing something useful, but honestly, Dave, I can't eat a thing. I feel sick.'

'Yeah.' The word felt inadequate.

'I rang the funeral director today. I guess you know I can't organise a date until the autopsy's been done.'

He nodded. 'I don't know how long it will take for it to happen, but I'd think he'll be back before the end of the week. I could ring and ask, if you like? I know the pathologist up there. Shannon, her name is; she's actually been to Barrabine. When Spencer and I were looking into the body-down-the-mine-shaft case.' He knew he was rambling.

'Thanks, Dave, but there's no need. You won't be able to hurry anything up. I know how these things work.' She swallowed. 'I've been a copper's wife for quite a few years now.'

'Have you . . . have you thought about what you'd like?'

'The Inspector was here this morning and he said it would be a full-honours service.' Kathy stopped and put her hand over her mouth to hold in the sobs.

Dave reached for her other hand and squeezed it.

Gathering herself, she took a few shaky breaths. 'Would you give the eulogy?'

Freezing, Dave stared at her. 'Me? What about the sarge down at the station? He worked with Spencer for longer.'

Cocking her head to one side, Kathy gave a watery smile. 'Come on, Dave, you know he used to annoy the crap out of Spencer.'

Dave gave a short laugh, remembering the way Spencer used to take the piss out of the sarge when he wasn't looking. *Walks around like he's got a carrot up his arse.*

'What about someone from dancing?'

'No, Dave, I want it to be you. Please?'

He took a breath. He really didn't want to. To do that would make Spencer's death real all over again. 'It would be an honour, Kathy. Thank you.'

'Good.'

Lapsing into silence, Dave imagined himself standing at the lectern, speaking to a crowd about his mate. It filled him with fear. What if he couldn't make it through the speech?

Looking at Kathy now, he wished Mel were alongside him; being a nurse, she'd know just what to say. Dave was struggling.

Then a thought filtered through that it wouldn't make any difference if Mel were here or not. She wouldn't be standing with him, in Kathy's kitchen.

'Have you thought, um, about anything else?'

'Like what?'

'What you're going to do?'

Tears pricked her eyes again. 'There's nothing else to think about. This was supposed to be our forever home. All our friends are here, and we haven't got kids. I couldn't leave Barrabine, it's my home.'

'Have you got any family?'

'No. Mum and Dad died years ago and I'm an only child. Nope, here is where home is. And I don't think Spencer would want to be buried anywhere else either. We'd always intended to stay here after we retired. And Spencer's family, well, there's not really anyone there either. He's got a distant cousin somewhere in the eastern states, but we both always felt like we were orphans, you know. We were each other's family.'

She got up and walked to stand before a wedding photo on the wall. Kathy was quiet as she traced the outline of Spencer's face behind the glass.

'We'd been married for forty years last year, you know. He was only a couple of years off retiring.'

Dave could see all the plans they'd made together tumbling down around Kathy. The trips they could have taken, the places they'd wanted to see.

Now Kathy was alone. The bubble of sadness in Dave's chest threatened to burst.

'How're things with Mel?' Kathy asked, coming and sitting back down. She wiped her hands along her jeans and straightened her head as if she didn't want to think about what was happening in her life anymore.

'Strained,' Dave said, honestly.

Kathy leaned forward and took his hands in hers. 'Dave, are you happy?'

He stared at her, not able to answer.

'It's so important to be with someone who makes you happy, who makes you laugh. I know that the kids are little and they need their dad, but if you and Mel aren't happy, those kids will grow up in a household that won't know how to make them joyful. What sort of an example are you giving them, relationship-wise, if you don't love their mother? Or if she doesn't love you?'

'I'm . . .'

'And as Spencer has just proven to both of us, life is very short. Neither of you deserve to be unhappy, and those kids deserve to know what it's like to be loved by two happy and content people, rather than parents who walk on eggshells around each other. Give them good examples of love, not just making do. You wouldn't want them to end up in relationships like yours, I'm sure. So, show them a good one.' She swallowed hard. 'Now, listen, I need to do a few things, so how about you take off and I'll catch you a bit later on today. Could you come and help me talk to the funeral director at about four?'

'Of course, I can,' Dave said, glad he didn't have to say anything in response to everything else she had just said. She'd said too much for him to know how to start.

He got up and put his hand on her shoulder, before giving it a squeeze.

❧

'What are you doing?' he asked Bob, who was sitting outside the motel with the troopy packed up.

'I'm heading back to Perth. You need to stay here and make sure Kathy is okay. You can work from here. I've organised for you to have a desk at the Barrabine police station.

'I'm going to head back to try to find this Kendal fella and see if I can have a yarn with him. Plus, Parksey called—there's been another case come in that I need to oversee.'

Dave nodded.

'Major Crash are back in town.'

'Already?'

'Yeah, they must've got back in late last night. The car's down at the compound. They'll finish off going through it this morning. Getting the last of the forensics and so forth. You should try to get a look at it.'

'Why?'

Bob regarded him for a moment then said, 'I think it will help you to come to terms with the accident.'

'Right.' He let out a sigh and sat on the dusty park bench. 'Kathy's asked me to do the eulogy.'

'Thought she would.'

Dave's head jerked up to look at him. 'Why do you say that?'

'Well, you were close. I don't know, I just thought she would.'

They sat together in silence, the sun warming their faces.

'When will you be back?'

'For the funeral. There'll be coppers from all over the place coming. It'll be massive. All coppers' funerals are.'

'Yeah.'

Bob gave him a sideways glance. 'You never said how you got on with Mel.'

'It really doesn't matter.' Dave paused. 'But not good.'

'Hmm.'

Dave watched him raise his eyebrows and decide whether to say something. He chose not to.

'Well, I'd better get on, son. I want you to do everything we discussed on the way here. Start by requesting the statements for the stock agent and Kendal. We should be able to work forward from there.' He stood up. 'I'm on the end of the phone if you need me,' he said, putting out his hand.

Dave shook it and nodded. 'Cheers, Bob. And thanks.'

His phone dinged with a message. Opening the flip phone, he read the text. 'Major Crash has finished going through the car,' he said.

Bob frowned. 'That's quick.'

'Maybe there was nothing to find.'

'You don't believe that and neither do I. There's always something.'

'Anyway, they're asking if I want to collect his personal effects to take to Kathy.' The weight of loss touched his shoulders again and they slumped a little.

'You're going to have a tough time in the next week or so,' Bob said. 'But you'll get through.'

'Guess I'd better go and sort that, hadn't I?'

'I've organised for you to have the use of a station vehicle. If you like, I'll drop you off so you can pick it up, then you can get on with what you need to do.'

Dave smiled for what felt like the first time in a long time. 'That was one thing Spencer always used to say: "You need to have a plan." And that sounds like one.'

Chapter 21

'Car's out the back,' Tez said quietly. 'It's been pretty bashed up. They reckon it rolled four or five times.'

'Fuck,' Dave muttered. Thoughts of tearing metal and screams ripping from Spencer as the car flipped again and again and again came into his mind. He knew what would have happened, because he'd seen vehicle accidents before. He had to push it away.

'He was thrown from the vehicle but not far enough. It landed on top of him. The bloke who found him said all he could see were legs sticking out from under the bonnet.'

'No chance, then?'

'None at all.'

Dave shook his head. What he really wanted to do was cover his ears and not listen, not have the images in his mind. But he couldn't do that. As a cop he was trained to see and hear and know, regardless of the victim or the suspect. He had to put his feelings aside and keep going.

'Right-oh, I'll head out and have a look. His effects are out there too?'

Tez nodded.

They walked to the door together and looked out into the compound.

The car was on a trailer, the front bonnet, windscreen and roof caved in. The spotlights were shattered and the antenna snapped.

From where they stood, the rear of the car looked untouched. Tez clapped his friend on the shoulder and left him alone with the vehicle.

Silently, Dave pulled open the door and walked out, still staring at the smashed vehicle. He circled it, coming to a standstill in front of the driver's door. Without touching anything he leaned forward and peered in, his heart giving an extra hard thud as he spotted the pen Spencer always carried in his top pocket on the dashboard.

Snapping on a pair of gloves, he prised the back door open.

Glass covered every crevice of the interior. The front seat was pushed back into the safe on the floor. The roof was touching the top of the passenger's seat.

He looked closely among the debris, checking for blood, but didn't see any.

Brushing the glass from the top of the safe, he checked the lock: open. Carefully he raised the lid and looked inside.

There was a plastic bag that looked empty, but as Dave moved forward a flash of colour caught his eye and he froze.

'Shit,' he whispered and lifted the bag from the safe.

Inside was a piece of indicator and a cut cable tie.

Dave stared at the black plastic for few long moments, then shook himself out of his thoughts and quickly searched the rest of the vehicle. He found the camera—an older style that still used film—under the passenger's seat, and a quick check showed that Spencer had taken fifteen photos of the possible twenty-four.

Gently, he placed the two items on the ground and went back to look for more.

He wasn't able to open the passenger's front door, so he leaned through the gap in the seats and tried to reef the glovebox open. It wouldn't move, so he banged it a couple of times with his fist before it fell open with a clunk.

Discarding Panadol, loose coins and the service manual, he rifled through the loose papers. Nothing of interest—a doctor's appointment card and the vehicle registration. Dave looked at the roof and then opened the drop down glovebox above the driver's seat. The leather wallet that Spencer carried in the back pocket of his shorts fell out, and all Dave could do was stare at it.

What hit home to him the most was the sheer mundane normality of it. All of Spencer's everyday possessions—his wallet, his watch, his pen, his notebook—were all still here in the present. People who were alive could see and feel them, they were tangible.

But Spencer wasn't here anymore. They were never going to see his smiling face or hear his voice again. Everything had changed in one moment in time.

'This is fucked,' Dave said to the trashed car. 'Fucked.'

He picked up the wallet and opened it. In the clear plastic pocket was a photo of Kathy and Spencer frocked up at a dance night. His credit cards were behind the photo, and there was one hundred dollars in cash.

Not a robbery.

Nor did Dave believe it was an accident.

Spencer's death had something to do with Bulldust, he was sure of it. Had he run Spencer off the road? If he had, there would be paint from the other vehicle and he hadn't seen anything like that.

Dave was about to shut the door when from under the felt pocket inside the safe he noticed the corner of something sticking out. Reaching in, Dave opened the pocket to reveal Spencer's notebook. Flicking it open, he stared at the familiar writing before turning to the last page.

He noted the date was the day that Spencer's death had been reported, then GPS coordinates. Then, a list:

Indicator light found approx. five metres from embankment.

Cut cable ties found approx. eight metres from embankment and three from indicator light.

No other physical evidence.

Cable ties would match the marks found on Victor Richardson's wrists.

Bulldust/Scotty?

Link between victim and POIs?

Search area to 30m from where indicator light was found.

No drag marks, broken branches; motorbike did not hit hard.

Victim bike did not veer over the edge in an accident. Victim was pushed. Injuries of rider confirm.

Did rider come across something he shouldn't have?

Camp—BD and Scotty? Other?

Dave re-read Spencer's notes, adrenalin beginning to run through him.

Spencer suspected that Bulldust and Scotty had something to do with this, which meant they could be camped close to where this accident happened.

Dave had been right all along. They wouldn't be anywhere but in the bush.

Looking at the camera, he knew he had to get the film developed ASAP. He should also let Major Crime and Crash know, but he wasn't going to just yet. He had his own investigation to do.

Pocketing the notebook and tucking the camera and evidence into his backpack, he walked out of the station and down the main street to the chemist.

'Could you get these done in an hour?' he asked.

'Yes, of course.'

'Thanks.'

Walking out, his mind whirling, it took everything in his power not to get in a car and head out to the Great Central Road. The two brothers were so close, Dave could feel it now.

If only Spencer hadn't died, they could have solved this case together, he was sure. One last case for old times' sake.

Not to be.

Dave found a park bench under a large tree and took out his phone. Dialling Bob, he watched a couple of cars drive lazily down the street. In the distance, he could hear the constant hum of the mine.

The noise had been hard to get used to when he'd first moved to Barrabine. Always there, in the background. Mel had complained about it a lot, but it had only taken a short time before he no longer noticed it.

'Hello?' Bob's voice crackled down the line.

'You'll never believe what I found in the gun safe in Spencer's car.'

'His gun?'

'That would've been obvious. No, a cut cable tie in an evidence bag.'

Bob was silent and Dave could hear the car's engine as he drove towards Perth.

'And in his notebook were some comments about where he found it and the search path he'd taken.'

'Are you jumping to conclusions?'

'Only the same ones he did. Spencer had written their names in the notes: Bulldust and Scotty, and then he wondered what the link to the rider was.'

'Circumstantial.'

'Yeah, Judge. That's what he would've said too. But he was worried enough to make a note about them.'

'Hmm.'

'I found his camera in the car, too, so I'm having the photos developed. Wouldn't surprise me if there's something we can use in them. He would've taken photos of where he'd found the cable ties and piece of indicator light as well.'

'Does the indicator light look like something off a bike?' Bob asked.

'Hard to tell. It's only a piece, not the whole shield.'

'What else was there?'

'Nothing. He said in the notes that there weren't any broken branches and so on. That the bike must've landed relatively softly.'

'So, it might not even be the place of the accident.'

'I'm going to head out and have a look a bit later. I'll just see what's in these photos first.' Something niggled at the back of Dave's mind. 'What did you say about his gun before?'

'What? Oh, I thought you might have found his gun in the safe.'

Dave thought a moment, then his heart rate picked up. 'It wasn't there. I didn't see it anywhere in the car.'

'No doubt Major Crash will have secured it in the station.'

'I'll call you back.'

Dave jogged back to the station and went to find Tez.

The station had a quiet, shocked feel as he entered. The normal laughter and chatter weren't there, and when he found Tez, he was staring aimlessly at his desk.

'Tez, mate, did the guys who got the car secure Spencer's gun?'

Tez looked up. 'What?'

Dave repeated the question.

'Don't know. Why?'

'I've just been through the safe and it's not there.'

Tez blinked a couple of times as if to focus. 'I guess they did. I'll check the register.'

He picked up the phone. 'Yeah, Bucko, Tez here, mate. Did you find a Glock in Brown's car when you recovered it?'

Pause.

'Yeah.'

Pause.

'Right. Okay. Nah, nah, was just checking. Thanks. I'll get back in touch if there's a problem.' Tez hung up and looked at Dave, shaking his head.

'No, there wasn't a gun in the vehicle.'

'So, where's his service weapon, then? I can't believe they overlooked it!'

'Maybe he didn't take it with him. Would he have had it locked up at home?'

'Even if it was, surely someone would've gone and got it?'

'I don't know. This isn't my call, Dave.'

'No, I understand, I just . . .' He raised his hand in a wave which indicated his thanks. 'Look, it's all good. Thanks for checking for me.'

Dave walked out and headed straight to the chemist, his mind racing. Sure, Spencer's service revolver could be in the safe back at Spencer's house, but Dave doubted it. Spencer never went too far without the Glock.

Guns are a bit like toilet paper, he'd always said. *Always good to have on you, just in case.*

Outside the chemist, Dave quickly opened the packet and looked carefully at each photograph. There were three of the piece of indicator in situ, the same of the cable tie and four of the bush around the scene.

He flipped to the last two: Spencer had photographed the evidence bag in the gun safe and also his notes.

That was odd. Why would he have taken a photo of his notes? Another record, Dave suddenly realised. He'd not known Spencer to do that in the whole time he'd worked with him.

Dave went back to the evidence-bag photo and held it closer.

That's when he saw it. The plastic bag was on top of the Glock. He could tell because the handle was sticking out from underneath. The Glock that had vanished.

Chapter 22

'Spencer was murdered.'

Bob let the silence extend for a few moments. 'You've got proof?'

'No, but—'

'Son, you and I both think that's a possibility, but it's a fairly serious accusation to throw around without anything to back it up. Major Crash are still investigating and so far they haven't raised any red flags. What's got you all burred up?'

'His gun. I've got a photo showing the Glock was with him when he took the photos of the evidence. It's sitting in the gun safe underneath the evidence bag. And now it's nowhere to be found. No way Spencer would've let his gun be taken from him if he was alive. So, where is it?'

'You're still thinking Scotty and Bulldust are behind this?'

'That's my gut feeling. I don't know how he came across

them, or what happened but, yeah, I'm sure that's where it's at.'

Silence.

'You know, son, this could be something as simple as a roo jumping out in front of his car and him overreacting.'

'Yeah,' Dave agreed, 'it could be. But what if it isn't and we haven't done anything about it? I'm not going to let my mate down if there's more to this than what we're seeing on the surface. Surely you can see there're some problems with the scene?'

'I'm not disagreeing with you.' Bob paused and Dave heard road noise down the line. 'What do you want to do?' Bob finally asked.

'I want to talk to Lemming. Tell him what I've found. They need to know that it's possible Bulldust and Scotty are in the area.'

'You'll have to tell Major Crash, too. And they're not going to be happy with you implying their investigation isn't up to scratch.'

'How no one has thought about his gun and its where-abouts is beyond me.' He stopped. 'Still, I wouldn't have thought about it either, unless you'd mentioned it.'

'Making sure that gun was secure is protocol; someone fucked up,' Bob said. 'Now, Lemming isn't going to be thrilled to hear from you.'

'Too bad. Once I've talked to them, I'm going out to the scene.'

'Now steady on there, son. I'm not sure that's a good idea. It seems to me we've got two accidents and one death of people who went out on the Great Central Road by themselves. Richardson didn't die but he's not exactly in good shape. If you believe in old wives' tales, then bad things come in threes. Let's not make you number three.'

'We can't leave this, Bob.'

'I agree. Maybe let me ring Lemming. I'll get back to you when I've spoken with him.'

Dave fidgeted.

'Mate, I mean it. I don't want you out there by yourself. Just give me an hour, okay?'

'I don't like it.'

'I know, but it will be better this way.'

❧

Dave was poring over the photos when his phone rang.

'Burrows.'

'Dave, it's Shannon. Shannon Wood. From Perth.'

Dave's eyebrows shot up as an image of the young pathologist came into his mind. He hadn't seen or heard from Shannon for a couple of years.

'It's great to hear from you. How are things?' His curiosity was piqued.

'Good. How about you? I hear you made it to the stock squad.'

'I did. Earlier this year. How did you hear that?'

She laughed. 'I always keep my ear to the ground.'

There was a pause as Dave remembered how she'd asked him for a drink as she'd left Barrabine, forgetting he was married. She'd been embarrassed and there hadn't been a lot of conversation since. He'd always thought they both knew there could have been something between them if he were free.

'Are you going okay? Still in pathology?'

'Yeah, I am. Actually . . .' She paused and Dave heard her adjusting the phone. 'Actually, Dave, that's why I'm calling.'

'Okay . . .' He drew the word out, wondering what he was about to hear.

'I know you and Spencer Brown were really good friends as well as partners, which is why I'm breaking protocol and calling you.' She stopped and Dave waited. 'I think he was dead before the crash.'

Dave blew out a breath and rubbed his hands over his face. 'Why?'

'He took a blow to the base of his head; I don't think it was caused by the impact, because there's no bruising anywhere else. Also, around his other injuries, his legs, where the car crushed him, there isn't any bleeding, which would indicate his heart stopped beating before they occurred.'

'No bruising?'

'No.'

'What about from the seatbelt? Surely—'

'No, Dave, there's no lineal bruising across the chest either. That could be because he wasn't wearing one, but the rest of the body isn't showing forensic evidence that he was alive when the crash happened. You know, it's funny because the sort of injuries he sustained in the crash would have made sure he died quickly, which could have stopped the bleeding and the bruising from forming. But the blow to the base of the skull? That would have killed him instantly, and I'm sure it wasn't sustained in the accident.'

'What caused the injury at the base of his skull?'

'A blunt instrument. I don't know what exactly because I haven't finished collecting all the evidence from the body. I've been over it once, and found enough inconsistencies to do another pass. That's when I decided to call you. I've got serious concerns.'

Dave's mind raced. 'What will your findings be?'

'I'm certainly leaning towards murder. Once I've finished, I'll know conclusively.' She paused. 'I know I'm breaking protocol, but I felt you needed to know.'

'Have you told anyone else about this?'

'It's not formal yet. I haven't finished my report, but when it's finished it's going to Bucko over at Major Crash.'

'I see. Did you find anything else that could help me, Shannon? Anything that might indicate there was another person in the vehicle with him . . . or who touched him?'

'I've picked some splinter-type fibres from his neck and I'm running tests on them. I haven't found any indication there was another person with him. I'm waiting for forensics to come back to me. I thought they might have finished by now, but I haven't heard from them. I'll let you know when they come through, if you like?'

'That would be great. I'll try to head back out to the crash site and see if I can pick anything up.'

'I'm sorry to be the one to tell you, Dave.' Her voice was soft through the phone and Dave imagined her long black hair touching his arm the way it had when she'd leaned over in the police station to show him something she'd found.

'I'm glad you did. Thank you.' He sighed. 'This is fucked.'

'I'm sorry about Spencer, too. I know you guys were close.'

'Yeah, we were.' Dave wanted to share his thoughts about what was going on—he knew she would listen and understand.

'You sound very calm about this. Were you expecting that he'd been murdered?'

'What? No. Yes. Maybe.' He sighed. 'I found something else that made me suspicious, but I hadn't finished working it through.'

'Uh-huh.'

'The guys who shot me when I was undercover, they're over here somewhere and I felt they could be involved somehow. Is there anything else you can tell?'

'No fingerprints, no nothing. But don't forget, I haven't got the car. Hopefully, they'll find something in that.'

'I looked at it this morning. I got a few things out of it—Spencer's camera and notebook, and his personal effects, which I'm going to give to his wife.'

'I hope you find who did it.'

'I will, there's no worries about that. They won't know what hit them, when I turn up.'

Silence hummed down the line.

'How have you been, since . . . you were shot?' Shannon asked quietly.

'I still get a bit of pain in my shoulder but mostly I'm fine.'

'That's good to hear. I wondered. You know, so many people would've had a reaction to an incident like that.'

'Oh, don't get me wrong, I had nightmares for a while afterwards, but I'm back on track now. Took a bit of work.'

'And how's your wife?'

'Mel's fine. She and the kids are away at the moment. Holidays.'

'Nice.'

'And you, Shannon? Do you . . . Ah, have you . . .'

Shannon laughed quietly. 'No, still footloose and fancy-free. Not too many blokes understand my job. Makes it a bit tricky to have a relationship when I tell them I cut up dead bodies and they want to puke.'

'They don't know what they're missing,' Dave said, a smile in his voice. Shannon would have been a great partner. She understood the job, and he was beginning to learn how important that was.

'Such is life. Anyway, I'd better get on.'

'Shannon,' he stopped. A trickle of nervousness ran through him. He wasn't sure where his relationship with Mel was going to end up, but the words tumbled out before he could stop them. 'Maybe when I'm back in Perth we could have that drink?'

'Um, yeah, if you like.' Her tone held curiosity.

'Good. Let's make it work.'

'Okay. And Dave?'

'Yeah?'

'Be careful. If it's taken you three years to ask me for that drink, I'd like to make sure it happens. Don't go playing dangerously, okay?'

~

'I didn't get on with Lemming very well,' Bob said when Dave picked up his call.

'I'm shocked.' Dave navigated a corner and watched the road in front of him as he drove. He had one last thing to check—if it was what he thought, he would be convinced that Spencer had been murdered.

'Yeah, you sound it. He basically said it was nothing to do with him and I should go talk to Major Crash.'

'Not even when Bulldust and Scotty were brought into it?'

'Something about finding the cows that needed chasing.'

'Fuckwit.'

'Yeah. He wanted to know if we could link Bulldust and Scotty to this other than by the cable ties, and if there was any link with the motorbike rider. Which of course we haven't found yet.' Bob sounded as frustrated as Dave felt. 'You sound like you're driving.'

'I'm going to Kathy's. And I had a phone call from Shannon Wood—the pathologist.'

He went on to tell Bob what she'd told him.

'You're fucking kidding me?'

'No.'

'We've got enough to go back to Lemming now. We know Scotty and Bulldust are here.'

'Yeah, you and I do, but Lemming's going to tell us that it's all circumstantial again. Could be a cranky prospector who got the shits.'

'How do you reckon Spencer came across them?' Bob ignored Dave's comment.

Dave shook his head, then realised Bob couldn't see him. 'I'm not sure, but knowing his investigation methods the way I do, I think he would've gone back up to the road from the scene and looked around trying to see if there was a camp anywhere nearby. Maybe he came across it accidentally.

'Or maybe they were driving down the road and he recognised them and got them to stop. I don't know. All I know is if the bastards have killed my friend, then they're not going to get away with it.' Dave glanced down at the speedo. His anger had pushed his foot down harder than it should be. 'The biggest piece of information is that Shannon thinks Spencer was dead before the car crashed. Now, to know whether that's enough to prove murder or not, we'll have to see the report. That's number one.

'Two, cable ties. We know that's their MO.

'Three, Spencer's gun is missing.

'Four, sighting in Perth of Bulldust, which puts him in WA . . .' Dave trailed off.

'Victor Richardson's crash didn't look like an accident either,' Bob added. 'There are questions hanging over how that happened. And now Spencer's in an accident that perhaps wasn't either.' He paused. 'But it's still too flimsy. You know as well as I do that if we didn't have that sighting of Bulldust in Perth, we'd have nothing to link any of this to them.'

'But the cable ties. I know I keep harping on about them, but . . . Shit! I know it's them, Bob,' Dave said through gritted teeth as he pulled into Kathy's driveway.

'I feel that you're right, too. But until we get something more concrete . . .'

'I've just pulled up at Kathy's. I want to check the gun safe and make sure his service revolver isn't here.'

'You told me it isn't.'

'I know, but I have to see for myself. Make sure there wasn't a second weapon.'

'Right-oh. I'll talk to you tomorrow. How about you put this aside for a bit and follow up on that information I need for Nefer Station?'

'No worries, that's tomorrow's job.'

They said their goodbyes and Dave got out of the car, noting that there were three cars parked in the quiet street and he could hear voices coming from the house.

He knocked and called out before pulling the screen door open. 'Kathy? It's Dave.'

'Come in, Dave. We're in the kitchen.'

Following the passage down to where it opened up into the bright kitchen, he stood in the doorway and smiled at women he didn't know, all busy washing and drying the good teacups and saucers.

'Hello,' he said, taking in the large bouquets of flowers covering the kitchen table.

'Just getting the cups ready for the wake,' Kathy said, coming out from behind the counter. She looked as she had when they'd organised the funeral a few days before: tired and grief-stricken. But there seemed to be something a little more peaceful about her, Dave thought. The beginnings of acceptance, perhaps.

'Ah,' said Dave. 'Doesn't the church have enough?'

Kathy kissed his cheek. 'We're going to have the wake at the dance hall. He would've liked that. And they've only got enough for thirty people. I'm trying to round up a few more.'

'Can I have a word in private?'

'Sure,' she said, wiping her hands on her skirt. 'Come into the living room.'

'Flowers now, not food this time,' he said as they sat.

'Yes, another gesture when people don't know what to do,' she said quietly.

'How are you holding up?' As soon as he asked the question, he wanted to kick himself. He could see how she was.

'Existing,' she answered. 'That's all.'

He nodded. 'Do you have a key for Spencer's gun cabinet?'

'He kept one in his desk in the top drawer. Do you want to have a look?'

'Yes, please.'

Dave followed her to the back of the house, where a small room had become Spencer's study. On the walls were framed certificates and awards he'd won—Bravery and

Service Excellence hung closest to his desk. In the corner was a filing cabinet and behind the door was the gun safe.

Kathy opened the drawer and felt around the top, before pulling her hand out and handing him the key.

Slipping it into the lock, Dave pulled open the door and saw what he knew he would.

It was empty.

'Kathy, do you remember Spencer taking his gun with him to work the day he left? I know he'd been away for two or three days by the time he went out to the crash site. He'd been in Wallina.'

'Yeah, that's right. I didn't see him take it, but I know he would have. He never went anywhere without it.'

'Had he been working on anything that was worrying him?'

'Not that I know of. He always joked that after you left, Dave, there wasn't anything exciting happening in Barrabine.' She smiled, and so did Dave. 'Not that he minded. Spencer loved policing, but as he got that bit older he was happy enough if it was quiet. Most of his work involved helping people rather than solving crimes and high-risk takedowns.' Kathy's voice trailed off. 'Not that it made much difference in the end.'

'He hadn't been concerned about anything in particular?' Dave asked.

'Not that I know of. And he did talk to me about work, you know. Not in detail, but I always knew when something was bothering him, and I'd have noticed if there was anything in particular. In fact, he was happy. Excited about the grand final. Pleased to see you.' She shrugged. 'Life was going well.'

Dave looked back into the gun cabinet and felt along the shelf to make sure there was nothing hidden there. 'Okay, right, that's good.'

'Why the questions, Dave? What's going on?'

'I'm just following up on a couple of things, Kathy. His gun wasn't in the safe in the car and I wanted to make sure it wasn't here.'

'Well, where would it be, then?'

'My guess is Major Crash have got it, but I haven't been able to catch them on the phone yet.' As he said the words, he felt his stomach constrict. He didn't want to lie to her, but he certainly wasn't going to tell Kathy what he suspected. 'Thanks for letting me have a look,' he said, and gave her a smile.

Chapter 23

In the small office that Tez had found for him in the police station, Dave typed into the computer: *cable ties.*

Waiting while the computer searched through the records for similar incidents involving cable ties around Barrabine and Wallina, he took a sip of coffee. His favourite cafe The Mug had closed since he left Barrabine and in its place Beans Means Business had sprung up. The coffee wasn't quite the same but it was drinkable, and he needed the lift.

No hits, the computer told him as he took another sip.

He wrote in his notebook: *No incidents in Barra/Wallina for three years.*

After expanding the search to all of Western Australia, he got three hits, but after skimming through the files he could quickly put them aside. One was a woman who had been tied to a tree outside her house by her partner when he was high on drugs and wanted a public bondage session. The second involved bikies, and the third was a man who'd been found on the side of the road, bound and gagged. That had piqued Dave's interest until he read the conclusion: a drug sale gone wrong.

Changing tack, the next search was for motorbike crashes that were not accidents.

Again, so few. Dave knew it wasn't impossible to make a murder on a motorbike look like an accident, but it was harder than your average murder. It took planning. Victor Richardson had survived, but for the Perth cops to ask Spencer to go out and investigate the scene? Well, clearly there was some uncertainty about what had happened with the crash.

He made a note to ask Bob if he would go and speak to Victor while he was in Perth.

Leaning back in his chair, Dave narrowed his eyes as he thought about Bulldust. What did he know about the man that fitted with these incidents?

Bulldust could be calculating and strategic, but they weren't his strengths. Neither of these 'accidents' felt like that. Rather, they felt like someone was rushing to cover up a problem.

Scotty was capable of covering up problems, but with planning. He had been the fix-it man of the operation in Queensland. These incidents didn't feel like him.

Perhaps Bulldust had started to unravel since they'd last crossed paths?

Dave grabbed his pen and made a list of things, in his notebook, that had happened to Bulldust.

One, lost the mustering business.

Two, POI to police—warrant out for his arrest. Does he know this? I'm sure he would.

Three, no contact with Shane, daughter. Shane wanted nothing more to do with him.

Four, hiding/on the run for twelve months.

Five, approached Mel in the supermarket.

Dave stopped there. He didn't need to write any more. That was the sign that Bulldust had started to unravel. To approach Mel so openly—well, it looked like he was becoming nothing short of a loose cannon, which would make Scotty furious and Bulldust even less careful again.

That meant they were dealing with someone extremely dangerous. Dangerous enough to risk killing a police officer. The threats Bulldust had made previously, to kill Dave, seemed even more real and more menacing than they had before.

Dave thought about Scotty and was prepared to bet that nothing had changed there. It was his ability to wait and be patient that made him a high-risk POI.

'What's going on, Dave?' Tez put his head through the doorway and held out another coffee. 'You in need?'

'Thanks, mate. I'm always up for a good brew.' He got up and took the coffee before leaning on the desk. 'What are you up to?'

'Chasing a little bastard who's stolen a car and headed south.'

'What's the story behind that?'

Tez shook his head disgustedly. 'Just being a little prick, as far as I can see. He's known to us. Done some B-and-Es around town before. Had the normal sad childhood. Mum and Dad were absent parents, yada, yada, yada. You know the story.'

'Any chance we can get him into the youth centre that Spencer started back when I was stationed here?'

Tez cocked his head as he thought about it. 'Hmm, he'd fit the bill. Leave it with me, I'll have a think.'

'It is still going, isn't it?'

'Yeah, yeah. Got heaps of kids attending. That's the trouble: there's more need than there is funding and people to help out with the kids.'

'That's the normal story, too, isn't it?'

'Oh yeah. Youth Justice is just the same.' He paused. 'So, you're doing the eulogy for Spencer?'

'Yeah.' As he answered he realised there were only two days until the funeral, and he hadn't tried to write anything.

'Brave man.'

'Gotta do what you gotta do.' Dave looked back down at his notes. 'Better get back to this.'

Tez glanced around and then walked into the office and shut the door. 'I've got a bad feeling about Spencer's death.'

Dave took a breath. 'Why's that?'

'There's something not right, but I can't put my finger on it. The gun, to begin with,' he said, raising his eyebrows.

'Yeah.'

'I think he's been targeted.'

Crossing his arms, Dave asked, 'What was he working on before he went north? I mean, I know he went to ask a few questions for me, but did he have anything else on that would've taken him up there?'

'Nope, these ones were from around here. A couple of cases; nothing too nasty. One bloke he was trying to track down had stolen some gold from one of the mines—he was working there, so it was a stealing-as-a-servant case.

'The other was a couple of prospectors who were found on a tenement that wasn't theirs. He'd tried to arrest them, but they'd got away and there was a BOLO out on them. He'd said that neither of them seemed dangerous, just breaking the law. Nothing wild west like there can be out here.'

'Are there any mining leases around where the car was found?' Dave suddenly wondered if, with all the flimsy evidence he had, he might be barking up the wrong tree.

'Not that far up, but he wasn't chasing prospectors when he went up there, was he?'

'No, he told me that morning the blokes in Perth wanted him to do a scout around the crash site of the motorbike. See what he could see because they didn't think it was an accident.'

'Hmm. Well, look, all I know is that something is wrong with this whole scenario. Major Crash are telling us fuck-all. The rumour mill is in overdrive.'

'Bound to be.'

'You don't know anything you can tell us?'

'I've got some problems with what I've found, too, but I don't have enough to go to Major Crash or Major Crime with yet. I'm making some discreet enquiries, and as soon as I know anything more, I'll let you know.'

'Those fuckers in Major Crash, he's just a number to them. Even though he's a copper, he's just a number. They seem to forget we worked with him and he's our mate.'

'You're not telling me anything I don't know. Leave it with me, Tez. I won't let this slip through the cracks, I can promise you that. And neither will you. We'll both have to do our best for him by keeping an eye on the investigation.'

'Cheers, Dave.' Tez left the office.

Dave sat down, closing his eyes and putting his head in his hands. Whether Bulldust and Scotty had killed Spencer, or someone else had caused his death, there was something off about it, and Dave wasn't the only one who thought so. This gave him some comfort that he was on the right track.

His phone dinged with a text message.

Found Dunstan Kendal. Feedlot manager in Katanning. Will interview him on way to funeral. How are you getting on with your side of things?

He put the notes he'd made aside, knowing he had to do some work on the new case that he and Bob were investigating.

He picked up the phone and called the Major Fraud squad.

'G'day, it's Detective Dave Burrows from the stock squad,' he began. 'I'm looking for some information.'

'Sure, you're speaking with DS Lewis. How can I help?'

'I'm investigating a case which has seen cattle stolen from a property. Need to check on a few accounts.'

'Right. Name of POI?'

'First one is Peter William.'

'Got a DOB?'

Dave reeled off what details he had, then made another request.

'I'd like to see if we can access every bank account and credit card owned by a Dunstan Kendal and Peter William.'

'Reasoning?'

'Need to track the sale of cattle and the funds that would have come from it.'

'Need the DOB for Kendal, please, and your contact details?'

Dave read out the extra information and recited his email address before thanking DS Lewis. After he hung up, he got onto the business register and looked up Nefer Station. The business name of the parent company turned out to be Aurora Agriculture. Under that, the rest of the properties were listed: Nefer Station, Jupiter Downs, Canning Plains.

As Dave read through the information, he appreciated what Bob had told him when they first went to see John on Nefer Station. Even though this was a family-owned business it was run like a corporate company.

George Windy was the Chair, and seven of his cousins sat on the board.

Dave put George's name into the computer to see if he had any priors. Nothing. He did the same for the rest of the cousins, but they were all clean. Deciding he wanted to take that a little further, using his two pointer fingers he typed an email to DS Lewis asking for information on all the board members as well.

Then he turned his attention to Peter William.

The stock agent had a drink-driving conviction, but that was all Dave was able to find. Not that unusual. He tapped the pen against the desk, staring at the screen, willing more information to appear. Clicking on the tab that showed all of William's connections revealed only that William didn't have any ties with the underworld or criminals.

'Damn.'

He tried Dunstan Kendal's name.

'Interesting,' Dave muttered as he leaned forward and started to read. 'Conviction for stealing-as-a-servant.' Dave ran his fingers down the screen, making sure he took in every major point.

'Working at an engineering business in Wagin, Western Australia. Charged with three counts of theft: one trailer, one welder and four thousand dollars in cash.' Dave's eyebrows shot up as he read. 'Well, well, well, you might be exactly who we're looking for.'

Chapter 24

The day of Spencer's funeral dawned cool and clear.

Dave woke with a feeling of dread in his chest and lay in bed, his arms behind his head, staring at the ceiling for a long time. Part of him wished that Mel was alongside him. That he had someone, a warm body, to hold. To remind him he was still alive. The other part knew that considering how things were in his marriage at the moment and the way Mel was feeling, she might not be able to do that for him.

His thoughts turned to the children. Bec's gorgeous smile and Alice's chubby cheeks. The hurt in his heart made him realise how much he missed them. Hearing Bec's laugh. Even Alice's cries were part of him.

What would his children feel as they grew older if it were him inside that coffin instead of Spencer? He knew that the police family would close in around them, make sure they understood their dad was a hero, but would it really matter?

The girls were still so small—if he died in the line of duty tomorrow, would they even remember him? Bec might recall flashes, but Alice would never know him. Perhaps Mel would move on with someone else, and his daughters would be raised by a new father. One who got to share in every part of their childhood and on into their adult lives. A father who was there, who came home every night.

As he lay there, he realised that bothered him. A lot.

If his family were with him now, today would be much easier, he was sure. Instead, he had to rely on his police family; the people who understood the job, the feelings and the situation. And that wasn't a bad thing. It was all he had.

He threw the covers off and plodded to the shower. His dress uniform had been shipped to him and it now hung on the cupboard door handle.

Spencer would be in his dress uniform, inside the coffin, he thought. Kathy had told him yesterday that's what she wanted. He knew he wouldn't be able to look at the coffin without imagining Spencer lying there cold and unresponsive, dressed to the nines. If he'd been alive, he'd have complained about the formal dress.

'*Can't breathe in this bullshit*,' he would've said.

Turning on the cold tap, he stepped into the shower, letting the chill water run over his body. He wanted—needed—to feel alive, and the iciness of the water would make him feel that. He'd dreamed the night before that it had been him lying in the coffin. He'd woken with panic spreading through his chest, his hands trying to push the lid off and claustrophobia crawling over him as he felt the satin that lined the inside of the coffin and smelled arum lilies.

Sweat had covered his face as he moaned fearfully.

Then, as he'd opened his eyes and seen the streetlight outside, he'd known it was only a dream.

Not a dream.

A fucking nightmare.

He'd dragged in deep breaths and tried to slow his heart rate; all the while, the claustrophobia still clawed at him.

As the sprays of water hit his face now, he thought of Kathy. She had only her friends to support her today. If something happened to Dave, Mel would have her family and the kids, as well as her friends.

Kathy would be on her own in weeks, if not days, after the funeral. When all the people who were coming today dispersed back to where they'd come from, her house would be empty, the flowers would dry up and the food deliveries would stop.

He wondered if Mel would mourn his death as much as she kept saying she would. In the dream, he could see her sitting in the church as he tried to lift the lid from the coffin; she couldn't hear his cries for help over the noise she was making.

Then the tears had cleared and relief had spread across her face.

That's when he'd stopped banging to be let out.

Dave shut off the water and towelled himself dry, before carefully dressing in his uniform. The eulogy was folded in his pocket; he could feel it burning against his breast as his breathing quickened.

It had taken six beers and a pocketful of memories to write this speech.

He'd remembered the day he and Mel arrived in Barrabine. Spencer had shown up at their door with coffee, milk, butter and bread—the essentials, so they wouldn't have to shop—along with a hearty welcome and an invitation to dinner with him and Kathy.

How he'd called Dave 'my man' for a while, until they got to know each other better, and how Spencer had introduced Dave to Ernie, his new Aboriginal neighbour.

And the words he'd said to Dave as they sat on the hill above Barrabine listening to the roar of the mine: *The miners work hard, especially the ones underground. And they play hard, too. In a sense, Barrabine is like the last frontier. I hope you're prepared.*

There was a bang at the door, and Dave strode towards the noise, yanking it open, trying to push all his thoughts and feelings aside.

'Morning,' Bob said. He twirled the hat which matched his uniform.

'You must've got here late. I waited until eleven for you.'

'It was about one a.m. when I finally rolled in. Spent a bit more time talking to Kendal than I thought I would. That information you got me was really good, son. Helped frame a lot of the questions and I managed to trap him with a couple of them.'

Dave nodded. 'Yeah, priors are always good.'

'But that's a conversation for another time. Ready to go? I've got the car waiting.'

Dave glanced at his watch. 'Guess we'd better. This is really happening, isn't it?'

'Yes, son, it is. It's real.' Bob stepped back from the door and let Dave out.

❧

Inside the church, Spencer's coffin was already at the front, displayed on the trolley. Dave made out a glimpse of walnut-coloured wood underneath the Australian flag that covered the coffin.

The large photo of Spencer gave Dave pause. It was a publicity photo—one the police force would use in the media. Spencer was sitting on a stool, half turned towards the camera, smiling, his police hat glinting in the flashlight.

To the side of the coffin sat the Honour Guard, who hadn't left Spencer's side since his coffin had been wheeled into the church.

'Had a few medals, didn't he?' Bob muttered as they sat in the row behind Kathy.

Dave nodded and reached forward to touch Kathy's shoulder. She turned to acknowledge him, then looked back towards the front. On either side of her were friends Dave recognised from the visit to her house a few days before.

'The media scrum is big enough,' Bob said quietly, glancing towards the back of the church. 'I hate the way they let them inside. This should be a safe place for the family to mourn without cameras and shit in their faces.'

'But that's the whole point of the media, isn't it?' Dave said with loathing. 'To catch the family at their weakest moment and show the widow crying.'

'Bastards. Ah, here's the Inspector and Commissioner.'

The two men walked past, standing tall and upright. They saluted the coffin, then Kathy, and took their seats as the rest of the church filled with mourners, other police officers, friends and acquaintances.

Dave turned around to have a look and caught a glimpse of the young woman who'd served them in the pub that first night they'd found out about Spencer's death. She looked uncomfortable, dressed in a skirt with high heels, and she had tears on her cheeks.

Dave wondered how many other young people were here because Spencer had made an impact on them.

The organ started to play and quiet crept over the church as the police chaplain stepped up to begin the service.

'We are here today to honour the life of Detective Sergeant Spencer Brown,' he said.

Dave bowed his head and tried not to listen. Instead, he thought about the first time he'd met Spencer.

It was three years ago, and he and Mel had just arrived in Barrabine. Dave had been doing his best to placate her— Mel had been horrified by the town she'd landed in. Having lived in Bunbury and Perth all her life, she hadn't been prepared for the roughness of the place. Spencer had got out of the police car, hoisted up his shorts and held out his hand, with a large smile on his face.

He'd taken Mel's iciness in his stride. Her statement that her name was *Melinda, not Mel* had made him stumble, but only a little, and he had recovered, all the while trying to make Mel feel at home. He'd just kept talking, telling them both about the house they were moving into and how it had been renovated. Spencer had been so proud to show them around.

Later, Spencer had sat next to Dave after he'd belted his father-in-law, Mark, and Mel had left to drive back to Perth, leaving Dave in Barrabine.

Then there was the night Spencer had turned up with two beers and Dave had joked that the beers were flowers and Spencer must have done something wrong. Spencer had just smiled and after a little while said, 'I've got an opportunity for you. I think it's come at a good time.'

With those words and the knowledge that Mel was making a new life in Bunbury, Dave had gone undercover.

And discovered Bulldust and Scotty.

Whom he'd brought into Spencer's world. The domino effect.

A ferocious anger swirled around in his stomach. They would not get away . . .

Bob nudged him. 'You're up, son.'

Dave blinked and looked around. The chaplain had sat down and the lectern was empty.

Standing up straight, Dave walked past the coffin, stopping briefly to put his hand on it, then he turned and faced the crowd. He was momentarily stunned by the amount of people in the church and outside. There were dozens of police officers in uniform, sitting upright, staring to the front. Their faces grim. Some, Dave recognised, but it was the expressions he read more than the faces. Every man and woman in the church, who were police, were glad they weren't him right now.

'Spencer was not only my partner, he was my friend and mentor,' Dave began after he'd cleared his throat. 'I met him three years ago, when I was stationed at Barrabine. We worked many cases together. I never once saw him lash out in anger. He prided himself on being able to talk himself out of any situation.

'Spencer was a career policeman. He was short and large, and if there was ever going to be a fella with two left feet, it would have been him. But he was a surprise package.

'Kathy was the love of his life and together they navigated their way around the dance floor. I would never have believed he had any real skill at ballroom dancing, but I went and saw Spencer and Kathy dance one night after he'd twisted my arm. To be really honest—' Dave looked up and shared a smile with the crowd '—I hadn't wanted to go and see him embarrass himself.'

There was a little laughter.

'But, like I said, he was a surprise package. They danced beautifully together. Ballroom dancing was his passion and he was excited to have made the grand final.' Taking a breath, Dave looked at the coffin.

'Spencer's sole purpose in life was to help people. That's why he became a copper in the first place. His passion was young people. The inroads he'd made in Barrabine with wayward youth was impressive, and one of his proudest achievements was the youth shed he opened to encourage kids to come in and talk or just to hang out. A safe place.

'Mate,' Dave turned to the coffin, 'you won't know how much I'll miss you.'

He left the lectern and sat down, his heart pounding. It took a couple of seconds before he could lean forward and put his hand on Kathy's shoulder. Instantly, she covered his with hers.

Silence rang out across the church, before the chaplain stood to end the service. It wasn't long before the haunting sound of a single bagpipe rang out through the church walls and the Commissioner stood up and walked to the coffin.

While 'Amazing Grace' played, the Commissioner collected the flag, folded it, then put Spencer's police hat on top. Slowly, carefully, he walked to Kathy and presented them to her. As she reached out to take them, Dave heard a sob escape from Spencer's widow.

Her friends closed in around her as the Commissioner stood back and the pallbearers lifted the coffin to their shoulders, and they started the slow march down the aisle out into the bright sunlight.

Chapter 25

'I need you to tell me about the motorbike rider.' Scotty towered over Bulldust, glaring at him.

'Nothing to tell.'

'You never said anything about there being an accident.'

''Cause I dealt with it. You wouldn't even have known about it if that fucking copper hadn't turned up here. Anyway, we've sorted out the copper. Won't be any issues from him.'

'You're a space cadet sometimes. I don't know how we're related.' Scotty leaned in and spoke slowly, as if he were explaining something to a small child. 'The cop was sent out here to investigate the crash. The cop dies. More cops will come out to investigate the cop's death.' He raised his voice. 'They'll be coming. So, *tell me what you know*.'

Desert set up a round of barking at Scotty's tone, pulling against the chain that tethered him to a tree.

Scotty turned on him. 'And you can shut the fuck up, because if there's anyone around, they'll hear you.'

Bulldust walked over and put his hand on Desert's head.

'Quiet.' Turning to Scotty, Bulldust said, 'The bloke turned up here.'

'Who?'

'The bike rider. I heard him coming down the track. He had a flat tyre and he was going real slow.'

'And?' Scotty stood back and crossed his arms, still glaring at Bulldust.

'He got off the bike and came in here. He must've seen the tracks in or something. I don't know how he found us, but he did.'

'Where were you?'

'Down at the creek. I heard him coming and shot through. Snuck in behind him when he was standing at the drying racks and knocked him out.'

'Then what did you do?'

'Got rid of him. Strapped him to the bike and pushed him over the edge just up the road a bit.'

'But he didn't die?'

'Doesn't sound like it.'

'Was he conscious?'

Bulldust paused and Scotty groaned.

'He was, wasn't he? And he would've seen your face.' Scotty got up and walked the perimeter of the camp, then came back to stand in front of Bulldust.

'Right, we haven't got any other option. I know I wanted to wait until we finished the next harvest, but I heard on the news that the dead cop's funeral is today. This place will be swarming with them soon.'

'They've already been out and collected the car. There's no reason for them to come back.' Bulldust shooed the flies away from his face and frowned. 'Where are we going to go?'

'I don't give a fuck where you go, but we're not going together. I'm going to get the rest of the product out, we'll split the money and then we go in different directions. I don't know what's got into you, Bulldust, but fucking hell, you're a problem to have around.'

'Yeah? And who made you god?'

Giving a mirthless snigger, Scotty turned and walked away. 'I'm god because I have the brains. Get over here and start dismantling everything. Burn what you can.'

Seething, Bulldust stood up and went across to get the sledgehammer. 'You know what? You're a fuckwit. I've lost everything and you had nothing to lose. I've lost Shane . . .'

With four quick, angry steps, Scotty was in front of him, grabbing his shirt. 'Listen here, you worthless piece of shit. You've obviously forgotten how all this started. We were going fine with the cattle side of things until you—fucking *you*—brought that copper into the operation.

'You were the one that fucked it. And just in case you've forgotten, I lost my station. The cattle I had there, my income. You're not the only one who's lost out, but you *are* the only one who caused it.'

Bulldust brought his arm down onto Scotty's, breaking his grip. 'Don't. Touch. Me.' He turned and walked away, his head spinning with anger. All he wanted to do was grab his stash of dope and Desert, and get in his ute. Bulldust hadn't given any thought as to where he would go, but he knew he needed to get away from Scotty. This bust-up had been coming for a long time. A lifetime.

Well, Scotty wasn't the only clever one around here anymore. Bulldust gave a mean smile as he thought about how much marijuana he'd stolen so far . . . And Scotty didn't have any clue about that. Not as smart as he thought he was.

Grabbing the hammer, he swung it over his head and brought it down on the drying rack. Splintering under the weight of the hit, the legs fell from it and he let the hammer drop.

Collecting up the wood, he threw it onto the fire, a tower of sparks shooting up into the sky. Using a claw hammer, Bulldust picked out the staples from the wood and detached the wire netting from the rest of the frame, tossing everything that would burn into what was turning into a bonfire.

He folded up the netting and took it over to the cave. Turning his headlight on, he made his way right to the back and placed it neatly on the ground.

Scotty came in behind him with an armful of shade cloth.

'You get the retic and drums in here and we'll use them as a wall to block the rest of this gear in,' Scotty instructed.

'Yeah, when I've finished the racks.'

'No, start getting some of that stuff in here. I want to get it stacked.'

'I don't reckon there's as big a hurry as what you think there is,' Bulldust grumbled. 'Reckon you're jumpy for no reason.'

'Do I look like I care what you think? No, just get on and do what I say. If we get this packed up quick enough, we can be out of here tonight and far away by the time they show up.' The urgency in Scotty's voice was obvious.

Walking back to the entrance, Bulldust asked, 'Where are you going to go?'

'Tonight? I'm going to get all the gear to the suppliers. If we can get the seedlings loaded up, I'll negotiate with the buyer to see if they'll take them, too. Then I'm going to get in my ute and fuck off way up the top and find me another bush camp.'

'Wouldn't mind finding myself a little sheila for a bit of fun.'

'You do that. Good idea. Show your face in a town where the cops are looking for you. Clever as fuck, you are.'

Bulldust stopped and turned around. 'Shut the hell up.'

'Why?' Scotty sneered at him. 'You know I'm right. You'd be better off listening to me. I might end up saving your arse.'

'Prick,' Bulldust muttered, trying to stop the red-hot anger hissing around his brain. It was making his head fuzzy. He couldn't let Scotty get the better of him. There were things to do and it would only be a few hours before he would be free of him forever.

'You know what?' Bulldust asked, turning to look at Scotty, who was coming out of the cave and heading over to the generator.

'What?'

'Nah, nah, doesn't matter.' He stomped off to collect the drums. Then he stopped and turned around. 'Yeah, actually it does matter, you arsehole. If we go back to the beginning in this, the whole fucking thing was your idea. You had the land and came to me about setting up the mustering business and then getting a few illegal things happening on the side. It was you who suggested Shane should go away to school and left me with the huge private-school bills.'

Scotty looked at him. Bulldust glared back; he wasn't as strong and both of them knew that. Scotty kept Bulldust in line with fear and intimidation.

Not any longer.

'So, don't give me any shit about this all being my fault. 'Cause you've let me believe that for all this time and, yeah, I know I made some mistakes: we thought we had Joe on-side to vet all the new people we brought into the business. I mean, for fuck's sake, he's a copper and he couldn't find anything on Burrows. If he couldn't suss him out, then none of us had any hope of realising he was undercover. All right? Just fuck off with the accusations.'

'Ah, you're getting yourself all wound up there, little bro,' Scotty laughed. 'Reckon you should take a couple of deep breaths and calm the fuck down. You really don't know when you're on a good wicket.'

Bulldust clenched his jaw. He wanted to yell and scream and push Scotty around, but the last time he'd done that, he'd come off worse than when he went in. 'Stop it,' he snarled. 'Just shut up.'

'Ah, Bulldust, still the same old pissed-off angry ant. You know, when Dad kicked you out he did us all a favour. I shouldn't have gone out and found you. Should have just left you to your own devices. You wouldn't have got this far without me.'

Bulldust scrunched his fists to his side and held onto his T-shirt to keep his hands from touching Scotty.

Scotty came in close and put his nose close to Bulldust's. 'But I didn't, see, 'cause I felt sorry for you. My little brother and all. But you weren't worth protecting. Dad was right: you're a weak, pathetic little runt. Just like you were when—'

Scotty didn't get to finish because Bulldust threw his fist into his nose and his brother staggered backwards.

'I've had it with you, *brother*. I've covered for you, put up with your lies and secrets. Telling me how fucking stupid I am. You can get royally fucked. I don't care if I never see you again. This is on *you*.'

'You—' Scotty growled and launched himself towards Bulldust, who side-stepped until Scotty caught his ankle and flipped him over, landing heavily on top of him.

'Oomph.' Bulldust was winded, but he knew he had to keep fighting. He tried to send punches to the side of Scotty's head, while Scotty connected with his stomach.

Bulldust stopped moving, his eyes watering with pain.

'Don't think you can ever put one over me,' Scotty puffed as he got to his feet and reached down to haul Bulldust to his. 'I own you. Show some respect or next time you won't get back up.'

Bulldust doubled over, trying to catch his breath. He wanted to kill the bastard. Finally he was able to stand up and look Scotty in the eye. But instead of saying anything he turned and walked towards the drums and picked four up.

'Whatever you say, *boss*,' he said.

They worked quickly and in silence until most of the gear was packed away. Together they lifted the canopy onto the back of Scotty's ute and stacked in the trays of seedlings, along with the vacuum-sealed drugs. There was no point hiding it in the drums today. If he was pulled over, the seedlings would be enough to get Scotty arrested.

Bulldust went over to the campfire and sat down, his head in his hands. All he could think of was Shane and getting as much money as he could, for her. He needed to get back to her and make sure she was okay. If he was cashed up, surely she would talk to him.

Then he'd be back for Burrows.

'Right, I'm off.'

'Yeah,' Bulldust said without looking at him. He got back up and went across to Desert. He let him off the chain and the pup bounded away, running in circles, trying to chase his tail.

'I'll meet you ten kilometres off the road in two days' time. Next to that mine where we've been before.'

'Yeah, I know where you mean.'

'For fuck's sake, try to stay out of trouble. And move on from here tonight. Get up the track a way.'

'I know. You've said.' The intensity of the fury came back and hit Bulldust with so much force he almost staggered. Instead of reacting, he tried to smile.

Desert ran across to Scotty and gave a little bark, looking up at him, his tongue hanging out as if he were smiling.

'Fuck off,' Scotty said and aimed his boot at the pup's stomach. 'You're always in the way.'

Desert flew through the air and landed with a yelp. He didn't get up.

Bulldust didn't think. He picked up the log of wood that was alongside the fire and charged at Scotty, who had his back turned.

'Fuck youuuu!' he roared and slammed the branch into Scotty's waistline. 'Don't touch my dog.'

Scotty staggered and fell to the ground, smashing his head on a stone as he went.

Bulldust turned and ran back to Desert, who was lying still, whimpering.

'You'll be right, mate,' he said, picking him up and checking his legs. Gently he held him just above the ground and then let him down slowly to see if Desert could hold his own weight.

The pup wobbled a bit, then held himself up and walked gingerly back to his bed, where he lay curled, not looking up.

Bulldust watched him for a couple of seconds, making sure he was okay, then turned to where Scotty was lying.

Blood was trickling from his forehead.

'Ah, for fuck's sake, get up. You're not as weak as that.'
He walked over and put a boot into his brother's side, but
he didn't move. 'Scotty?'

This time Bulldust bent down and looked more closely.
Then he stood up and took a few steps backwards. 'Scotty?'

No answer.

'Shit!' Dropping to his knees, Bulldust crawled quickly
to him and felt for a pulse against his neck.

Nothing.

'Scotty, mate.'

Sitting back on his heels, Bulldust knew he'd killed his
brother. A long, low howl rang out from him, echoing off
the hills.

Chapter 26

Dave's head thumped with a hangover.

He didn't remember much about the previous evening. The wake had been packed with coppers until Kathy had gone home, then most had left. He and Bob had come back to the motel, shed their dress uniforms and hit the pub with the rest of the force, who had come to town for the funeral. The coppers had been driven to Barrabine in two large buses. Dave knew those buses were licensed to carry sixty passengers each and there could easily have been that many men and women at Spencer's funeral.

As he sipped his coffee and punched two Panadol out of the packet, Dave thought he remembered a bottle of rum, and then leaving the pub a little later, but the memory was so hazy he wasn't sure.

'How's the head?' Bob asked, walking into the makeshift office and shutting the door behind him.

'Mate . . .' Dave couldn't form any more words.

Bob sat down and brought out his notebook.

'I don't think . . .' Dave started but his mouth dried up and he reached for the glass of water sitting next to the coffee.

'Try one of these,' Bob said, handing over a bottle each of hydrolyte and Berocca.

'I don't remember . . .'

'Not surprised. Do you remember trying to kiss me when I put you into bed?'

Dave reared back. 'What the fuck? I didn't!'

Bob let out a loud laugh. 'Nah, you didn't, son, but I could tell you anything this morning and you wouldn't know whether it was true or not, would you?'

'I'm sure the memories will come back. They're just a little . . . foggy at the moment.'

'Yeah, well, you keep working on remembering. I think you'll have your work cut out for you.'

Dave ran his hands over his face and realised he'd forgotten to shave. 'Shit, I hope the Inspector doesn't look in on me this morning.'

'I think he'll have seen it all before. Don't forget he came up through the ranks, too. This is how we move on, son. I've told you, solidarity at your comrades' elbows. Someone who's been through whatever you're going through is the only one who can truly understand.'

'I don't think I need any more understanding for a couple of days,' Dave said.

There was a knock on the door and Tez walked in without waiting for an answer. 'Geez. You look like death warmed up,' he said by way of greeting.

Dave stared back him, noting his stubble and bloodshot eyes. Tez's shirt was crumpled, as if he'd slept in it.

'I wouldn't be throwing stones if I were you,' he answered.

Bob let out a cackle. 'You boys need to get in training. I don't seem to have a problem and I stayed until everyone went home.'

'Were you drinking like we were?' Tez asked.

'Does a bear shit in the woods?'

'You must have pickled insides, then.'

'Tetchy, tetchy,' Bob answered, a smile on his face.

Tez frowned, then seeing the packet of Panadol on the desk, grabbed it and took two, swallowing them without water.

'Help yourself,' Dave said.

'One question,' Tez said pulling out a chair and flopping down into it. 'Spencer's gun.'

'What about it?' Bob asked.

'We haven't managed to account for it. You said it wasn't in his home safe, Dave, so I'm wondering if it's been thrown clear of the car when it crashed and Major Crash didn't find it.'

Dave nodded. 'It could have been. That would be preferable to what I've been thinking.'

Tez frowned. 'Why, what do you think?'

'Oh, mate, I don't have enough to substantiate what I think, so I'm keeping my mouth shut for now.'

Tez regarded him for a moment. 'Come on, spill the beans.'

Dave shook his head. 'Look, I know you think there's something that doesn't add up about his death and so do

Bob and I. But out of respect to Spencer, and given the lack of help from Major Crime, I'm not opening my mouth until I've got more evidence.'

Frowning, Tez looked like he wanted to ask more questions, but refrained. 'Well, I want to go back out there and have a look for it.'

Dave nodded. 'Can I tag along?'

'Hey! Boys, settle down. Have you forgotten this is Major Crash's investigation?' Bob said holding up his hands, his eyes wide. 'This is outside your jurisdiction.'

'Actually, it's not. Sarge has said I can head out,' Tez said.

'Why?' Bob drew the word out.

'Just to cast our own eye over things. After all, Spencer was one of us.'

Silence filled the room.

'So, can I tag along?' Dave asked again.

'Son, we've got our own work to do.' Bob frowned and spread his hands towards the paperwork covering the table.

'I know. But like Tez said, Spencer was one of us. And I was one of them.'

Bob pulled out another chair and sat. 'Give us a minute would you, Tez?' he asked.

Without a word, Tez got up and walked out of the room.

Bob waited until the door was shut and he could hear the clip of Tez's shoes walking away.

'Son, we've got shit to do, yeah? We need to focus on what we've got on.'

'I know, but there's something . . .'

Bob threw his hands in the air. 'For god's sake! I can see I'm not going to get anything useful out of you until you get rid of the bee in your bonnet. Have you got anything more you need to tell me about this thing with Spencer?'

Dave looked down at the table. 'I don't think I've got enough to go to Major Crime with,' he admitted. 'Anyway, they're not interested in hearing from me—Lemming has made that clear. It's the cable ties that make me think it's them. I'm sounding like a broken record.'

Bob nodded.

'I want to go out there, Bob. Look around where Spencer was killed, then go to the motorbike site. The two are linked, I know they are.'

'You might be right,' Bob said. 'But you're not going out there by yourself.'

'Let me go with Tez, then. He's going out there anyway.'

Bob leaned forward with a frown on his face. 'Right, son, here's the deal. You are becoming obsessed with Bulldust. Obsession is not a good attribute for a detective to have. But I get that it involves your family, and because this is Spencer I'm going to let you go, just so long as you go with Tez.

'Put this to bed. Either solve it or let it go when you get back, because we've got our own shit to do here and I'm not going to carry you for much longer. All right? You need to get this over and done with, then get back to the investigation we've already got going.'

'Thanks, Bob.'

'Right. And Mel?'

Dave sighed. 'I haven't called her since I rang to let her know about Spencer. And she hasn't rung me either, so I'm leaving it for a bit.'

'You haven't spoken to your kids?'

Dave shook his head. 'I asked once and she wouldn't put me on to Bec. I don't want to have to beg to speak to my own children.'

'Ring her before you go,' Bob said firmly. 'Make sure you talk to Bec and to Mel. Surely Spencer's death has taught you something, son.' Bob turned and left the room, Dave staring after him.

Speaking to Mel was the last thing he wanted to do. The adrenalin coursing through him made him want to get on the road right now. To head out there and find what Spencer was looking for. Find out for certain if Bulldust and Scotty were involved. Find out exactly what happened to Spencer.

Instead, he picked up the phone and dialled Mel's number.

'Hello?' she answered on the first ring.

'Hi, it's me,' Dave said, his stomach flip-flopping at the sound of her voice. It didn't seem to matter how many differences they had, whenever he heard her voice he realised he loved her.

'How are you?' Mel's voice sounded strained.

'Fine. And you?'

'Okay.'

Silence stretched out between them.

'And the girls?'

'They're fine, too. Alice isn't sleeping very well, but I guess newborns never do.'

Dave felt a pang of sadness that he was missing out on Alice's first months of life. Remembering her little face as she slept deeply in the cot before they left, he pressed his hand to his chest.

'How many times are you having to get up to her?'

'Three or four, depending.'

'Is she feeding okay?'

'Oh yeah, that part of it's fine. And it's good having Mum here to help. She entertains Bec, which frees me up. I don't think I'd be coping without her.'

With her gentler tone, Dave wasn't sure if that was a shot at him for not being around, or simply an observation. He decided to take it as an observation.

'Are you still in the same spot?'

'Yeah. The yacht just makes me sick. I'm not sure how I'll get home, because I don't really want to sail. Maybe I'll fly. Mum could come with me and help with the kids. You know how much Bec would love to go on a plane.'

'Yeah, I reckon she would.' He paused, the words *I love you* on the tip of his tongue, but he couldn't quite get them out. Instead he asked, 'Are you coming home soon?' Dave tried not to let the hope come across in his voice; he didn't want to be disappointed by her response.

'I don't know. I haven't heard an update on the situation for a few days.'

Sighing, Dave said, 'I don't think there is one. Spencer's funeral was yesterday. Everyone was consumed with that.'

'Was it large?'

'Huge.'

'And Kathy?'

'Coping. Just.' Anger welled up in him. 'I miss him.'

'What do you want me to say, Dave?' He could almost hear her shrug. 'I can't help what's happened and I stand by what I said before: if he hadn't been on the job, he would still be alive.'

'Mel, I can't understand your thinking. This was someone's life. My friend's life. Someone you knew. Kathy is distraught, and you just brush it off like Spencer dying doesn't matter.'

'Oh, it matters,' Mel said. 'But I'm not going to let myself be drawn into this—the hurt and grief of it all—because it's taken me a long time to get myself back on track after you were shot. You know how much I struggled with the thought that you might not come home. I don't want to feel like that again, so I won't be thinking about this at all. I won't be contacting Kathy and I don't want to hear about it. I have to protect myself.'

Fiddling with the pen in front of him, Dave couldn't think of a damned thing to say.

In the background Bec started to laugh. Dave's heart leapt. 'Can I talk to Bec?' he asked.

There was a muffled sound as if Mel were turning to look towards her daughter. 'No, she's with Mum, just going out for a swim. Alice is asleep. That's the only reason I answered the phone; it's too hard to do anything when she's awake. As much as I love her, she's a very demanding baby. Wants to be held or fed all the time that she's not sleeping.'

'Please, Mel, just let me say hello to Bec.'

'They've just gone out of the room.'

Dave leaned his head against the wall and breathed deeply. 'How's your father?'

'Why do you ask? It's not like either of you hide your mutual dislike. I would have thought you'd be happy to never speak to each other again.'

'Mel, I'm making conversation. If you hadn't noticed, I keep ringing you, even though you've said some pretty nasty things to me. I keep wanting to have a relationship with you. But you're not making it very easy.'

'And, Dave, you keep leaving us, your family, when we need you most, so you're not making it easy either.'

Another long silence.

'Right, well, I'm out bush for a few days,' Dave finally said. 'I'm going out to the scene of Spencer's accident, so you won't be able to get me.' He added silently: *Not that you want to, by the sounds of it.*

'Okay.'

'See you later, then.'

'Bye.'

Dave slammed the phone down. *No 'Be careful' or anything*, he thought. *Don't know why I'm bothering with this.*

Tez stuck his head into the office. 'Can you be ready in about half an hour? I've got the sarge's permission to take you.'

Dave nodded, glad of the distraction. 'I'll grab some clothes and meet you at the troopy. We going to both sites?'

'Yeah, but the first port of call will be where Spencer was killed. I really want to look for that gun.'

Dave nodded. 'Me too. So maybe we should go to the motorbike accident scene first.'

'Why's that?'

'Because that's where I last clocked the gun. There's a photo of it, under the evidence bag.'

'Yeah, we can start there.' He eyeballed Dave. 'You going to be okay? On your full game? 'Cause if something happens out there, we're going to need to cover each other with a clear head.'

'I'm good, man,' Dave said. *I hope we do come across something*, he thought. *Bulldust and Scotty.*

Chapter 27

Dave held the photo up and surveyed the scene, while Tez looked over his shoulder.

'The GPS coordinates are saying it's here, but this doesn't look like the area. See? I can't work out where that group of trees are,' Dave said, spinning slowly around. He tapped the photo where a clump of trees were in the distance.

Tez shooed the flies away from his face and looked up at the sky. 'I don't know how you can tell too much out here. It all looks the same to me. I'd be afraid I'd get lost.'

Dave pointed to the sky. 'First off, you can work out what direction you're looking by seeing where the sun is. The bush can look similar but there're always small things that can help you. So, in this photo you can partly see the road but most of it is mallee trees and spinifex. Obviously Spencer was down an embankment.' Dave paused and took out another photo. 'Ah, this makes sense now. I reckon we need to walk on a little to the east. See here? There's that cluster of big gum trees. I bet there's a waterhole over there.'

'But they'd be about three or four k away,' Tez said, squinting into the distance.

'Yep, that'd be about right. But they've given us a land-mark, you see? Just like that hill over there.' He pointed to the north. 'You pick something that's high or easily seen on the horizon and use it as a landmark.' He gave a bit of a laugh. 'It's much easier since GPS was invented. No way of getting lost now.'

He walked down the red road, his feet sinking into the soft dirt. 'These sorts of roads cause that many problems for truck drivers. See, look here.' He pointed to the middle of the road.

'Looks like a road to me,' Tez said.

'Yep, stick your boot into it.'

Tez frowned and looked again, before kicking the dirt gingerly so he didn't stub his toe. The red dust covered his shoe before he'd felt the bottom.

'It's a pothole but it's filled with what they call bulldust. The driver can't always see them. Travelling up this way can make for uncomfortable driving and plenty of break-downs and flat tyres.' He turned around with a smile on his face. 'I love it, but travelling up here, you need at least two spares with you, and a tyre-fixing kit.'

A swarm of budgies flittered in the distance and Dave watched them fly towards the group of trees. 'See, now that's how you can tell where water is. Birds know. Roos and all the other animals know. If you observe nature, you'll never die out here.'

'Well, I'll let you be Steve Irwin because I don't plan on dying out here and you know more than I do. There's been enough of that shit going on in the last couple of weeks.'

Dave gave him a look and then flicked through the pictures. 'Okay, so here's the photo with the gun in it.' Dave handed it over. 'Taken in the back of his car, inside the gun safe.'

Tez tapped the photo. 'Yeah, you can see the handle sticking out here.'

Dave nodded. 'And this.' He glanced around and then back at the satellite phone he was holding to check the coordinates. 'Maybe he walked to the edge of the road, then along a little further . . . Nope. Try here . . .' He back-tracked five metres. 'Yeah, look here. When you know what you're looking for. See?' He pointed to a couple of slide marks. 'This is where he was!' The excitement in Dave's voice caused Tez to jog back from where he was standing and peer over the edge.

Dave didn't wait for him, but went over the edge and down the steep cliff, using the mallee tree trunks as hand holds. Stones skittered out from underneath him until he got his foot hold. Then he stopped and looked around, comparing the bush to the photo. Sweat broke out across his brow and his heart accelerated. He was getting closer!

'This is the place,' he called back up to Tez. 'I can match the spinifex to the photo. I'm just going to . . . *Fuck*.' Dave caught sight of a blue-and-silver glint to his left and gingerly made his way over to it.

'What is it?' Tez called down, his voice tense.

'Pocket knife. Spencer's. It must have fallen out while he was searching. This is the exact spot. Can you pass me the camera? Why didn't Major Crash come out here?'

Tez leaned over the edge and dangled the camera on the strap to Dave, who grabbed it and took several photos. With gloved hands picked the knife up and carefully passed it up to Tez, who bagged it. ''Cause the bike accident wasn't what they were here for. This will be a Major Crime investigation when we prove he was murdered.'

Dave pushed his way into the bush a little more, his eyes scouring the covered ground.

'Get snakes down there?' Tez asked.

'Yeah, but you can't think about that!' Dave called back. He came across a couple of empty Coke cans, scrunched up and faded by the sun. He took more photos but his instinct told him this bush rubbish wasn't connected to either Spencer or the motorbike rider. Dave had never witnessed Spencer drink Coke, and it was hard to drink a can of soft drink while riding a motorbike. The faded cans looked like they had been out in the elements for a lot longer than two weeks.

He kept searching, but after a few more minutes he had to accept that there wasn't any sign of the gun.

Just about to turn back, a scrap of faded paper caught his eye, lying on top of a small scrubby bush. It hadn't been heavy enough to fall through to the ground.

He picked it up and his heart gave an extra hard thump.

'Tez!' he yelled. 'Tez, I've got something. I've got something!'

He turned and scrambled up the embankment as fast as he could.

'What's going on?' Tez asked, alert.

'It's Shane,' Dave said, waving the piece of paper. 'It's an old photograph of Shane. They're here somewhere.'

'Who? What the hell are you talking about?'

Dave handed the photo to Tez. 'We've got to bag this and get it back to test for fingerprints. This is what I've suspected the whole way along. Bulldust and Scotty are involved.'

'You've obviously been holding out on me. Fill me in from the start.' Tez looked at the photo. A young woman sat on a jet ski, her long hair tumbling down her shoulders, a wide smile on her face.

'That girl is Shane, Bulldust's daughter. Bulldust and his brother Scotty were the two I was tracking when I went undercover to Queensland. Spencer was my handler.'

As Dave finished the whole story, Tez shook his head. 'That's why you left town so quickly. I always wondered.' He looked down at the photo again. 'So, you reckon Bulldust had something to do with Spencer or the motorbike rider?'

'I'd say both.' Dave spun around, looking for what, he didn't know, but some sign that Bulldust was close by.

'They'll be camped out here somewhere. I always knew they would be. There was no way they'd stay in the city.'

'What are we looking for?' Tez asked.

'I don't know. A camp off the road, tracks that go off into the bush, that sort of thing. And I guess they might not be too near here because it would be stupid to try to kill the driver right near the camp.'

'So, these fellas are dangerous.'

'Like you wouldn't believe.'

'Want me to call in back-up? Maybe we should get fixed wing up here so we can spot from the sky. Looking for a camp on the ground is going to be like looking for a pothole under bulldust,' Tez quipped.

'We haven't got time. They might disappear at any moment. They probably know we'd end up back out here having a look, so they might even be expecting us.' Dave jumped in the car. 'Come on, let's have a drive and look around. I've dealt with these two before when they've been camped out, and they know the bush. They'd find somewhere on a creek, where there was water. Maybe that outcrop of trees over to the north, but I couldn't see a track . . . Where's the map?'

'Mate, you're being a bit gung-ho, don't you reckon?'

'Maybe, but these pricks aren't going to get away from me this time. Where's the map?'

Tez unfolded the map on the seat next to him and found their spot. 'What are we looking for?'

Dave traced his finger along the road, his eyes searching for a river system or another source of water.

'See here, there's a creek and just a little further on there's a lake. It's not far from here. They'd be able to dig down and get water, but they won't be near the lake because that's on Aboriginal land and there's a likelihood of them being discovered. They'll still be out here . . .'

He put the car into gear and started to drive slowly on the wrong side of the road. 'Keep an eye out for any type of vehicle tracks that look out of place, you know ones that turn off the main road here. A dead tree that doesn't fit into the landscape or a two-wheel road going off to the side, that sort of thing,' he instructed.

Both men peered out the windows on either side of the vehicle as they drove slowly along, searching.

'Stop!' Tez yelled. 'Back up about three metres.' He flung his door open and jumped out. 'Something like this?'

Dave joined him and looked carefully at the tracks that had veered off the road and into the bush. He followed them for a little way, then shook his head. 'Nope, see, they come back onto the road. Someone has just had a little trip off the edge.'

Back in the car, Dave drove on, seeing nothing but small scrubby bushes and long waving grasses. As they turned a corner, an outcrop of larger trees came into view and he brought the troopy to a standstill. 'Okay,' he said slowly, still a little way back from it. 'Something like this . . .'

'What are you looking at?'

'See how the country we've come through hasn't had a lot of tall timber? This is the first bit we've come across, and according to the map there's a creek behind here. And see that ridge of hills? That would make for a really sheltered spot in there. Let's take a look.'

They got out of the vehicle, Dave making sure he had the camera and his service revolver. 'Got your gun?' he asked.

Tez nodded, and they set off walking along the edge of the road.

'Mate, check that out,' Dave said quietly, stopping.

Tez walked over to him and they both stared at a set of vehicle tracks coming out from the bush and across the grader ridge. Dave stooped down and shot some photos while Tez went out into the bush and checked how far in they went.

'There are dying trees in here. Looks like they've been pushed over. Maybe trying to get in? Or out.'

Staying away from the tracks so he didn't compromise them, Dave skirted along the edge of the bush to stand next to Tez.

'Whoever this is has pushed their way out,' Dave said. 'The trees are pushed towards the road, not away from it, so they've come from in further. There must be another way in.' He started to walk, following the broken branches. 'I bet they've had a camp in here.'

'Dave, we should get back-up. Don't be a freaking cowboy. Spencer is dead, remember.' Tez's tone was agitated.

Unbidden, the sight of the police vehicle rolling, spinning in the air, came to Dave. He could hear the shattering glass. The screeching of torn metal. Spencer being thrown from the car. In among it, he heard Bec and Alice. Saw the hurt and fear on Mel's face, before the pure fury. No, he wasn't waiting for anyone.

'I'm not going to be this close and not have a crack at finding them, Tez,' Dave said, his voice terse. 'If you want to call in back-up, you do it, but I'm checking this out. Now, keep your voice down and stay close. We need to be quiet in the bush—noise travels a long way. They might have dogs that can hear us further out, too.' He continued to walk as quietly as he could, picking a track of least resistance.

After ten minutes of walking through tall timber and along a sandy creek bed, Dave saw the remnants of a camp-fire on the riverside.

He stopped and took a photo before looking around. 'Look here, footprints.'

Standing tall, he tried to see if there was another camp nearby, but there didn't seem to be. He withdrew his gun and indicated for Tez to do the same and slowly, slowly they walked towards the range of hills.

Chapter 28

'Check this out,' Tez said, pointing to a patch of earth. The red soil was powdered up, as if it had been walked over many times. There were footprints, but none of them were clear; they were all blurry from where the wind had started to cover them.

Dave looked around and took more photos. To his left was an upturned rock lying next to a hole in the ground. Again, there were scuffed footprints and turned-up dirt, as if something had been hidden there but later removed. Above him a shadow crossed over—a wedge-tailed eagle flew high in the blue sky, circling over their location. The buzz of flies filled his ears, and the gentle breeze brought the smell of eucalyptus.

A glint in the tree caught his eye and he went over, seeing a nail belted into the trunk. Looking harder, he found another three. He followed the tree line and counted five trees each with nails embedded at the same height, as if a shelter had been fixed to them.

The camera clicked as Tez called out, 'Dave, you'd better come and see this.'

'Coming,' he called back, standing still and searching the landscape. He clocked the eagle again and watched it circle high on the thermals. 'What are you doing up there?' he muttered.

'Dave?'

'Yep, on my way.'

Tez was standing at the entrance to a low cave set back in the hills, red rocks around the entrance and few spindling bushes growing out.

'Check out what's in there,' Tez said with a jerk of his head.

With raised eyebrows, Dave let Tez lead the way, his torch light flashing against the walls. A little way in, Tez stopped and trained the light onto the back stone wall.

Large drums of fertiliser and trace elements were lined up neatly against the rough wall, a generator next to them. The cave was musty, and when Dave flashed the torch around the edge he could see bat shit on the ground. As he turned the torch towards the ceiling he saw little black-winged mammals lined up, their wings curved around their bodies.

Back down on the ground, Tez was reading the backs of the drums. 'Looks like they've been doing this for a while. There's a shitload of stuff here.'

'So, they've been growing the green stuff. That's how they've been living,' Dave said, quickly walking over to look at the drums. 'That's what the shade would have been for. I bet they ran some shade cloth along the trees so the seedlings wouldn't get burnt and the crop wouldn't have been seen from the air. Bastards!'

He turned around and marched outside. 'We've missed them, though, haven't we? Can't see any sign of them here now.' He handed the camera to Tez. 'Get some more photos of that and we'd better call it in. I'm going to see what else I can find.'

Getting his gun out from his waistband, he walked along the edge of the hills, all the while keeping a sharp eye on his surroundings. Both Spencer and Victor Richardson had had injuries to the back of the head, meaning someone had snuck up behind them.

Sounded like fucking Bulldust. Cowardly bastard.

The bush gave way to an open breakaway and Dave saw where their main camp had been.

A campfire, a chair and a pile of branches for the fire were still there.

'God damn it,' he swore. Following the tracks, Dave noted two types of vehicles—one heading out the way they'd come in and the other in the opposite direction. He also noted dog prints—small ones, so they had a pup with them. Or a small dog. Not one that was going to be a problem if they came across it. That made Dave breathe easier. He remembered the ferociousness of Bulldust's dogs back in Queensland as they chased him. The snapping and barking had been almost as frightening as the fact that Scotty and Bulldust had been taking pot-shots at him in the dark.

He focused back on the tracks, which indicated that the vehicles—and the brothers—had gone their separate ways. Perhaps that was why there was only one of everything: one brother was staying here and the other had left, taking his camping gear.

The shadow of the eagle passed over him again, this time much lower. Dave glanced up, and his blood ran cold.

'Tez,' he called. 'Tez?'

No answer.

Turning, with gun held skywards against his chest, he ran back to cave. 'Tez?'

'Yeah, mate?'

'Better come with me,' Dave said.

Out in the sunlight, Tez asked what was wrong.

'Eagle,' Dave muttered, walking in the bird's direction.

'And?'

'Bird of prey. It's been circling over us since we got here. And it's not that far away from the camp.'

Silent, Tez took in what Dave said and glanced at the sky.

'Told you, watch nature. Never know what you'll find. I reckon we need to follow these tracks here.' He pointed to those heading in the opposite direction to the way they'd arrived at the camp.

Together they walked along the tracks until Tez stopped. 'There you go. Ute.'

With their guns drawn, they approached the vehicle, which was parked under a tree. The Toyota tray-back wasn't brand-new, and it had the coating of red dust that everything had out here. The doors were shut and the windows up. It looked just as if its owner had parked it and gone for a walk.

To Dave, the scene spelled trouble.

'Police!' Dave called out.

'I can't see anyone,' Tez said quietly.

'Hello? Anyone there? Police!' Dave called again. He jogged over to the ute and peered inside. Nothing.

He pulled another set of gloves from his pocket and opened the door, then pulled down the sun visor and checked behind it. Nothing.

Tez started on the passenger's side, going through the glovebox. 'Dave?' He held out a piece of paper.

Taking it, Dave felt a thrill of fear run through him. 'That's my address in Perth. This must be Bulldust's vehicle. So, where is he? And where's Scotty?'

Tez dialled the station on the satellite phone. 'Yeah, Sarge, we've found the camp of two POIs in the case of Dave Burrows. We're requesting back-up and a forensic team ASAP.' He turned and looked at Dave, who was now away from the vehicle and looking around in the bush.

'Negative, no sign of either of them.'

'Jesus,' Dave said quietly as he saw a suspiciously shaped mound in front of him. Carefully he kicked away a bit of the soil. 'Tez?' he called. 'You better tell them we've got a body.'

Still on the phone, Tez ran over as Dave crouched down, gently moving dirt aside. 'Yes, sir, we have one deceased. Ah, I don't know. Hold please.' He looked down into the grave and saw a lifeless face with a beard appear as Dave worked quickly. To Dave he said, 'Who is that?'

Dave stared at the lifeless features, saw dried blood smeared through the hair. 'That is Scotty.'

Tez looked up as the shadow of the eagle passed over again. 'Watch nature,' he muttered.

❧

Dave put his fists on the table and stared angrily at the Superintendent, head of Major Crime. 'I've been trying to tell Lemming that these guys had gone bush and he kept dismissing me.'

'I understand that, Detective Burrows, but that doesn't mean he's not been doing his job.'

'We could've found these pricks back when this first started and now a cop is dead and Bulldust has shot through again, all because you lot didn't listen.'

'Calm down, Dave.' Bob put a hand on his shoulder. 'The Super understands the problem here.'

'What I'd like to know, Dave, is why you were out there in the first place,' the Inspector said. 'You'd been told to stay away from the investigation. And yet here you are, the one who found Scott Bennett's body.'

'I've told you, I went out with Tez to help look for Spencer's gun. It was unaccounted for. Yes, I certainly wanted to see the site where Spencer died. I've been suspicious that it wasn't an accident and Shannon Wood's post-mortem report confirmed it. He died before he was put in the car. Major Crash haven't said there was anything strange about the site, but there has to be. Scotty or Bulldust killed Spencer, there's no doubt.'

'And,' Bob interjected, 'now we have three incidents where people have been hit with a heavy object to the back of the head. Two are dead, one isn't talking. It's highly probable the same person has done all three, I'm sure you agree.'

'You think it's Ashley Bennett?'

'I don't think, I know,' Dave said before Bob could say 'Most likely'.

The Superintendent leaned back in his chair and looked at Dave. 'You know, Burrows, I don't like mavericks. Taking it upon yourself to investigate a case that's outside your jurisdiction isn't the right way to go about things. You're a hot-head, and even though you're a talented detective, you still have a lot to learn about working within a team. I like all of my boys and girls to work together. There's a reason for that—we're stronger when we've got each other's backs.'

'I would've happily worked within a team if your blokes had listened to me in the first place,' Dave said, feeling the heat on his cheeks.

Bob turned to Dave and frowned. 'For fuck's sake, shut up and listen to the man, son. Do you want to get kicked off the force?'

'Hmm, you should listen to your partner, Burrows,' the Superintendent said.

'Sir, I'm with Dave on this, though,' Bob said. 'Both of us have tried to speak with your men. They've done nothing but belittle us and the work we do. Dave has certainly broken protocol, but he has also got the closest lead we have on Bulldust in the past couple of weeks, and that needs to be acknowledged.'

'Yes. I do acknowledge that and the fact that it appears my team has dropped the ball. However, neither of you need to worry about that now because I'm aware of the situation. You fellas need to go back to your work and let us now track Ashley Bennett. Both of you are too close to this case and you need to step away.' He let out a sigh and spread his hands. 'Look, I'm sorry but we've got a BOLO out on Bennett, and so far we've got nothing. So unfortunately it looks like he's disappeared again. We've missed him.'

Dave wanted to shout at the man, instead he just stared at him. What a wasted opportunity.

'We will do our best to find him, Dave, you must believe me. I will oversee our communication with you myself.' Dave had to admit, the man did sound sorry.

'And we should have listened to you more when you obviously know the people we're dealing with better than we do.' The Super nodded towards Dave.

'Thank you, sir,' he said grudgingly.

'Well, it's back to your jobs now, boys. We'll be in touch.'

Glancing at each other, Dave and Bob walked out of the office.

'What a load of shit,' Dave spat.

'No, son, he's understood you knew the two POIs better. That's as good an apology as you're going to get. Now, I've got some news for you.'

'What's that?'

'Well, it appears that our little friend in Wallina, Mister Peter William, has some business interests in a feedlot where Dunstan Kendal is.'

Dave did a double-take. 'You're kidding?'

'No, I am not.'

'They not only know each other but they're in business together?'

'No, not as such. Peter William owns the feedlot that Kendal is managing. He's been there since he left Nefer Station. I reckon we should head back up to Wallina and have a yarn to him.'

Dave nodded, then after a pause he said, 'There's something I need to do first.'

Chapter 29

Dave stared at the phone for a long time. This was one call he didn't want to make.

Still, there was no point putting it off.

He flipped open his phone and dialled the number. There wasn't any answer. Toying with the idea of leaving a message for a moment, instead he hit the end button, telling himself he would try again before he left.

Half relieved, he put down the phone and started to pack his bag. He still couldn't quite believe that Bulldust had killed Scotty. What sort of an argument could they have had to cause that? When Dave had been undercover he had considered the brothers to be close—he would have called them mates. Good mates. He'd seen arguments between them while they were chasing him, but that was amid high tension and stress. They were fearful of being caught and needed to silence Dave, so he could understand the anger between the two men then.

Dave could only imagine how much more dangerous Bulldust would be now. He would bet that Bulldust hadn't meant to kill Scotty. Maybe hurt him a little if they'd had an argument, but not murder his own half-brother. As far as Dave knew, now, other than Shane, Bulldust was alone in the world. No one would like that.

Damn it, he should have thought to tell the Super to get some men on Shane. There was every chance Bulldust would head to her now.

His phone rang and Dave dropped the shirt he was holding before answering. 'Hi, Mel,' he said quietly.

'Hi. You rang?'

Sitting down heavily on the bed, Dave sighed. 'Yeah, yeah, I did. How are you?'

'Like I was when you called a few days ago. Fine. So are the kids and so are Mum and Dad.'

'Good,' he said. No small talk here. 'I need to tell you something.' He heard her breath catch.

'Yes?'

'I found Bulldust's camp when I went out bush just after I talked to you last.'

'Oh.' Excitement came through her voice. 'You've found them? We can come home?'

'Not quite. I found the camp but Bulldust wasn't there. It looks like he killed his brother, Scotty.'

There was a sharp intake of breath.

'The positive thing about this is, we're now only looking for one person. Scotty—well, he's in the morgue, so we know where he is.'

'And Bulldust? Do you know . . .' Her voice trailed off, almost as if she didn't want to find out the answer.

'He got away. I think we only missed him by a day at the most. Scotty's body wasn't decomposed, and the wildlife hadn't got into him yet. He was buried in a shallow grave, but the dogs and birds of prey would have found him if he'd been there for much longer . . .' He realised Mel had drawn in a loud breath. 'Sorry, I shouldn't be telling you that. I went into copper mode.'

'That's okay. What happens now?'

'Major Crime are searching for him. There's going to be a bit more publicity—I heard that Lemming is going to go to the media again, looking for the public's help with sightings. You'll need to be prepared for that. They're showing his photo on TV and we've got a better idea of the vehicle he's driving from the tyre tracks we found. So, there's a bit more information this time round than when he first approached you.'

'That's got to be helpful, doesn't it?'

'I'd like to think so.'

In the background, Dave could hear the sound of waves. 'Are you on the beach?'

'Yeah, I'm down here by myself. Needed a little bit of me time.'

'Hmm.'

'You know what, Dave?'

'What's that, sweetie?' Dave lapsed into his pet name for her without thinking.

'I'm sick of living out of a suitcase and I'm sick of being away from home. It's so hard to have any type of routine with the kids when we're away, and any type of schedule I start is only a fake one because it'll change when we get home.' Her voice fell away.

Dave stayed quiet, not sure where this was headed.

'I don't want to hide anymore, and you and I really need to work out what we're doing with our marriage. This uncertainty is unfair on both of us. I'm going to get Dad to bring us home.'

'Mel, I don't think that's a good idea until we find Bulldust,' he said quickly. 'I understand that—'

'No, you don't. You can't possibly know what it's like living in a hotel with a baby and toddler.'

'But Bulldust is still in the wind.'

'Yeah, but it could take you years to find him, couldn't it?'

Dave didn't answer.

'I'm right, aren't I? If Scotty's dead and Bulldust knows there's a murder charge hanging over him, then he's not going to be stupid enough to appear anywhere where there're heaps of people, is he?'

'I can't answer that, Mel. Not with any authority. I mean, who can know what's going on in that bloke's head at the moment.' He paused as he ran through the possibilities in his head. 'You could be right, but you might not be. It may take time to find him. I wish I had a crystal ball to tell you long it would be.'

'We can't hide out here forever. I just want to go home.'

Scratching his head in concern, Dave got up and walked around the room. 'I understand why you want to come home, sweetie, I really do, but I'm not sure—' He broke off. 'It's up to you. Whatever you feel comfortable doing.'

'Good, then I'll get Dad to bring us home tomorrow. See if we can get flights.'

'Are you going to go to our house?' He asked the question with trepidation.

'Where are you going to be?'

'I'm in Barrabine at the moment and we're heading to Wallina after I've finished talking to you. I can be home in a couple of days tops, I reckon.' He broke off. 'If I'm at the house, will you come and stay there?'

'Only if you're able to help me.'

'I'll see if I can get leave.' He didn't have to think about it. He just wanted to be with his family.

'Okay. I'll text you the flight details when I know them. And Dave?'

'Yeah?'

'What I said before still stands. It's the police force or us.'

'I hear you.' Dave hit the end button and stared at the floor. Crunch time.

❧

'Okay, so I've found something in the finances,' Dave said as he looked up from the paperwork on his lap.

Bob was driving to give Dave a chance to search through the bank and credit-card statements forwarded by Major Fraud.

'What is it?'

'Okay, on 8 July, Kendal had thirty thousand dollars go into his bank account from Primaries Stock Agents in Barrabine.'

'They weren't the stock agent of choice.'

'No, but then fifteen grand is withdrawn and . . .' He flicked through a few pages and started to read again. 'Yeah, just as I thought. Turns up in Peter William's personal account a few days later. Huh, they didn't cover their tracks very well.'

'Are there any other big amounts that go into either Peter William's or Dunstan Kendal's account?'

'As in, above ten or fifteen k?'

'Yeah, something like that. Make it above five k.'

Running his finger down the page, Dave shook his head. 'No, this goes through until November and there's been nothing at all like that.'

'What's the largest amount deposited?'

'Nothing huge. Two k, but I can see that's from the company he works for. Wages. Comes in every two weeks.'

'Hmm. What about the feedlot income?'

'No, nothing yet. That won't come through until February or March when the stock is ready to sell. Wrong time of year.'

'Of course. You're right,' Bob said.

'What are you thinking?'

'I don't know yet. I went back through sales at Scotty's place out of Barrabine—the legal ones—and I can see he'd been buying cattle privately. I wondered if perhaps he'd bought off Kendal or William.'

'That would be a funny coincidence, wouldn't it?'

'Stranger things have happened.'

Dave went back to the paperwork with fresh eyes and continued to trawl though.

'There're a couple of bigger withdrawals out of William's account just recently,' Dave said suddenly. 'Not cattle-like sums, but two lots of two and a half grand in a week.' He marked the date with a highlighter. 'And another one, this time three k.'

'How has it been withdrawn?'

'Says cash.'

'ATM or in the bank?'

A quick glance told him ATM.

'Should be camera footage of him getting it,' Bob said.

'But what would it be for? Could be anything. Might've bought a body of beef off one of his clients or given out cash as a birthday present,' Dave said.

'Let's ask him,' Bob said with a smile.

'I don't like it when you're like that,' Dave said with a grin. 'It's like you've worked it all out but you need the proof.'

Bob glanced across at Dave. 'Son, you always need proof.'

❧

Dave and Bob walked into the Wallina Stock and Station Agents. The shed was cold and dim and there was no one in sight.

'Hello?' Dave called out as Bob walked over to Peter's office and looked inside.

'Anyone around? Peter?'

There was a shuffling behind them and Peter William appeared from behind some of the large pallets of merchandise further towards the back.

Dave took in his dishevelled appearance and held back a grin. 'Interrupt anything did we, Pete?'

'G'day, fellas. Nah, nah, just doing a bit of a stocktake on the gear I've got out the back. Bit dusty and dirty out there.' He grinned and ran his hand through his hair, then patted it down. 'Didn't expect to see you guys back here so soon. Found something?'

'Well, we have, Pete, and we'd really like to chat to you about it. Can we go into your office?'

'Course.' Peter indicated for them to go ahead. 'You know the way.' He glanced back to where he'd come from, and Dave and Bob exchanged glances.

Bob gave Dave a little nod.

'After you,' Bob said to Peter and let the man walk in front of him.

Dave waited until they'd entered the office then casually walked to the back of the shed, from where Peter had appeared.

He smelled the marijuana before he saw it. In the corner underneath a large, heavy-duty shelf was a woman sitting with her shirt hanging from her shoulder and buttoned up incorrectly. There was an ashtray beside her and a bowl containing green leaves next to the rollie papers.

'You right there, love?' Dave asked.

The woman jumped and stared at him in surprise.

'Where's Pete?' she asked.

'Just answering a few questions of ours,' he said. 'What's your name?'

'Why? Are you the cops?'

'What makes you say that?'

'You're asking questions.'

Dave laughed. 'Well, if that's going to give us away, guilty as charged. Detective Burrows from the stock squad. And you are?'

The woman glanced around nervously as if she'd just remembered the drugs were sitting in front of her.

'Um . . .'

'We can do this the easy way or the hard way,' Dave said, taking a step towards her. 'Now, what's your name?'

'Julia. Julia Stone. I'm a . . . friend.'

'Ah. Not Peter's wife, then?'

'Friend.' She looked at the ground.

'Where'd you get the dope from, Julia?'

Dave strained to hear her low voice and asked her to repeat what she'd just said.

'Pete gets it for us. We don't do a lot of it. Just a little bit.'

'Of course, personal use only,' Dave agreed. 'Can I get you to stand up for me?'

Julia eyed him warily. 'Why?'

'Well, even though it's personal use, I can see there's a lot more than what's allowed for a couple of people. I'm going to have to take you into custody, and confiscate the drugs.'

'Oh.' She blinked a couple of times as if trying to understand what Dave had said. Her bloodshot eyes told Dave she was still stoned.

'Come on, Julia, on your feet.' Dave reached forward to help her get up.

'Don't suppose you've got something to eat?' she asked. 'I'm really hungry.'

'I'll see what I can do.' He walked her back into the main area of the shed and sat her on a chair next to the bench. 'Sorry to have to do this, Julia, but I do need to make sure you don't go anywhere.' He took out his handcuffs and cuffed one wrist to the arm of the chair, then did the same to the other one. 'We won't be long.' He left her staring at the cuffs as if she were unsure what had just happened.

Chapter 30

'Peter, could you tell us about the fifteen thousand dollars that hit your account in July, please?' Bob asked just as Dave came into the room.

He saw Peter William's eyes narrow for a moment before he arranged his face in a neutral expression.

'Fifteen grand? What?' He craned forward and tried to look at the page Bob had in front of him.

Dave leaned against the wall and crossed his arms.

'Yeah, you can see here . . .' Bob pushed the statement across in front of the man and showed him where the amount was highlighted. 'Now, we think we know where this has come from, but we'd like you to tell us.'

'I didn't even know there was that much in my account. The wife handles all the money.'

'Does she?'

'Yeah. Better at the business side of things than I am.' He gave a laugh and spread his hands in a helpless gesture.

'I wouldn't know how much is in what account or when! I don't pay the bills or—' he glanced up at Dave '—or anything really. Just use my card and assume the money's going to be in there because I earn it.'

'Right, so you can't tell me what the withdrawals of the large cash amounts are for either?'

'How big are the amounts? Guess she's buying something again.' He sounded bitter. 'She does love to spend money.'

'So, you know she likes to spend, but you don't check the bank accounts?'

'Well,' Peter shrugged, 'there're always things turning up in the post. Clothes, books, stuff for the house, that sort of thing.'

'So, you can't tell us how the fifteen thousand got into your account?' Dave changed the subject back quickly and leaned forward to look Peter in the eye.

'No, mate, I told you! I don't.'

'Know a lady called Julia, do you, Peter?' Dave asked. This time Peter dropped his head.

'Yeah, I thought so.' Dave turned to Bob. 'She's not the wife.'

'Ah. Well, then, son, perhaps you'd like to tell us exactly what the money is for.'

'Will you tell my wife?'

'That depends on what you tell us. Want to start from the beginning?'

'It's like what I just said. She likes to spend. I never made enough for her.'

'And so Kendal offered you a way out of this, did he?'

Peter's eyes widened at the mention of Kendal's name, then Dave saw the realisation that he wasn't getting out of this hit him. 'No, that was my idea. He's so stupid he didn't realise what I was actually doing until the company questioned him and he got scared.' Peter sounded resigned to what was coming next.

'Scared?'

'Yeah, he's already got form and he was worried he'd go back inside.'

'Tell me how it all worked, Pete,' Bob said.

'Kendal'd get the cattle in, I'd sell them in his name. Money would turn up in his bank account and then he'd give me half.'

'So he was stealing the cattle from the owners of Nefer Station and selling them in his own name?' Bob double-checked he understood what Peter was telling him.

'Yeah.'

'Ah. And how much did you make out of this little scheme?'

'God knows. Enough to keep the wife happy and off my back.'

'Peter, you've sold nearly fifteen hundred head of cattle. At today's prices, that's a lot of money. Nearly a mil. Didn't she question where it came from?'

'Not when she got a new car.'

'And you gave Kendal a job when he left?'

Peter half stood up but sat down as Dave moved towards him.

'It's okay, I was just going to walk,' he said. 'Doesn't matter. The heat was getting too much for him. I own a feedlot. My dad left it to me. I needed a decent bloke to help and he's good with stock, even if he is a bit thick. I put him on there.'

Dave breathed out and shook his head. 'And the drugs.'

'That's what the cash is for.'

'Really. And where do you buy it?'

'Some bloke turns up here every couple of weeks. Don't know his name. He sends me a message when he's coming, and I meet him. I try to buy a reasonable amount so I can sell some on. Get some of my money back.'

Dave stood up straight and looked at Bob.

'What does this bloke look like?' he asked.

'Dunno. Tall. Bald. He drives a Toyota LandCruiser.'

'When did you meet him last?'

'Last night. Said it was his last run and I'd have to find someone else to buy from.'

'Where'd he go?'

Peter looked puzzled. 'How would I know?'

Bob leaned forward. 'Listen, son, this is very important. What road did he take when he left you?'

'Looked like he was heading for the big smoke.'

'Perth?'

'Yeah, Perth.'

'Get onto Lemming and tell him that Bulldust is headed for Perth,' Dave said urgently to Bob as he moved towards Peter, who was looking confused. 'Fuck, Mel decided to come home yesterday. They'll probably be there now.'

Dave hauled Peter to his feet and handcuffed him. 'I'll get these two to the cop shop here and explain what's happened.'

Bob hurried towards the door. 'I'll make the calls, then we'll get on the way home.'

'Shit, we're still ten hours from Perth,' Dave said.

'Which puts us not that far behind him. Go on, get going with these two and then come back and pick me up.'

'What's going on?' Peter asked.

'Mate, you've just solved a little problem for us. When you get out of jail for stock theft, I'll buy you a beer,' Dave said, jerking him upright. 'Now, come on.'

'What about Julia?'

'What about her?'

'She didn't do anything wrong.'

'She was in possession of drugs when I found her and she's implicated you in buying them. You're both going into the police station.'

'But my wife . . .'

'Pete, you should've thought about all of that before you decided to party with Julia.'

'You said—'

'Come on.' Dave shut down the conversation and dragged Peter towards the car. 'I'll be back for you,' he told Julia, who was still staring into space.

'Did you get me something to eat?' she asked.

'Sorry, love, you'll have to ask them at the cop shop,' Dave said with a grin.

Ten minutes later, Dave was pulling up in front of the police station and explaining to the local sergeant what he was doing there.

'Geez, Pete, didn't think you were into that sorta thing?' the sarge said, looking at him incredulously.

Peter dropped his eyes to the ground and let himself be led away, while Dave waited with Julia.

'I'm still hungry,' she said.

'Lemming says there's no one at either house,' Bob said as they left Wallina.

'Was he going to put a guard there?'

'Not at this stage. He's got a BOLO on the roads into Perth. He reckons they might be able to apprehend him outside the city. If we think about this, he'll have to get rid of all the dope he's got. I've got no idea how much he'd have to sell, but it might take him a little while.'

'It was a big set-up,' Dave said quietly. His heart was beating much faster than usual and he was struggling to concentrate.

'Don't worry, son. I'll get you there,' Bob said, glancing over at him.

'I'd rather there was a guard on the house.'

'He mightn't even go there. He might know you're up here. Spencer's funeral and all.'

'How would he know that?'

'Those blokes seem to know things. And we don't know if he spoke to Spencer. What do you reckon happened there?'

Dave shook his head. 'All I can think is that he caught Spencer in the camp. Like you said, he was good detective and had been around the clock a few times. He was never going to put himself at risk. Maybe Bulldust surprised him.'

'Or Scotty.'

Dave shook his head. 'I've been thinking about this. I reckon all of these "accidents" are Bulldust. I think he's unhinged. He's lost contact with his daughter, he's been on the run for a year and he knows we're after him. And Scotty's death will have pushed him over the edge.' Dave looked across to Bob. 'Which means right now he's capable of anything.'

❧

Bulldust pulled up in an underground car park in the city centre of Perth. He'd driven ten hours, stopping only for fuel and food, and he was ready for a shower and a camp. From the back of the LandCruiser he took a bag, made sure Spencer's gun was inside, along with a wad of notes, and zipped it up. Desert gave a small bark, and Bulldust patted his head.

A car pulled up next to him, and Missy's pretty face stared out at him.

'You're looking good, stranger,' she said, her smile large.

'And I'm pleased to see you, too,' he said, getting in and giving her a kiss. 'Mmm, just as good as I remember. I brought a friend.' He indicated Desert, who was squirming under his arm, trying to get to Missy.

'Well, aren't you a bit cute?' She held out her hand and let the pup smell her before looking back at Bulldust. 'My place?'

'That's the plan.' He put his seatbelt on, laid the bag between his legs and pushed Desert gently on top.

'How long are you here for this time?'

'Couple of days, I reckon. Just a few things to tidy up, then I'm going to head back across to Queensland and see if I can find Shane.' Bulldust tried to swallow the tension that had hit him the minute he'd entered the outer suburbs of Perth. He was here to finish the business that Dave had started when he'd betrayed him, and Shane was part of that.

'Have you heard from her?'

Bulldust blinked as Missy drove out into the sunlight. She eased onto the road and suddenly there were cars either side of them. Bulldust felt hemmed in and looked out, trying to spot any police cars.

'Nah, I haven't tried to call her yet. Thought I'd get away from here first.'

'You got some trouble?'

'Why'd you say that?'

She glanced over at him, a smile playing on her lips. 'You're looking around as if someone's after you. Doesn't matter if you are. You know you're safe with me.'

'Nah, Missy,' Bulldust said, forcing his body to relax, 'just nervous in the city. All these people . . . You don't see a lot out in the bush. They make me twitchy!'

'Yeah, I know what you mean. Trouble is that this is where most of my work is. I'd much rather be out in a small country town somewhere.'

'Only place I'd be.' Bulldust lifted Desert onto his lap and held him close.

'How's Scotty?'

Bulldust froze. 'Um . . . he's okay. Still out bush. Headed off last week. Not sure where he's gone to.'

Missy frowned. 'You boys split up?'

'Yeah. For the best. He does things different to me and I've got things I want to do that are different to him.'

'All good things must come to an end. Still, I'm sure you'll miss him.'

Bulldust looked out the window to hide the tears that had sprung into his eyes. 'Yeah,' he said quietly. 'I know I will.'

He swallowed a couple of times then pretended to sneeze so he could wipe his eyes before he looked back over at her. 'Hey, I might go and sort out this shit I have to first. Then I'm free and we can spend all the time we want together. Can you drop me at the bus stop. That one where you dropped me last time. I know how to get back to yours from there.' Bulldust tried to keep his voice neutral but, even to him, it sounded tight and tense. He hoped Missy wouldn't notice.

'Honey, I can do whatever you want, just so long as I know you're coming back to shag me senseless.'

'Won't be missing out on that,' he said, reaching over to run his fingers over her breast. 'I'll be there as soon as I can—promise you.'

❧

'Mummy! Come and look. Granny's got new flowers in the back yard.'

Melinda put down her bag in the hallway of her parents' home and allowed herself a small smile. She wasn't in her own home, yet, but it wouldn't be long. She'd heard from Dave yesterday and knew he would be driving back today. She held a little bit of hope he was coming home to tell her he was giving up the police force. After all, why wouldn't he? He wouldn't give up his two girls for work; he couldn't.

Mel only wished she'd given him the clear ultimatum sooner than she had.

'What colour are they?' she called back to Bec as she stepped into the kitchen.

'Pink and yellow.'

'All right?' Mark came to pick up her bag and smiled at her. 'You look a little peaky.' He put a hand on her shoulder and squeezed.

'I'm fine. Just a little tired from the flight. But, gee, it's good to be here.'

Ellen bustled in. 'I've got ham and cheese in the fridge and lovely Mrs Atkinson from across the road is going to drop off fresh bread and a few groceries, so we shouldn't have to go out tonight. I'll be pleased to have a home-cooked meal.'

'Me too. There's only so much restaurant food you can take,' Mel agreed.

'When is Dave going to be here?' Ellen asked.

'I think it will be early evening,' she said, helping her mother butter the bread. She took out the ham and laid it in the sandwich for Bec. 'I'm looking forward to seeing him.'

'Darling, don't get your hopes up that he's going to leave the police force,' Ellen said. She turned to look at her daughter. 'You know I don't agree with what you've done there. Couples have to work through things together, not give each other ultimatums. He loves his job.'

Mel turned to her mother. 'You can't seriously think that what we've just had to do was all right, Mum?'

'I'm not saying it is. But Dave didn't bring this on us purposefully. Making enemies is part of being a policeman. It's that criminal's fault, not Dave's. He did his best to make sure we were going to be okay. And, as he's said before, he has people who rely on him.'

'I understand that, I really do. But I'm not prepared to go through life being frightened and having to protect my kids every time some crook takes against him.' She put the top piece of bread on the sandwich and called Bec.

Alice gave a little cry from the pram where she was sleeping in the sitting room.

'I'll get her,' Mark called from his office.

'Bec, come in for lunch, please,' Mel called.

There was a knock at the door.

'I'll get that,' Ellen said and disappeared into the passageway. 'It'll be Mrs Atkinson.'

Mel placed the sandwich on the table as Bec ran inside. She climbed straight up on the chair. 'No, Bec, you've got to wash your hands first,' she said. 'Hop down and go to the bathroom.'

Bec groaned, but she did as she was told.

'Mummy?' she stopped. 'Mummy?' Her voice rose a little.

'What, darling?'

'Who's that with Granny?'

Mel spun around. Her mother was being pushed into the room by a man in a beanie, jeans and a dirty jumper. She frowned, not understanding, but somehow recognising the man's eyes. Then her mouth dropped open.

'Oh . . .'

The man's eyes were on Mel as he smiled a slow, cruel grin and raised his gun to Ellen's head.

Chapter 31

'Bec,' Mel said, trying to keep the panic out of her voice. 'Bec, come to me right now, darling. Quickly.'

The little girl ran to her and hid behind her legs.

'Mum, are you okay?'

Ellen nodded, the fear in her eyes clear as she stood stock still.

'Who are you?' Mel asked, her voice taut. She needed to be sure.

'Oh, you don't recognise me, little lady? You'll have to forgive my bad manners.' The man reached up and took off the beanie to reveal his bald head.

Taking a few steps backwards, Mel let out a little moan and clutched Bec to her.

'We've met before. Bulldust's the name. I'd really like to see your husband. He around?'

'What the hell is going on—' Mark strode out into the kitchen and stopped when he saw Bulldust and Ellen. 'What

305

the—?' The realisation dawned on his face, and his gaze skimmed over Mel and Bec before flashing back to Ellen and the unwelcome stranger standing in his kitchen. 'Are you him? What the fuck are you doing here, you parasitic criminal?' Mark took a step towards Bulldust, who waved the gun at him.

'I wouldn't do that if I were you.'

Mark stopped, his eyes on the gun. Slowly, he put his hands up and moved backwards.

Bulldust gave a grin. 'Much better.'

'Mummy, Grandad swore!' said Bec from behind her.

'Shh, Bec. Just be quiet,' Mel said, still staring at Bulldust. 'Dave isn't here,' she told him. 'He's out bush. Where he always is. He's hardly ever with us.'

'Don't lie to me!' Bulldust yelled suddenly. 'I know he's with you!'

Bec flinched and Alice started to cry. Mel moved towards the pram but stopped when Bulldust barked, 'Stay where you are!'

Alice's cries grew louder and Bec buried her head in Mel's legs.

'He isn't,' Mel said, trying to make her voice strong. 'He's been at Barrabine. One of his old partners was killed and he was at the funeral. You can check the whole house. You won't find him here.'

At this, Bulldust cocked his head, and a slow unpleasant smile spread across his lips.

Mark moved forward again, this time staring at the gun in Bulldust's hands. 'Let my wife go,' he instructed.

Bulldust laughed. 'Why? I need some insurance.'

'Take me.'

Narrowing his eyes, Bulldust shook his head. 'Come on, all in one room.' He pushed Ellen towards the sitting room and Mark quickly grabbed her hand and yanked her towards him, putting his arm around her protectively.

Bulldust waved the gun at Mel and she followed his instructions, picking Bec up as she went.

'Now, let's all get nice and cosy while we wait for Dad to come home,' Bulldust said, looking at Bec with a strange smile as Mel pulled her closer and stood next to Alice's pram, trying to rock it enough to make her daughter stop crying.

'I haven't seen my daddy for a long time,' Bec said. 'Why have you got a gun? Is it real?'

'Shh, Bec,' Mark said, frowning at his granddaughter.

'Yeah, it's real, kid. In fact, your dad knew the man who owned this gun.'

Mel's head snapped up. 'What do you mean by that?'

Bulldust didn't answer, just smiled again to reveal yellow teeth.

Mel drew in a startled shaky breath. 'Did you kill Spencer?' she asked quietly.

Fixing her with his cold eyes, Bulldust said, 'Now, why would you think that?'

Mel stared back, willing herself not to react. She couldn't deny the trepidation that was seeping into her.

'Why, you—' Mark threw himself across the room at Bulldust. Their bodies collided and Mark bounced off the giant man without making an impact on him.

Bec started to cry. 'Granddad! Don't do that.'

'Mark!' Ellen leaned forward trying to stop him from going again, but Bulldust just laughed.

He put the gun in the back of his jeans and put up his fists. 'Let's make it a fair fight,' he said as he landed the first blow onto Mark's nose.

Mark stumbled but regained his footing and aimed a couple of right jabs at Bulldust's stomach, but only one connected.

Bulldust brought his meaty fist down on the back of Mark's neck.

Mel watched in horror, the slow motion of her father falling to the floor without a sound. He didn't move.

Ellen screamed and ran to her husband's side, while Bulldust got up and stood in the doorway.

'Anyone else want to have a go?' he asked, bringing the gun back out into everyone's vision.

Ellen sat next to Mark, sobbing, while Mel brought a shaking Bec closer to her and reached for Alice's pram. Neither woman made eye contact with Bulldust.

'I guess now we wait,' Bulldust said, drawing a chair into the doorway.

Ellen tried to wipe the blood away from Mark's face. His eyes flickered and he let out a loud groan.

'Are you okay, Granddad?' Bec asked. She turned to Bulldust. 'Why did you hit him? You don't have to be mean. Mummy always says you shouldn't be mean.'

Bulldust grinned. 'You're right, little lady. I don't. But it's what I'm good at. Now, you keep your mouth shut or I'll shut it for you.'

Mel put her hand over Bec's mouth and leaned down to whisper in her ear. 'I know this is going to be really hard, darling, but you must be quiet. Please don't say anything until I say it's okay to. This is very important. All right?'

Bec nodded, her eyes wide as she stared at her grandfather, who still wasn't moving.

Bulldust fiddled with the gun while the silence, interspersed with Ellen's sobbing, stretched out for what seemed like hours. He repeatedly cocked the gun, checked the bullets in the chamber and clicked it back into place. Glancing up, he sneered at Mel and Bec, before running through the same routine.

Daring to look at Bulldust, Mel saw his rough workhardened hands stroking the gun lovingly.

'Won't be long,' Bulldust said softly, 'and I'll have you.'

Finally, there was movement and Ellen let out a relieved sob as Mark came to. He groaned and put his hand to the back of his neck, before managing to pull himself up to a sitting position. Mark glared at the intruder in his house.

'You're nothing but scum,' he said. 'Going into people's houses and terrorising innocent people. The bloke you're looking for doesn't even live here.'

'I sort of feel like he's going to come by here,' Bulldust said casually.

'And so he might, but none of us are who you want.'

'Maybe not, but you're all draw cards.'

Mel spoke up. 'Look, why don't I ring him? Get him to come over.'

Bulldust looked at her. 'But you just told me he wasn't going to be home until this evening.'

'Let's see where he is.'

'Go on, then. But don't you fucking tell him I'm here. You tell him to hurry home because you're missing him and can't wait for a bit of dick. Yeah?' He got up and moved over to the pram. 'Don't do anything silly, little lady. I've got something you want.'

Mel took a breath and got up. 'The phone is over there.'

Bulldust nodded, waving the gun at her in a hurrying motion.

Taking a breath, she slowly walked over and picked up the receiver. She looked at Bec and put her finger to her lips to make sure she stayed quiet. Then she dialled Dave's number.

Dave looked at his phone as it rang and saw Mark's house number.

He frowned. 'I thought they were going straight to our house,' he said to Bob. 'Hello?'

'Hi, darling, it's me.'

'Mel?' Dave took the phone away from his ear and looked at it. 'Mel, is that you?' He listened as she gave a tinkling laugh. 'Of course it is, honey. I'm just wondering how far away you are? Mum's just about got dinner on the table and Dad's looking forward to seeing you and having a catch-up beer.'

Dave was silent. What the actual fuck? Fear spread through his body and he looked across at Bob. He put the phone on speaker and indicated to Bob to listen.

'Are you okay, Mel?'

'Oh yes, everything is just great. It's just we all can't wait to see you. And,' she lowered her voice a little, 'we've been apart so long, Dave, I've got a few needs, you know?'

Dave's eyebrows shot through the roof and Bob's face went pale.

'Is Bulldust there with you?' Dave asked.

'That's right. Just so long as you're not far away. I don't want to have to wait too long.'

Bob put his foot down and indicated ten minutes.

'We're about ten minutes away. Do you want to stay on the phone?'

'No, no, that's fine. We'll see you in ten minutes. I can tell Mum to put the garlic bread in the oven. See you soon. Love you.' She hung up.

Bob flipped the siren on and yelled above the noise. 'Ring Lemming, he needs to be in on this. Tell them to get Tactical Response Group out there.'

Dave relayed the message and hung up.

'Jesus, they're about twenty minutes away, at best. Shut the siren down. I don't want him to know we're coming.'

Bob turned it off. 'Son, you are not to go in. You need to wait for the TRG. You'll only cause more trouble if you go at it alone.' He looked across at Dave. 'Do you understand me? You're not to go in.'

'I'll just get around the edge of the house and have a look. I'll be able to help direct them when I can work out what room they're all in. I'd say she was calling from the sitting room or the kitchen. Pull up here.'

'What's this? Two blocks from the house?' Bob flicked on the blinker and jerked the car to a halt.

Dave ignored the question. 'You think I'm going to leave them in there by themselves?' He reached into the back and pulled out his radio and clipped it on his shoulder. Reefing open the door, he ran low and quickly, his gun drawn, ignoring Bob's quiet cries to stop.

He had to get to them. To Mel and the girls.

And Bulldust. Bastard! How dare he go after them.

His heart was pounding after the long sprint when he reached the house. He leaned up against the fence and crept along it, trying to keep himself hidden. Crawling along on his stomach, he stopped underneath the front window and listened.

Everything was quiet. Or was that sobbing?

He strained to hear. Yes, someone was crying.

Anger flared through him at the very thought of Bulldust laying a hand on his wife or daughters. He couldn't even imagine how scared they must be. Bec would never forget this. What else would she be forced to witness before this was all over? He couldn't bear the thought. Somehow he had to get inside.

Before he could make a plan to sneak a look through the windows, he heard sirens in the distance. *Fuck!* he screamed silently. *Turn that bloody noise off!*

Just as he finished the thought, they were silenced.

Moving on, he went to the kitchen window, this time standing flush with the wall, and bent around to look in.

The first thing he saw was Bulldust in the doorway, facing the sitting room. His heart still pounding, Dave quietly spoke into the radio: 'They're all in the sitting room. Front window to the left of the front door.'

With his back to the wall, Dave crept back to the front of the house and stood to the right of the sitting-room window out of sight, before bringing his head around slowly to peer in.

Bec was fidgeting on the couch next to Ellen when she let out an excited squeal. Her eyes were trained on him. He only hoped she wouldn't say his name.

Bulldust jumped, and his voice carried through to Dave. 'For fuck's sake, shut that kid up! I'll shoot her, I swear I will.'

Dave flinched and his hand tightened on his gun as he heard Mel scream, 'Bec!'

Ellen was calmer as she stood and picked up Bec. 'Come on, darling,' she said firmly but quietly, 'you need to be nice and quiet until Daddy gets here.'

Mark muttered under his breath, and Bulldust trained the gun on him. 'You can shut the fuck up, too. You're much more dispensable.'

For the first time in his life, Dave was grateful that Mark was with his family, although from what he could see, it looked like Mark and Bulldust might have had a fight.

Mel sat on the floor near the phone. She was holding her face and Dave could see an angry red welt on her cheek. Violence threatened to burst out of him, and it was only the thought that he could be guaranteeing her death if he stepped in that allowed Dave to stay where he was and stay silent.

'But there's Daddy!' Bec yelled pointing out the window. 'He's just there.'

Dave whipped his head away from the window just as Bulldust shot to his feet, the gun aimed where he'd been, and Ellen turned around to see what Bec was pointing at.

Dave heard Bulldust yell out, 'Get in here, Burrows! I've got your family. You'd better come and make sure they're okay.'

Dave's heart started to race as he ran through his options. Before he could answer, Bulldust let off a gunshot, and everyone inside the house screamed. The bullet broke through the window and the sound of shattering glass swirled around as an echo of the gunshot.

'Come on, Burrows, I know you're there.' Bulldust's voice was muffled a little with his next words. 'You sure you saw him, you little shit?'

Bec didn't answer, and it took all Dave's strength not to charge in there and knee-cap him.

'Come on, Burrows.' This time Bulldust's voice was sing-song. 'Come on. You wouldn't want me to hurt anyone in here, would you?'

Silence.

Holding his breath, Dave resisted the urge to look and see what was happening.

He glanced at his watch, willing the TRG to arrive. As he looked up he saw movement in the bushes at the front of the house. Bob was crouched there, his weapon in his hands.

Dave tried to signal to Bob to look into the front room and see where everyone was, but he was talking quietly into his radio.

'Burrows, I can hear you.'

Snapping the radio off, Dave took a breath and crept down the side path towards the back door. He had to get inside, and he had to retain the element of surprise.

'I've got a present for you. Brought your mate's gun. Thought we could have a little chat about Spencer Brown.'

Freezing, Dave stopped and listened to what Bulldust was saying.

'Yeah, fuck, he was easy to take down. He thought he was gonna take Scotty in, you know,' Bulldust taunted Dave. 'Even had him all cuffed to the chair. Didn't know I was behind him.' He paused. 'Burrows, come on in so we can have a yarn. Sure your little wife here can't wait to see you.'

There was a scraping noise and then Mel cried out.

Dave dragged in angry, deep breaths through his nose and clenched his fingers harder around the gun, while trying to work out what to do. He wanted to be able to get Bulldust in his line of sight through a window and put a bullet in his heart.

'Leave her alone,' he yelled out. 'She's not who you want.'

'You are there, you fucker!' Bulldust spat. 'Get in here now. Or are you too scared?' he taunted.

Dave heard a slap and Mel cried out again.

'You bastard!' Mark's voice this time.

'What's that about my mate's gun?' Dave asked calmly.

'You'll see when you come inside. Show yourself!'

There was silence and Dave had to stop himself from looking in the window again. It seemed to last forever, then Bulldust started to speak once more.

'You really thought you were going to get the better of me? Thought you were going to put me in the slammer? You know what, you're a traitor. Just like the other bastards I had to kill.'

'I'm sorry I had to hand you in,' Dave said quietly, listening carefully to the silence in response. Bulldust wouldn't have been expecting him to be contrite. 'I know you trusted me.'

'More fool fucking me.' Agitated footsteps crossed the room again.

'Don't do this, mate. What about Shane?'

An angry roar came from within the house. 'Don't bring her name up, you arsehole! Her leaving was all your fault. Get in here now.'

Realising he'd broached the wrong subject, Dave took another breath. 'Back to Spencer, then.'

'Burrows, if you're not in here in ten seconds, one of them dies,' Bulldust yelled.

The sobbing from the lounge room was loud. Bec and Alice were crying and Dave thought Mel might have been as well. It made him shake with rage but at the same time it fuelled his focus, his determination to protect his family.

'Think about Shane,' Dave said quietly.

Silence.

He took a breath. 'If you do this sort of thing, Bulldust, you're probably not going to get to see her again. If you hand yourself in, you'll still be able to tell her everything.'

He clicked open the kitchen door just as Bulldust said, 'I've lost my patience.'

'No!' Ellen's voice rang out loudly.

At the sound of another gunshot Dave ran into the room just as Ellen pushed Bec to the floor and suddenly fell backwards.

Mel and Mark screamed as they saw blood spread across her chest.

Dave took aim. The shot hit Bulldust in the shoulder and he stumbled backwards, dropping his gun.

Mel rushed forward, kicking the gun away while Dave, yelling into the radio, ran towards Bulldust.

Dave heard the front door being rammed in and suddenly Bob was in the room, puffing, his gun raised to the ceiling. Taking in the scene he yelled into his radio. 'Two down, two down. Ambulance required.'

Dave wrenched Bulldust onto his back, ignoring the howl of pain.

'You're under arrest, you fucker,' Dave hissed in his ear as he slammed the handcuffs on. He then crawled quickly to Ellen, grabbing a cushion from the couch and pushing it down hard onto her chest.

Mark crawled over, weeping. 'Ellen. Ellen!'

Mel dropped to her knees next to her mother, then scrambled up to get Alice, who was screaming.

'Ellen,' Dave said. 'Ellen, can you hear me? Just hang in there. The ambulance is on its way.'

'Holy fuck,' Bob said quietly once he'd made sure Bulldust was secure. 'Bec?' The little girl had blood running from her mouth and her arm. She was deathly quiet, her face white. He raced to her, sat her on the couch and examined her, all the while talking.

'Hi there, Bec. I'm Bob, one of your dad's friends. You're going to be just fine . . .'

'Mummy,' she whispered.

'We're going to get a doctor to have a look at you, I think. Can you hear the sirens?'

'Jesus, Bec?' Dave looked at Ellen and realised there was nothing more he could do for her. He half crawled, half scrambled over to his oldest daughter.

Mel crouched over her mother, with Alice in her arms, staring across at her daughter, Bec, unable to move. Then suddenly she stood up, still holding Alice, and ran out of the house screaming. 'Help! Someone, please help! My little girl, she's been shot. Help!'

'It's all right, Bec,' Dave said, cradling his daughter in his hands. 'It's all right, princess. Daddy's here.'

Epilogue

Dave pulled on his suit coat and straightened his tie. He looked over at Mel, who still couldn't look him in the eye.

Bec walked into the bedroom, her arm heavily bandaged. 'Daddy?'

Dave bent down to hug her. 'Yes, princess?'

'Where's Gran gone again?' She looked up at him with large eyes as Mel let out a sob. Dave watched as his wife turned away and left the room.

'Well, honey, Gran has gone to be a star in heaven,' he said. 'To look out for you and Mummy and Alice. You won't be able to see her anymore, but she'll always be watching over you, and every time you look at the night sky, you'll be able to see her twinkle.' A lump in his throat made it difficult to talk. 'Come on, we have to get going.' He took her hand as they walked out together.

Mel was standing in the kitchen, Alice in her arms.

'Ready?' he asked.

She nodded and walked out in front of him.

In the car, Dave strapped the two girls in and got into the driver's seat. He reached for Mel's hand. 'Okay?' he asked softly.

'How dare you ask me that?' she said in a low voice. 'How dare you.'

This is how it had been since Ellen had been killed. Anger. Silence. Grief.

All of this had helped Dave make his decision. There had been so much to think about, so much to work through. It was nigh on impossible to come back from what had happened.

Mel stared straight out the front window, her head high. 'Once today is over, I don't want you to come home with us. I'll get Dad to get in touch about the legal side of things.'

'Mel, let's not do this today,' Dave said. Her words weren't unexpected. He'd been going to tell her after the funeral he was leaving. He knew that would be what Mel would want.

'No, I have to . . .' This time, she looked over at him. Her eyes were red and she looked like she hadn't slept in a week.

'Mel, I'm sorry.'

She held her hand up. 'Dave, I have nothing to say to you. My mother, your children's grandmother, is dead because of you. Bec was shot because of you. How could you even think this would work now?'

Tears welled in Dave's eyes. 'Mel, please, just let me—'

'No, Dave. We're done. No more.'

Letting the tears fall on his cheeks, Dave put the car into gear and they drove towards the church. He didn't have an answer, because she was right.

He thought about a future without his children living with him. Had chasing Bulldust been worth what he was about to lose? His heart felt as if it was being squeezed from his chest.

Glancing in the rear-view mirror, Dave saw his own blue eyes looking at him from Bec, and he dragged the back of his hand across his face, taking a few deep breaths.

Reflecting on what Kathy had said to him after Spencer had died, he knew he'd made the right decision.

'*Neither of you deserve to be unhappy, and those kids deserve to know what it's like to be loved by two happy and content people, rather than parents who walk on eggshells around each other. Give them good examples of love, not just making do. You wouldn't want them to end up in a relationship like yours, I'm sure. So show them a good one.*'

Life would okay, he decided. Hard, horrible, but okay. He would make it work.

Author's note

Fool's Gold, *Without a Doubt*, *Red Dirt Country* and *Something to Hide* are my novels that feature Detective Dave Burrows in the lead role. Eagle-eyed readers will know Dave from previous novels and it was in response to readers' enthusiasm for Dave that I wanted to write more about him.

In these novels, set in the late 1990s and early 2000s, Dave is at the beginning of his career. He's married to his first wife, Melinda, a paediatric nurse, and they're having troubles balancing their careers and family life. No spoilers here because if you've read my contemporary rural novels you'll know that Dave and Melinda separate and Dave is currently very happily married to his second wife, Kim.

Dave is one of my favourite characters and I hope he will become one of yours, too.

Acknowledgements

As always, the biggest thank yous and love go to Tom, Annette, Christa, Laura, Sarah and all those at Allen & Unwin. Without you, there wouldn't be any stories.

To Claire de Medici—I'm so grateful for your expertise and care of my books. Edits are a joy with you!

Gaby from Left Bank Literary—the best, most calm agent a girl could want. Fancy having fourteen books together!

DB, you're a legend. That's all there is to say.

Rochelle and Hayden—treasures. Rocket and Jack—dear, dear canine friends.

Cal and Aaron, Heather, Kelly, Robyn, Lauren and Graham, Ewin, Jan and Pete, Chrissy, Bev, Lee and Paul, Shelley, Lachie and the rest of my cheer squad—love you all so very much.

All the family. Plus, cousin Tanya!

To you, the readers—I've said so many times that I wouldn't be here if it wasn't for you all. During these crazy COVID times, I hope these stories have brought you hope and entertainment and perhaps some peace from the world. Thank you for your continued support, the buying, borrowing, giving of these books. I'm so lucky to be able to do what I love. And that is all thanks to you.

With love,
Fleur x

DVassist.org.au

DVassist (formerly Breaking the Silence) is an organisation I founded to support men, women and young adults who live in rural areas and are experiencing family and domestic violence. I'm so passionate about helping people in this area, I put my own money into starting this organisation before lobbying the Federal Government for a grant to continue the work I started.

DVassist has been created by me, as a rural woman for rural people. Life is so different out here to what it is like in the city. I've lived in the country all my life, so I know. We are here to help, with information, resources and practical support for those experiencing, or concerned about others who may be experiencing, domestic and family violence.

In September 2020, we launched a comprehensive website which explains what domestic and family violence is. It is not just physical violence. Domestic and family violence can often be hard to define and understand. Behavioural abuse, emotional abuse and psychological abuse can all be forms of domestic and family violence. This website is a resource to help you learn more about domestic and family violence, and to connect you to local domestic and family violence help.

If you require help, please go to our site at www.dvassist. org.au. This site is available to anyone.

In October 2020, we launched our telephone counselling services—if you call, you will speak to a qualified domestic violence counsellor who understands the unique challenges of living in rural areas.

Our counselling services are available Monday to Friday, 10 a.m. to 7 p.m. Please call 1800 080 083. (Also be aware the counselling services are only for those in WA at this time. Expansion into other states will happen over the next few years.)

If you would like to donate to DVassist we would be so grateful. You can do so by visiting the DVassist website and clicking on the donate button.

As Founder of DVassist, I'm proud to be able to help people across rural communities who need this type of assistance. One person experiencing family or domestic violence is one too many.